Murder Before Tuesday

An Inspector Reynolds of Scotland Yard Mystery

By Elaine Hamilton

Originally published in 1937

Murder Before Tuesday

Published by Resurrected Press

This classic book was handcrafted by Resurrected Press. Resurrected Press is dedicated to bringing high quality classic books back to the readers who enjoy them. These are not scanned versions of the originals, but, rather, quality checked and edited books meant to be enjoyed!

Please visit ResurrectedPress.com to view our entire catalogue!

For updates on future releases, LIKE us on Facebook:
http://www.Facebook.com/ResurrectedPress

ISBN 13: 978-1-943403-07-3

Printed in the United States of America

Resurrected Press Books in A. E. Fielding's *The Chief Inspector Pointer Mystery* Series

Death of John Tait
Murder at the Nook
Mystery at the Rectory
Scarecrow
The Case of the Two Pearl Necklaces
The Charteris Mystery
The Eames-Erskine Case
The Footsteps that Stopped
The Clifford Affair
The Cluny Problem
The Craig Poisoning Mystery
The Net Around Joan Ingilby
The Tall House Mystery
The Wedding-Chest Mystery
The Westwood Mystery
Tragedy at Beechcroft

RESURRECTED PRESS CLASSIC MYSTERY CATALOGUE

Journeys into Mystery
Travel and Mystery in a More Elegant Time

The Edwardian Detectives
Literary Sleuths of the Edwardian Era

Gems of Mystery
Lost Jewels from a More Elegant Age

Anne Austin
One Drop of Blood
The Black Pigeon
Murder at Bridge
Murder Backstairs

E. C. Bentley
Trent's Last Case: The Woman in Black

Ernest Bramah
Max Carrados Resurrected:
The Detective Stories of Max Carrados

Agatha Christie
The Secret Adversary
The Mysterious Affair at Styles

Octavus Roy Cohen
Midnight

Freeman Wills Croft
The Ponson Case
The Pit Prop Syndicate

The Uttermost Farthing: A Savant's Vendetta

Arthur Griffiths
The Passenger From Calais
The Rome Express

Fergus Hume
The Mystery of a Hansom Cab
The Green Mummy
The Silent House
The Secret Passage

Edgar Jepson
The Loudwater Mystery

A. E. W. Mason
At the Villa Rose

A. A. Milne
The Red House Mystery

Baroness Emma Orczy
The Old Man in the Corner

Edgar Allan Poe
The Detective Stories of Edgar Allan Poe

Arthur J. Rees
The Hampstead Mystery
The Shrieking Pit
The Hand In The Dark
The Moon Rock
The Mystery of the Downs

Mary Roberts Rinehart
Sight Unseen and The Confession

Dorothy L. Sayers

Whose Body?

Sir William Magnay
The Hunt Ball Mystery

Mabel and Paul Thorne
The Sheridan Road Mystery

Louis Tracy
The Strange Case of Mortimer Fenley
The Albert Gate Mystery
The Bartlett Mystery
The Postmaster's Daughter
The House of Peril
The Sandling Case: What Would You Have Done?

Charles Edmonds Walk
The Paternoster Ruby

John R. Watson
The Mystery of the Downs
The Hampstead Mystery

Edgar Wallace
The Daffodil Mystery
The Crimson Circle

Carolyn Wells
Vicky Van
The Man Who Fell Through the Earth
In the Onyx Lobby
Raspberry Jam
The Clue
The Room with the Tassels
The Vanishing of Betty Varian
The Mystery Girl
The White Alley
The Curved Blades

Anybody but Anne
The Bride of a Moment
Faulkner's Folly
The Diamond Pin
The Gold Bag
The Mystery of the Sycamore
The Come Back

Raoul Whitfield
Death in a Bowl

And much more!
Visit ResurrectedPress.com
for our complete catalogue

FOREWORD

Murder Before Tuesday is the final installment in the mystery series involving Scotland Yard's Inspector Reynolds. Written by Elaine Hamilton, the nine books in the series were published during the 1930's, that period of time often referred to as The Golden Age of British Mysteries. Other than her authorship of the series, there is little biographical information about Hamilton available.

Unlike the flamboyant amateur detectives that had been so popular during the previous decade, Inspector Reynolds is, at least on the surface, a professional policeman of the style of mystery that has been dubbed "Hum-drum" for their reliance on methodical investigative methods rather than intuition or inspiration. This style became popular in the 1930's in the works of writers such as Freeman Wills Crofts, A. E. Fielding, and Ngaio Marsh. Reynolds, far from being an eccentric character of quirks and moods as many of his predecessors were, is a thoroughly amiable chap, happily married, and not at all adverse to a good honest dinner when the opportunity presents itself. He is well respected by his colleagues and thought of fondly by those who work for him.

A central feature of all of the Reynolds mysteries is the presence of young women of good breeding and education who, due to circumstances, finds themselves caught up against their will in some criminal enterprise. The novels deal as much with how these young women manage, with Reynolds' help, to extricate themselves from this trap—and find romance in the process. The series was clearly aimed at a target audience who could identify with these heroines. As the series progressed, elements of melodrama were added and the books take on more of the aspect of a thriller. In many ways, they resemble Agatha Christie's *The Man in the Brown Suit.*

In *Murder Before Tuesday*, the young woman is Naomi Marsh, who takes a position as personal secretary to Vanda Quayne, an internationally famous dancer about to make her first London appearance as headliner at the Regis, a well known nightclub. While traveling to Paris to meet her new employer, Naomi Marsh finds her self shadowed by a shadowy figure in a long brown coat. Further incidents make it seem as though the dancer's mysterious past may be about to catch up with her. To top it off, Quayne has been receiving notes warning her that she will die before the end of the month, which happens to fall on a Tuesday, if she comes to London.

Inspector Reynolds is in the audience at the Regis when Vanda Quayne collapses during her performance. Taking charge of the situation, the inspector finds himself with and ample supply of suspects, all of whom seem to have secrets in their past, and none of whom seem willing to cooperate.

Murder Before Tuesday is a fast paced story, with plenty of drama–and melodrama–to keep the reader's attention. Clues dribble out slowly at first, but then become a torrent at the end, and the reader never has to wait long for *something* to happen. As a mystery writer, Hamilton is more entertaining than clever, though this seems to be by intention.

The works of Elaine Hamilton are hard to find these days, particularly the second through fifth books which are particularly rare, yet they are well worth seeking out. It is, therefore, with some pleasure that Resurrected Press offers this new edition of *Murder Before Tuesday.*

About the Author

Not much is known about Elaine Hamilton other than she wrote a series of mysteries in the 1930's featuring Inspector Reynolds of Scotland Yard. *The Westminster Mystery* published in 1930 was the first of these. Other titles in the series include *Murder in the Fog* (1931), *The Green Death* (1932), *The Chelsea Mystery* (1932), *The Silent Bell* (1933), *Peril at Midnight* (1934), *Tragedy in the Dark* (1935), *The Casino Mystery* (1936) and *Murder Before Tuesday* (1937).

Greg Fowlkes
Editor-In-Chief
Resurrected Press
www.ResurrectedPress.

TABLE OF CONTENTS

I. In Quest Of Adventure

Saturday, November 20th.

THE girl behind the desk in the Mayfair beauty parlour glanced up as the shop door opened and a tall, graceful figure entered.

"Naomi! What brings you to this den of robbers?" she exclaimed.

Naomi Marsh smiled at her friend's surprised question.

"That's a hard name for this elegant place, Phil," she replied. "I called for two reasons. One, a new job is practically mine; I go to Paris to-morrow for an interview."

Phil Ingram's eyes became thoughtful.

".H'm. What's the other reason?" she demanded in crisp tones.

"The same that all your clients have—I want to be made beautiful," Naomi told her.

Phil grinned broadly.

"Nature did that for you twenty odd years ago, my girl," she retorted. "We can do you over and make you look more *soignee,* perhaps, but it will cost real money: Casinier doesn't let his staff toil cheaply.

"Go ahead. I'll have the works," urged Naomi. "As the prospective highly paid secretary of a famous dancer I can afford to make a splash."

"As you wish, but remember you have been warned." Phil pressed a bell near the counter and gave a series of orders to the assistant who appeared.

"You'll only get a hurried polish-up, Naomi. It's Saturday and we close at one o'clock," Phil explained. "I must wait until then to hear your news."

She and Naomi shared a flat together in St. John's Wood. Although of totally different types, they were excellent friends. Naomi, slim, blonde and blue-eyed in appearance; calm and reticent in manner, adventurous in spirit. Phil, plump and auburn-haired, shrewd, capable and downright.

The two girls had been colleagues in Julian Casinier's office in the City for a while. Then Naomi Marsh had plunged into free-lance secretarial work, and Casinier—a man of widespread interests—had installed Phil Ingram as manageress of this beauty salon which he had recently acquired.

There again the two girls differed, for whereas Naomi loved her work, Phil frankly detested the beauty parlour and its clients.

She cast an appraising eye over her friend when the shop closed.

"Well, I hope you're satisfied. You look sleek and sophisticated, and it's cost you thirty bob, plus a tip."

"I'm not complaining," Naomi assured her. "It's given me self-confidence."

"Why you threw up a solid job with easy hours and good pay to play temporary nursemaid to semi-famous foreigners beats me," groused Phil as they waited for a bus. "Last time it was a pop-eyed Italian princess, and the time before a fly-blown Spanish author."

"Guess who it's going to be this time," Naomi had a mysterious expression in her eyes.

"Is he white or black?" scowled Phil.

"White, of course, and it isn't a man. It's Vanda Quayne."

Phil swung round and faced her friend with a frown.

"Vanda Quayne!" she reiterated blankly. "You don't mean that South American creature, the film star and dancer?"

"I certainly do," Naomi asserted. "She is coming to London for a few months. I shall get an incredible salary and some most amusing experiences."

Phil's lips met in a disapproving line.

"If one half that I've heard about Vanda is true, you'll get a whole lot of experience of a kind that you won't bargain for. Some man shot himself last month because of her."

"Lightning doesn't strike twice in the same place, Phil. Anyhow, I'll take the risk. It's a job with a kick in it. It will be something of an adventure to be secretary to such a glamorous person."

"Adventures can be dangerous and jobs shouldn't resemble cocktails," warned Phil. "Oh well, if your mind's made up, it's no use for me to talk as if I were the mother of seven. Come on. Here's our bus."

II. A TRIP TO PARIS

Sunday morning, November 21st

WARNE ROAD in St John's Wood was at no time a busy thoroughfare. On this chill Sunday morning in November it was deserted, save for one man, a drooping figure in a shabby brown overcoat.

He was standing near the railings, with an attache case in one hand, when Naomi and Phil came out of the house where they lived.

"I hate seeing people off on a journey: it always makes me discontented and irritable," Phil remarked.

"Yet you insisted upon coming," her friend reminded her.

"Yes, that's the 'mother of seven' spirit oozing out again. We'll take a taxi. I feel extravagant."

"We'll take a bus. I feel mean," Naomi retorted. "There's plenty of time. My train doesn't leave until eleven o'clock."

At the end of the road they boarded a bus bound for Victoria.

"Upstairs," urged Phil "I want a cigarette." Looking through the window, she peered down on the two or three passengers who were entering the vehicle. "Who's your pal, Naomi?" she demanded.

Her friend looked surprised.

"If it's a riddle, I don't know the answer."

"The riddle is an ugly, ferret-eyed bloke in a brown overcoat," Phil told her sharply. "I saw him from our window more than an hour ago. He was still there when we came out of the house. Now he's inside this bus, and I mean to see how far he travels on it."

"Perhaps he was early for some appointment and preferred to wait in a quiet place," Naomi suggested.

"H'm. He had what he wanted, certainly. Warne Road is desolation on Sunday mornings. Maybe I'm a fussy old hen, Naomi, but you happen to be a particularly attractive chick." Phil glanced apprehensively at her friend's blonde beauty. "Why did you allow Vanda Quayne to drag you on this ridiculous errand?"

"A two-day trip to Paris is not exactly a perilous journey, and it's reasonable for Miss Quayne to see whom she is engaging." Naomi patted her companion's arm. "Cheer up. I shall be home again to-morrow evening."

Phil gave no sign of being comforted.

"I wish you'd never seen or heard of the woman," she blurted out.

"I've not seen her yet, except on the films."

"She's got a rotten reputation," Phil snapped irritably.

Naomi laughed outright.

"You're talking as if you were a village spinster. Vanda Quayne's private life can't affect me, Phil. Where's your sense of humour this morning?"

"There's nothing funny about that nasty-looking merchant who was glued to our front railings and is now on this bus. Why couldn't you be satisfied to stay at Casinier's in a regular post?"

"Because being a free-lance secretary is more fun. It also brings in more money. I've been fortunate too in having interesting people to work for, in spite of what you think of them."

"I've a hunch this is where your luck will change," grumbled Phil. "Two to Victoria, please," she said to the conductor.

The man punched the tickets and cast a keen eye at the girls who were his only fares on the top of the bus.

"Excuse me, miss," he said diffidently to Phil, "but there's a fellow downstairs who asked me to let him know how far you were going. Is he with you?"

"No," Phil said decisively. "What did you tell him?"

"Nothing," the conductor replied with a grin. "And that's all he will be told."

"You see!" Phil remarked significantly when the man had gone.

"Only that an idle loafer has nothing better to do than try to pick up two, girls," retorted Naomi. "All the same I wish Bob Deane hadn't put that stupid paragraph in the *Evening Record* last night"

"So do I. If that bright young journalist minded his own business it would be better for everybody. He calls himself a crime expert, but isn't above scribbling gossip paragraphs."

"What exactly did he say?" Naomi asked. "I was too angry to read all of it."

Phil took a newspaper-clipping from her handbag and read it aloud.

Miss Vanda Quayne, the fascinating South American dancer and film star is expected in London shortly to fulfil various engagements. Miss Quayne is fortunate in obtaining Miss Naomi Marsh as private secretary, who, we understand, is going to Paris to-morrow to meet the dancer and discuss plans for her stay in this country. Vanda Quayne owns some enormously valuable jewels which she often wears on the stage.

"That's the lot," Phil commented cynically. "A positive gold-mine of information to any hard-up burglar. I could choke Bob Deane. Meanwhile, you watch your step, my girl."

On the train at Victoria, the loafer got into a compartment not far from that which Naomi was occupying.

"Don't worry, Phil," she urged her friend. "There are four other people in here. By the way, you look as if you were off on a trip to the Arctic. Why the heavy coat and attaché case if you're going back to the flat?"

"Who said I was?" Phil's tone was sullen. "If I like to spend my Sunday in Brighton, it's nobody's business but my own."

"Of course not," her friend agreed smoothly. "Sorry I butted in with a question, only you're always so frank about your movements that I wondered. The train's moving. Good-bye. See you to-morrow night."

On the boat Naomi's spirits rose. There was no sign of her shadow.

She took a place in the queue of passengers waiting outside a cabin to have their passports stamped. They were admitted in couples. Naomi's companion was a tall young man, obviously English, wearing a fleecy grey overcoat.

"Let me take your suitcase," he offered.

"Thank you, I can manage," was Naomi's aloof reply.

For a moment she struggled to open her handbag. It slipped from her grasp and was deftly caught by her companion.

"Pride goeth before a fall,' " he murmured with mischief in his eyes, and relieved her of her suitcase.

He held it while the official performed the stamping ritual and the girl had put her passport away.

"I'll carry this to your deck-chair," the young man suggested.

Naomi shook her head.

"It's too rough for me to risk staying on deck. I'm going to the ladies' saloon and hope for the best."

"A wise plan. I'll take your bag there for you."

Her fellow-passenger escorted her along the deck and down to her quarters in silence.

"Happy landings," he said, and left her.

Naomi retained an impression of grey eyes that held an amused twinkle, and a pleasant voice. She also had a vague impression that he was laughing at her aloofness. Then dismissing the subject, she slept tranquilly.

On the train to Paris, they met again in the corridor.

"Had a fair crossing?" he inquired.

"Excellent." Her manner was formal.

He raised his brows quizzically.

"I wonder what you'd say if I asked you to take luncheon with me."

"I should say thank you but that it would be a physical impossibility, as I've already had it," was Naomi's reply. "I took the first service."

"My luck seems to be out. Why not come and have coffee and watch me eat?"

Naomi shook her head and was turning away when she saw the man in the brown overcoat at the opposite side of the corridor.

"May I change my mind and have coffee with you?" she asked her companion, a little breathlessly.

A half-hour spent in impersonal conversation helped Naomi to regain composure, and she returned to her compartment calmly.

After all, coincidences often occurred in real life. Her supposed shadow might have a pre-arranged errand in Paris. Indeed, that must be so, or he would not have had his passport on him.

She decided to accept that solution, forgetting Bob Deane's paragraph in *the Evening Record*.

III. GENTLEMAN OR CROOK?

Sunday afternoon, November 21st.

NAOMI MARSH'S optimism was shattered on her arrival at the Paris terminus. There was no doubt now that she was being shadowed.

The knowledge did not cheer her. At no time was the Gare du Nord an exhilarating station. On this bleak November Sunday afternoon it seemed the epitome of dank gloom.

As she walked along the platform to the exit, she was acutely conscious of the individual in the shabby brown overcoat hovering near her. His watchful black eyes, set deeply and close together in a peaked and a pallid face, reminded her of some hideous bird of prey, waiting the chance to swoop down on its victim.

Whatever his purpose was, Naomi reflected, it certainly could not be centred on her, a girl with little money who earned her own living.

No, his objective must be Vanda Quayne and probably her jewels. Also, most probably he was following in the hope of learning Vanda's address.

That, Naomi determined, he should not discover, through her. Somehow she must contrive to throw this objectionable person off the scent.

An appeal to the French police occurred to her, but was instantly rejected as being impracticable. What a fool she would look if the man declared that he had not spoken to her nor noticed her existence! Doubtless he was prepared for such a contingency as he had not troubled to disguise the fact that he was obviously trailing her.

On a corner outside the station was a large hotel, which had a second entrance in a side-street.

Walking into the vestibule, Naomi booked a room and ordered her suitcase to be taken to it.

Then she left swiftly by the other door and, turning from the side-street, hurried down a narrow alley that gave egress to a broad boulevard.

She was more than half-way down the alley when the man overtook her, and seized her wrists. Silently she struggled, endeavouring to prevent a public scene, while the man tried to wrench her handbag from her fingers.

"You didn't track me from London to steal my bag," Naomi said desperately. "What do you want?"

The man made no answer. Suddenly he released her and ran away.

"What has that scoundrel stolen?" demanded a voice that she recognized.

"Nothing," gasped Naomi in relief. Before her stood her companion of the luncheon-car. Relief changed to fear as the thought flashed into her mind that perhaps these two men were working together. "How—how curious that you happened to come along this narrow alley," she said with an evident touch of suspicion.

"Fortunate but not curious." The newcomer's eyes showed amusement. "I have imitated Mary's little lamb ever since you left the station."

Naomi thawed at his confession.

"Why?" she inquired.

"Because you didn't tell me your address when we were having coffee together. So I padded after you. I'm glad I did, in the circumstances."

"So am I," admitted Naomi. She studied him thoughtfully, and liked what she saw. A clean-shaven, lean, eager face, not too handsome; and grey eyes that she was beginning to know fairly well. For the rest he appeared to be the average, inconspicuously well-dressed Englishman of about thirty years of age, with a cultured speech that denoted education. "By the way, about that

man who attacked me, have you ever seen him before?"
She watched him keenly as she put the question.

"Yes." He paused and then added with a grin as he
observed the girl's startled look, "I saw him on the boat
after you had gone to lie down. Did you think he and I
were accomplices?"

"I am relieved to know that you are not," she fenced.

"You don't know it now. Perhaps we followed you to
Paris so that one of us could snatch your hand-bag," he
suggested.

"An expensive method it only contains a few pounds.
Maybe, like you, he wanted to know my name and
address, for some obscure reason." There was a challenge
in Naomi's last sentence.

"Forgive me, but I don't want your name. I noticed
that while your passport was being stamped. Couldn't
you decide better whether I'm nice enough to know over a
cocktail or tea? We might go back to your hotel. I'm
staying there too".

For a moment Naomi hesitated. Promiscuous
acquaintances were always to be accepted with wise
reservations. On the other hand, this young man had just
done her a considerable service. Also, her appointment
with Vanda Quayne was in less than an hour. If she went
there at once, he could easily follow; whereas in the hotel,
she might slip away unobserved.

"I'd like some tea, thank you, Mr.—" She glanced at
him questioningly.

He supplied the answer at once.

"Stephen Talbot. Most folks shorten it to Steve."

"I think I can manage two syllables, Mr. Talbot,"
Naomi told him dryly.

"I can manage three—Naomi is a delightful name, if
you'll allow me to use it."

"I'll let you know if ever I do," she retorted.

His conversation during tea, which they took in the
hotel lounge, was chiefly about books and plays. He
neither asked questions nor volunteered information

concerning himself, and for all Naomi gathered, he might have been an artist, author, man of leisure or gentleman crook.

"Shall we go to a movie and then have dinner together?" he asked as she crushed but her cigarette and rose.

"There's plenty of time. I'll decide after I've seen what sort of a room they've given me," she said, assuming a casual air.

"Don't be too long. And don't forget that you haven't told me your London address yet."

"You haven't given me yours either," was her swift answer. "Meanwhile, we're both staying in this hotel. Thank you for my tea."

Stephen Talbot lighted a fresh cigarette and watched her move gracefully across the room.

A few minutes passed, but Naomi did not return. With a frown, Stephen hurried to the reception bureau.

"Miss Marsh cannot be in her room," he was told. "Her key is still here."

The observant hall porter settled the point.

"A tall fair young lady, m'sieur. *Une Anglaise*? She asked me to call her a taxi about ten minutes ago."

IV. THE ATTACK

Sunday afternoon, November 21st

THE taxi finished its mad course through the brilliantly lighted Paris streets and, with a triumphant screech of brakes, stopped abruptly in a sombre road on the south side of the Seine.

"Here is the Convent of St. Marie-José, mademoiselle," announced the driver, opening the cab door for his passenger.

Naomi Marsh cast a dubious look at the grim grey building with a high stone garden wall on one side. From the forbidding exterior, it resembled a prison.

"I want the hospital of that name," she told the, man in excellent French, "not this place."

"It is a Convent Hospital," he explained. "The nurses are nuns. They are very kind and skilled. Mademoiselle need have no fear under their care."

The girl smiled.

"I am only going to visit a patient," she replied. Crossing the pavement, she pulled the bell-chain. Its clanging summons was answered by an elderly nun in black garments.

"May I see Miss Vanda Quayne?"Naomi inquired. Adding as the woman hesitated: "She is expecting me. I am Miss Marsh."

"Please follow me," the nun directed. Conducting the visitor to a sparsely furnished waiting-room, she left her.

Naomi glanced at the bare floor and wooden chairs with a touch of amusement. Surely this was the last place where one would expect to find the gay South American dancer! What was such a sophisticated and exotic creature doing in this atmosphere of austerity?

In a few moments the mystery was unravelled by another nun, white-robed and young.

"Miss Quayne has had a slight attack of *la grippe*," she informed Naomi. "There is no risk of infection now. I will take you to her."

In silence she led the visitor along polished corridors until they came to a door at the end of the building.

"Kindly ring when you wish to go," she said, and pattered softly away.

Naomi drew in her breath with a resolve not to be depressed by this cold reception, and opened the door.

The amazing difference inside Vanda Quayne's room gave the English girl a shock of surprise. Masses of expensive flowers were grouped in vases, bizarre shawls and cushions, flung across the couch and chairs, glowed richly against the drab painted: wails, and signed photographs in ornate frames stood on table and mantelshelf. The only light was from a reading lamp near, the couch.

French windows, half open, led to a verandah, beyond which Naomi caught a glimpse of a walled garden, barren and desolate in the dusk of this wintry day.

The room was empty but presently there was a step on the verandah and Vanda Quayne appeared. Framed in the open window, she stood appraising the figure of the visitor.

"I expected you earlier than this, Miss Marsh," she said in slow drawling tones that expressed annoyance.

"My train was late," Naomi replied evenly but without apology. She had no intention of cringing to her new employer.

Flinging aside the fur cloak and scarf she was wearing, Vanda sank languidly on to the couch. With a touch she adjusted the shade of the reading-lamp so that it shed a becoming glow upon herself, leaving the rest of the room in semi-darkness.

"Sit down," she ordered, scanning critically the slim tailored elegance of her caller.

Naomi selected a chair facing the dancer, who had her back to the window.

"You have a determined character, I fancy," Vanda remarked.

"I need it in my work, Miss Quayne."

"Also you are better looking than your photograph," continued the other, rather grudgingly.

Naomi was silent, feeling that in truth she could not return the compliment. Vanda's eyes that looked so dark and lustrous on the screen merely appeared hard and rather dull now, and the black 'shining hair' seemed heavy and lifeless. Vanda Quayne, however, had undeniably beautiful features and an alluring quality in her personality.

"We are absolute contrasts," she observed after a close scrutiny of Naomi's pale gold hair, blue eyes, and delicate proud face that matched the English girl's air of distinction. "I wonder which type men prefer?"

Naomi raised her eyebrows. "Is the point in question, Miss Quayne? I am here as your prospective and temporary secretary and not your rival. You have your world, and I have mine."

"That is true." The dancer studied her speculatively. "By the way, what is your world, Miss Marsh? Where do you live? With my jewels and money, I am exposed to many dangers, so I like to know something about those whom I employ."

Naomi felt that the argument was reasonable, although she was a little sceptical about the suggestion of danger.

"I sent you my personal references," she reminded Vanda. "When I am in London I share a flat with a girl friend who runs a beauty parlour."

Vanda leaned forward.

"Can you mind your own business?" she demanded in a low, provocative tone.

Naomi smiled.

"You mean can I hold my tongue about yours? Yes, Miss Quayne."

"Good. I've had secretaries who were prigs and lectured me on my habits, and I've had others who were spies and sold lying information about me to the press and elsewhere," explained the dancer. "A woman of my looks and position attracts men. I have many admirers, Miss Marsh. Publicity is necessary to my career, but notoriety can be damaging. I am willing to pay extra for your silence. Do you understand?"

Naomi bowed frigidly.

"Loyalty to my employer is included in my salary, Miss Quayne," she replied, with inward contempt for the *naiveté* of this woman.

There was nothing dull, however, in the astute glance that Vanda turned upon her.

"You English are naturally a truthful race, so I believe you," she said. "Your cheque will date from to-day, although I shall not want your services until I reach London."

"When will that be?

Vanda thought for a while.

"This is Sunday. I will cross on Thursday with my maid," she stated. "Go back as soon as possible. I shall book a suite at the Ritz. Meet me there when you receive my cable. My business manager, Mr. Ferrari, will arrange for suitable publicity concerning my arrival. I have cabaret and music-hall engagements and then I am to star as dancer in an English film. I shall need you for four or five months."

The desolate garden was no longer visible in the growing darkness, Naomi noticed subconsciously, while Vanda Quayne was speaking. Only the outline of the French window behind the dancer could be seen in the narrow circle of light from the lamp.

Suddenly Naomi peered across the room uneasily. No one could have passed along that verandah without being seen by her, yet the window which had been ajar was now wide open.

"It is getting dark, Miss Quayne. Shall I close the shutters?" she asked, forcing herself to speak normally.

"No. This room is overheated," Vanda replied.

"By the way, I suppose you have decent evening dresses. I like my secretary to be—Why, what's wrong?" she demanded as she saw the girl staring at the window.

Naomi's eyes dilated as she noticed a black shadowy form in the open window. Could it be the curtain swaying in the breeze?

The shadow moved, loomed larger. For the fraction of a second Naomi watched a shrouded uplifted arm rising, as if with menace, above the dancer on the couch. Then with a deft movement she dragged Vanda to the floor, knocking the table-lamp over.

There was a crash as the electric bulb exploded.

In the darkness Naomi heard stealthy stumbling movements, the sound of quick breathing.

Then the window was closed and there was silence.

V. A Date For Murder

Sunday afternoon, November 21st.

VANDA was the first to speak.

"Put on the light. There's a switch by the door," she ordered.

She glanced composedly around the room when Naomi had obeyed her.

"Is anybody in the corridor, Miss Marsh?" Naomi opened the door and looked.

"No," she reported. "Shall I ring for the nurse?"

"Certainly not. Even nuns can talk. This is not the kind of publicity I want. What did you see?" Naomi bit her lip.

"I thought I saw something behind you. I can't be sure. It was very dark behind the reading-lamp. Perhaps it was only a shadow on the wall caused by the curtain blowing in a sudden gust of wind."

"You were wise to act quickly," the dancer remarked. She lifted a small dark object from the floor. "The wind didn't blow this in."

Naomi examined it—a man's glove containing a large lead weight.

"You didn't believe me when I said I was exposed to danger." Vanda's voice had an acid tang in it. "Well, it's true, you see. From threats I've received recently, I expected something of this nature. It was a feeble effort. My opponent may be more successful next time."

Against her will, Naomi was forced to admiration of the actress's coolness.

"You are very plucky, but if you know who your enemy is, why not obtain police protection?" she asked.

"Can I go round the world with a tame detective?" demanded Vanda scornfully. "Probably I have dozens of enemies with varying grudges against me."

She paused as someone knocked on the door. A dark-haired maid in uniform entered.

"Can I do anything for you, mademoiselle?" she inquired. "I am free for an hour."

Vanda thought for a moment.

"Yes, Henriette. Get me a bottle of cognac," she said, taking out some money. "You may keep the change."

"I am not supposed to leave the hospital, mademoiselle, but I can go out by the garden door and no one will see me," the maid replied. "It is only a few steps from there to the wine shop."

"Very well," Vanda agreed. "Slip on my fur wrap and scarf or the nuns might notice your white cap and apron."

Henriette's face beamed with pleasure as she drew the expensive coat round her and tied the scarf over her head. This indeed would be something to boast of to her friends.

She went along the verandah and Naomi heard her footsteps as she ran down the gravelled path.

"Henriette is a wardmaid," Vanda explained. "She has made quite a bit by doing my errands. I was going to tell you about my life. I was born and brought up in Rio; my father was Spanish and ran a gambling house. My mother was of fine old American stock. She was a brave woman who was stabbed while trying to save my father. She didn't succeed in doing so. He deserved his fate."

Vanda lighted a cigarette as if dismissing the matter.

"At fifteen I started to make my own way in the world," she went on. "I am beautiful, successful and rich. Men of all ranks and races have been in love with me." She shrugged her shoulders. "I tire of them and pass on. They naturally become angry and jealous. Apart from them, there are those rivals in my profession who hate and envy me. Also," she smiled cynically, "I have a circle of special enemies, most of them in England."

"It certainly complicates the difficulty of tracking down your most potent enemy," admitted Naomi. "However, you will be safe in London."

The dancer shook her head.

"On the contrary, Miss Marsh, I am assured that I shall not be safe there." Her lips curved in contempt. "There is sufficient of my mother's blood in my veins to make me determined to go there."

"Won't you be inviting further assaults on your life if you advertise publicly that you are staying at the Ritz?"

Vanda sat silently considering the point for a while.

"Find me a furnished house in a quiet locality where there's a large room with a parquet floor," she said. "Nicola, my, new dancing partner, can come there to practise with me."

"There's a house to let nearly opposite where live, Miss Quayne. It lies back in a walled-in garden and has a huge ground-floor studio. The furniture is quite nice. One of my employers took it for a while last year so I know the landlord."

"Fix it up with him and engage the necessary servants," was Vanda's request when they had discussed the terms. "Take it in your name. As a precaution, only you, Nicola and my manager shall know my address."

"I'm afraid it will soon leak out."

The dancer shrugged her shoulders complacently. "That is so. After the end of this month there may be no need for secrecy—perhaps in a grim sense."

She paused and demanded sharply: "How did you know that I wanted a temporary secretary?"

"Through my employment bureau."

Vanda nodded.

"I see. In my peculiar circumstances I have to be sure that you are not in league with my enemies. Ah, here comes Henriette with the cognac," she exclaimed as she heard quick steps from the garden

"You must drink to my success in London before you go."

The footsteps came nearer. Suddenly they merged into a scuffle, followed by a thud and the crash of glass.

"My poor brandy!" Vanda raised her hands in mock despair.

"Your poor coat!" Naomi said practically. "Let me see if it escaped the deluge."

Vanda checked her.

"No, I'll go. In case any of the nurses have seen Henriette, I can explain why she went out against the rules."

Naomi listened intently as Vanda went slowly along the verandah and down the steps. The clip-clop of the dancer's heels were the only sounds that broke the stillness.

It might have been one minute or two before Vanda returned bearing the coat. Shivering slightly, she closed and fastened the window.

"It's turning colder," she remarked. "I'd rather have one good fire than all these radiators."

"Your fur wrap is not stained, I hope." Naomi felt her heart beating more quickly. Was it her fancy that Vanda's face looked hard and strange?

"It's all right." The dancer spoke indifferently as though her thoughts were elsewhere.

"Was the girl cut by the broken glass?"

"Oh no. A bit ashamed of her carelessness. She has gone round to the kitchen." Vanda gazed steadily at Naomi. "I suppose you thought that my enemy had come back and mistaken the girl for me. If you're afraid of being mixed up in anything unpleasant that might happen, Miss Marsh, you'd better back out of our engagement now."

"I'm not at all afraid," Naomi declared. And I think you will be in no danger in London."

"We shall see. I'll put this coat away and get my cheque-book."

The dancer went into the adjoining room. In a few minutes she returned carrying a small parcel.

"Here's a cheque for expenses, Miss Marsh," she said. "Lock this packet away carefully until we meet in London."

Naomi took the cheque and the small sealed parcel which Vanda gave her.

"In case you cherish any ideas that I am imagining this threat of murder," Vanda continued calmly, "you may be interested to know that a date, or rather a time-limit, has been more or less fixed. To-day is the twenty-first of November. I have been advised that my friends can order wreaths for the end of this month." She held out her hand. "Good-bye. *Bon voyage.*"

VI. THE MYSTERIOUS PARCEL

Sunday evening, November 21st.

NAOMI MARSH came down the hospital steps and looked up and down the unlighted, depressing street. It was evidently not a bus route and there was only one vehicle in sight, stationary, a few yards away.

She was walking towards it when a voice made her jump.

"Taxi, miss? Carry your parcels?" was the hopeful inquiry.

With frowning brow she faced the speaker. "You again, Mr. Talbot," she remarked icily.

"Me again," he agreed with a cheerful gin. "Isn't it a coincidence?"

"A trifle too fortuitous this time, and in very bad taste."

The man stroked his cheek pensively.

"Not bad taste," he objected. "Let me drive you back to the hotel."

"I prefer to take a taxi, thank you."

"I'll bet one won't pass through this benighted neighbourhood for hours. Besides, I've been waiting ages for you."

"I can't think why." Naomi's tone expressed indignation.

Stephen Talbot was unabashed.

"Can't you?" he asked easily. "Do you see who is just passing that lamp across the road? If that's not your pal who tried to snatch your handbag I need strong spectacles.

Undoubtedly, Naomi saw, it was the man in the shabby brown overcoat.

"Perhaps you and he are hunting in couples," she suggested, trying to speak calmly although her pulse was throbbing in hard beats.

"My dear Miss Marsh, you do me wrong," Stephen declared dramatically. "He needs dry cleaning before we go poaching together."

"Why not have him sent away then if you take such a kindly interest in me?"

"Have I said that I do." Stephen demanded. "In any case, there are limits to my generosity considering that you won't even tell me your London address."

Naomi gave an exasperated laugh. "You know so much that I dare say you've discovered that too."

"You may be right. I'm a clever bloke," he observed complacently.

"You're an intolerable nuisance, and a complete humbug," Naomi retorted with heat.

"Now that shows we're real friends since you've started abusing me. Come along," Stephen urged as the taximan hooted, "cabby is getting impatient. Do I have to carry you or will you go quietly?" he added as she drew back.

His strong grasp on her arm made her realize that further resistance would be futile and ridiculous. Also that strange experience in Vanda Quayne's room had unnerved her. Could the man in the brown overcoat have been Vanda's assailant? The garden door was almost opposite where he was standing. Yet surely he would have made his escape at once, instead of hanging about like this.

Another solution occurred to her: might it not equally well have been Stephen Talbot who had slung that weighted glove at Vanda?

"How long were you waiting here?" she asked him as the taxi moved off.

"Long enough for me to get very hungry."

"Did you see anyone enter the garden door?"

"What garden and which door?" he inquired.

"The convent garden. There's a door in the wall."

"Where have you lived all your sweet young life, child? There are doors in walls everywhere. People use them, you know, to get into their houses. What's in your parcel?"

Naomi felt it would have been a great relief to slap his unperturbed face as he prodded the sealed packet which Vanda had given into her care.

"Leave it alone," she snapped irritably, tucking it under her handbag.

He sniffed at his finger for a moment and then grinned broadly.

"Nice girls shouldn't have nasty habits," he commented. "Give it up before it's too late."

"Give up what?"

"Brandy." Stephen touched the packet again. "Have you soaked a sponge in it?"

"Of course not: neither have I drunk any."

"Then I suppose you poured some into a paper bag. That packet is quite damp." He pulled down one of the turn-up seats in front of them. "Put it there or you'll stain your skirt."

Naomi did as he suggested, her mind occupied with a curious question. What had Vanda placed in that small parcel?

Suddenly as a street lamp lighted the taxi, she noticed that her white gloves had a darkish stain. Brandy surely was paler than that. With a gesture of unreasoning repugnance she stripped off the gloves and thrust them into her handbag.

She heard herself replying normally to Stephen's remarks, while her thoughts turned back to the incident of Henriette's fall in the garden.

Bit by bit she tried to piece together all that had followed the crash of glass. Had the maid fallen accidentally, or had Vanda's assailant still been lurking in the garden? If so, in the darkness he could easily have imagined that the wearer of Vanda's coat and scarf was Vanda!

The coat Vanda had taken into her bedroom. But where was the scarf?

Naomi strove to shake off these questions which were hammering in her mind. If the maid had been injured, Vanda would have called for help, of course. Besides, she had said, and calmly, that Henriette had run round to the kitchen.

On the other hand, Naomi had heard no footsteps save those of the dancer, no word had been spoken, and Vanda had previously said that publicity about any attack upon her might be damaging!

Suppose Vanda had found the girl injured and unconscious and decided swiftly to let people think it was an accident! Suppose—Naomi's brain reeled at any further conjecture.

Straining every effort for composure, she forced the horrifying thoughts away.

"We're almost back at the hotel," Stephen Talbot was saying. "Shall we dine and go to a movie?"

"If you like." She felt that any company would be preferable to solitude.

He gave her an odd glance as the taxi stopped.

"Pull yourself together." His sharp tone braced her nerves. "Here's your parcel." He folded a newspaper round it and slung the seat back into its position. But not before she had noticed a reddish smear, on the light linen covering!

In her room, she locked the packet, newspaper and all, into her suitcase, without daring to look at it again.

Over dinner, which they took in the hotel, Naomi's courage revived.

"That's better," Stephen observed as he studied her face. "Was the glamorous Vanda too much for you?"

The glass nearly dropped from her fingers. "So you knew where I was going!"

Stephen's eyes twinkled with amusement.

"I read the papers at times, and I happen to remember what I read. Last night's *Record* told me that Vanda Quayne was engaging a Miss Naomi Marsh as secretary, and interviewing her in Paris today. I saw your name on your passport."

Naomi was not satisfied by his explanation.

"Do you know Vanda Quayne?" she asked.

"My dear child, didn't she tell you that she was hopelessly in love with me?"

"Do be serious, Mr. Talbot. Are you a reporter?"

"Heaven forbid."

"Then how did you find out where Vanda was staying? I went away after tea so that you shouldn't follow me."

He raised her hand and studied the slender fingers for a moment.

"I'm a persistent person," he told her. "You gave me the slip and I was annoyed. It was quite simple to telephone to the theatre where Vanda had been dancing before she was ill, get her address, and chase after you. You had a good start, but I know how to pull strings."

"How long were you there before I came out?" Naomi's eyes had an anxious look.

"You asked me that before. Long enough to develop a healthy appetite."

"Was the man in the brown overcoat there before you arrived?"

"Did you think we shared the taxi?" he parried in a bantering tone.

"Please tell me," she begged.

"It might have been a dead heat or he might have been on your heels when you ran away from the hotel." Stephen's eyes narrowed. "Does it matter?" he demanded keenly.

"No, no, of course not. I was upset after he had tried to snatch my bag, and it alarmed me to see him outside the hospital."

There was now a glint of steel in Stephen's grey eyes. "If that is all you have to be alarmed about," he said significantly, "you need not worry."

But that was not all. Locked in her case was a packet, with a brownish stain on the wrapping. "I've a headache and think I'll go to bed early," she said as they finished dinner.

"A good idea," he agreed. "In that case we'll have coffee here. It's quieter than in the lounge. Will you forgive me for a few minutes? I've an urgent call to make. You won't run away while I'm gone, will you?"

"Not this time," she promised.

Stephen returned after a while, looking extremely che'erful.

"Apparently you got your number quickly," Naomi observed as she rose to leave him.

"Yes; there was no delay at all. Good night," he said coolly.

A little piqued that he had not asked when they could meet again, she obtained her key at the desk and went to her room.

With her heart beating quickly, she went to her suitcase. It was unlocked and the packet had gone!

VII. Seclusion

Monday morning, November 22nd.

THERE was no sign of Stephen Talbot in the vestibule next morning, and no note from him.

A few minutes before Naomi was due to leave for her train, she asked rather diffidently at the bureau if Mr. Talbot was in the hotel.

"Monsieur left early this morning," was the clerk's reply. His bold eyes stared at her curiously. Had he not seen the couple have tea and dinner together yesterday? Presumably there had been a quarrel which mademoiselle was trying to patch up.

On the journey to London, she caught no glimpse of either Talbot or her trailer in the brown overcoat. It was highly possible that they were confederates who had followed her to Paris because of her connection with Vanda Quayne. One or both of them might have been responsible for the fruitless attack on the dancer, and it was certain that Stephen Talbot had taken the packet from her suitcase. That alone stamped him as a man whose actions were not above suspicion.

The question was, why had he taken it? Could he have imagined that it contained valuables with which Vanda had entrusted her?

Naomi pulled out her soiled white gloves and examined them. True, there was a faint odour of spirit, but those dark patches certainly never originated from brandy.

With a shiver she thrust the gloves into her bag as the train drew slowly into Victoria. At the first opportunity she would destroy them and forget the horrid incident.

On the platform stood Phil Ingram. Naomi felt she had never before been so glad to see her friend's cheerful face.

"What about that little ferret-eyed rat who was shadowing you?" Phil demanded on the way back to their flat.

"I soon lost sight of him," Naomi said evasively. She knew herself to be unequal to a discussion on that subject just yet.

Instead, she spoke of her new employer's intention to take a furnished house and keep the address quiet for a while.

"What an extraordinary idea!" Phil exclaimed. "Vanda Quayne always chooses publicity and the most luxurious hotel." Her eyes grew shrewd. "Is there any reason for hiding her highly coloured light under a bushel?"

Naomi was silent for a moment. Phil would be bound to know if Vanda Quayne took the house, opposite their flat.

"I'll tell you when we reach home," she said, feeling a need to confide her worries in someone.

After supper Phil listened attentively to the history of her friend's eventful Sunday in Paris.

"Nice goings on for a respectable lass like you," she summed up. "I smell trouble, Naomi, if not worse. Take my advice: cut the whole business and take a permanent job."

"No." There was an obstinate expression in Naomi's face. "I shall see it through after—"

"After what?" Phil demanded crisply as Naomi broke off.

"After Vanda's pluck on Sunday," was the lame reply.

"Listen to me, Naomi. That's not the cause of your confounded obstinacy. You can hold your tongue if you wish, but don't try to spoon-feed me with half-truths. I'm past that stage. For Vanda, I don't care two hoots; she'll deserve whatever is coming to her. Why were you so anxious to get this job with her?"

"Oh, it came along and I thought it would be fun."

Phil gave her an odd glance.

"Nonsense, it didn't come along. You ran after it—hard. I met your agent to-day and he told me that you had urged him to write to Vanda's manager in Paris and suggest your name."

"What if I did, Phil?"

"It doesn't tally with your statement that Vanda's manager applied to your bureau for a secretary," Phil retorted bluntly. She gave a broad smile. "All right, my pig-headed lass, go your own way, but don't expect me to pull you out if you land yourself in a hole."

"Try to keep Bob Deane off my track, and you'll do me a great service," replied Naomi in a subdued voice.

"If that reporter person shows his impudent nose round here, I'll give him a face-lift so that his own mother wouldn't know him." Phil's glance became keen. "What about this Stephen Talbot? Has he faded out of your young life?"

"Of course," Naomi declared with vigour. "I shall be too busy to think of inquisitive young men for the next two days. I must take the house and get necessary staff by Thursday. Dare I risk engaging our landlady's husband as chef, or will he talk?"

Phil reflected.

"Skinny Gibbs is an excellent cook, and he won't talk much while he's sober. On the whole, I believe you can take a chance on him. Put it up to his wife to-morrow. Flossie's a wise old bird."

Mrs. Gibbs—better known as "Flossie"—welcomed Naomi's proposal on behalf of her spouse, with whom she lived in the basement flat of her house.

"A job of work'll do Skinny a power of good, Miss Marsh," she replied. "I'll make him keep silent about who he's working for. I'm afraid he'll guess it's Vanda Quayne because he read that bit in last Saturday's *Record* about you being her secretary. I'll fetch him up."

Her ample form vanished to reappear shortly with the spare figure and melancholy countenance of her husband.

Skinny Gibbs sighed heavily as Naomi issued urgent instructions for secrecy.

"Not a word shall pass my lips, miss," he promised, adding an elaborate form of oath peculiar to his kind.

"See that whisky doesn't either," his wife warned him.

Skinny had no intention of breaking his word.

Unfortunately he felt that the prospect of his return to lucrative work called for suitable celebration with a select circle of friends. By Wednesday morning the news had reached the sensitive ears of Bob Deane, of the *Evening Record*.

Unable to find Naomi, he went to Phil Ingram's beauty parlour.

"What do you want?" she snapped ungraciously.

"There's a pretty rumour that Vanda Quayne has taken a furnished house," Bob remarked.

"H'm. Hoofed off your paper, and starting in the house-agency business, I suppose."

A grin spread itself across the reporter's impudent features.

"You won't escape me by that line, Phil," he told her. "Be a sport. Give me the news."

"You're a cheap gossip writer, not a crime reporter."

Bob Deane shook his forefinger to and fro.

"Vanda Quayne always makes a good story; not so far off my beat either. Last month her name was linked up with a man who committed suicide. Who knows, this time there might be a murder. Come clean, sister. Vanda's taken a house in Warne Road nearly opposite your flat, hasn't she?"

"What fantastic tales you weak-minded young men get hold of." Phil gave a bored yawn. "Now I'll tell you one. Have you heard that Vanda has taken a large place on the Thames?"

Bob stared.

"No. What's it called?" he asked eagerly.

The Houses of Parliament."

"All right, Phil. You had your chance," he said in meaning tones. "Skinny Gibbs gave me the works an hour ago, but I wanted to verify details. Watch the *Evening Record* to-night. All the world will love to read of Vanda gone as shy as the Garbo."

It was nearly seven o'clock that evening when Naomi entered her flat.

"Sorry I'm late, Phil," she said to her friend. "I've had a full day fixing everything up. However, it's all gone well. I've taken the house in my name and engaged two Scottish maids new to London, who, I am sure, have never even heard of Vanda Quayne."

"You could have spared yourself the trouble," observed Phil. "Look at this." She gave Naomi a copy of that evening's *Record* and pointed to an article:

VANDA QUAYNE'S RETREAT

A famous and beautiful South American dancer and film star, who is descending upon London, has chosen for her temporary home the seclusion of a house in St. John's Wood.

With her entourage, Vanda Quayne will take up residence at Briar Lodge, Warne Road to-morrow.

Is there a romance attached to this decision? It will be remembered—

Naomi scanned the lines and flung down the paper. "That's Bob Deane's fell work, of course."

Phil nodded.

"Yep. There's also a photograph of the house on another page. Skinny Gibbs got tight and talked."

"I ought not to have engaged him as chef," Naomi said in uneasy tones.

"Nonsense. As Bob says, Vanda is news. Anyone else on her staff would have talked sooner or later. You did your best, and if Vanda shows her teeth, I'll drop in and show mine."

Naomi gazed abstractedly across the room.

"I wonder," she said, "how many people reading this article to-night have a personal grudge against Vanda?"

"And I wonder whether your grey-eyed knight, one Stephen Talbot, will be interested?" remarked Phil.

VIII. CAMEOS

Wednesday evening, November. 24th.

AN elderly woman gave her son a pleased smile as he entered the sitting-room of a small house in Kilburn.

"You look tired, dear," she said in concerned tones. "Bank clerks work longer hours than they used to. For your sake I wish we could afford to live nearer Westminster."

"I don't mind the distance, mother," the young man replied; shirking any further fiction on his part about being delayed at his bank.

The mother studied his haggard face anxiously. Cyril had never looked the same since his year at the Berlin branch. She watched him now as he moved aimlessly about the room as if something were troubling his mind.

"I'm getting short of cash for household expenses, dear," she remarked. "Has my dividend been paid yet?"

There was a flicker of hesitation before he answered.

"It will be along in a few days, I expect, mother. I can let you have a fiver meanwhile."

"There's no need. I'd rather wait for my own money. You pay your share weekly."

"Has the evening paper come?" he asked.

His mother passed him a copy of the *Record*, noticing presently that he turned from page to page before he had time to read anything.

"Cyril, if those shares you asked me to invest in have gone wrong, don't be afraid to tell me." Her voice was gentle.

The young man faced her with a hunted expression in his eyes.

"They have, mother. I had no right to sell your gilt-edged stock and put it into a wild cat mine. It may turn out all right one day, but I doubt it. You ought never to have trusted me to invest your money."

His mother smiled whimsically.

"I've been through worse troubles than that, my son. We'll manage somehow. You acted only in my interests."

If he could only tell her the whole truth, Cyril reflected bitterly, the reason for that mad investment!

Keeping back three hundred pounds of his mother's capital, he had bought some mining shares with the rest. The higher dividends they promised would have kept her income the same as before. And now—

His glance caught a headline on the paper he still held. Vanda Quayne! The cause of it all.

His brief infatuation for the dancer whom he had met when she was in Berlin was dead as ashes. It was for her that he had robbed his mother.

Vanda had coveted a pendant and asked Cyril to buy it, saying that she was short of cash but would pay him in a few days. Eager to please her, and flattered at the request, he had borrowed the money from a friendly German colleague in his bank. In her dressing-room at the theatre before a crowd of people, Vanda had kissed him effusively and thanked him for his—gift!

In vain he tried to see her next day; wrote explaining that he must have her cheque. She refused to see him and did not reply to his letters. The next week she had left Germany.

Cyril had returned to his London branch a little later, and in order to repay the German who was becoming importunate, had done this deal in shares with his mothers capital.

With clenched teeth, he fought back his rage as he read now of the dancer's forthcoming visit.

Vanda should pay him, he determined, even if he had to take it from her by force.

* * * * *

"Pint o' bitter, miss," demanded the man in a shabby brown overcoat.

He leaned against the counter in the Fox and Grapes and cast a wary eye round while waiting to be supplied.

From the far end of the bar a heavily built man lurched towards the newcomer, and grasping his arm, drew him to a quiet corner.

"Back from furrin parts, I see," the burly one remarked meaningly. "Who've you been working for, Weazel?"

"You've made a mistake," declared the other. "I've been laid up with the 'flu, Corney. Haven't been out of the house for nearly a week."

"Then it must have been your ghost, overcoat and all, that went to gay Paree last Sunday," Corney retorted. "It's no use stalling, Weazel. You never could keep your trap shut when you'd had a few drinks. We guessed you was up to some game when you didn't come on Sunday, so I put my gal on to you on Monday night. After a couple o' pints, you were boasting about your fine job and your trip to Paris."

"What if I did?" The Weazel attempted defiance. "I ain't tied to you and your bunch."

Corney regarded him with a menacing expression.

"You made a date to act as watch on Sunday night when we cracked that crib in Holborn. Two of us had to work it alone and nearly got nabbed."

"I'm getting scared of that sort o' business, Corney." The Weazel sucked in his breath, determined to act boldly. "Now I've got a straight job, I'm cutting out your stuff"

"Oh, you are, eh? All you were any use for was to act as spy while we took the risks, but you were mighty glad to share the dough. And another thing, what game are you up to with Filmer. You were in his café for hours."

The Weazel was apparently pained at the crude question.

"Can't a fellow have a meal in a resterong?" he countered.

"Yes, if he don't have heart-to-heart talks with the proprietor, who's a nasty squealer called Filmer. I suppose he didn't speak of Vanda Quayne by any chance?" Corney's eyes had a leering expression.

"Course not," the Weazel asserted. "Who's she?"

"Stow it." Corney's hand came down in a contemptuous gesture. "You know who she is, and everybody knows that Filmer hopes to get money out of her. He was in Rio for years. He's got something coming to him for squealing on me, only he don't know it yet."

"I swear I ain't working for Filmer." The Weazel's words had a ring of truth. "He was asking me a few questions about Vanda, now I come to think of it."

"You bet he was," Corney assured him. "Well, if you ain't working for Filmer—and I can't see what use he'd have for you—what are you doing?"

"Sort of following somebody," faltered the Weazel, and emptied his glass.

Corney slapped him on the shoulder.

"Fine!" he said heartily. "In the circs, we'll excoose you for a while."

Corney waited until the Weazel left the bar before he joined two of his companions.

"That little rat is watching Vanda Quayne," he informed them. "Some swell must have got hold of him. It's not Filmer, I'm sure."

"Phew!" exclaimed one man. "There's a bit about her in to-night's *Record*. Look." He pulled a newspaper from his pocket and showed the article.

"Warne Road," Corney remarked after reading. "Nice and quiet in that part. You follow the Weazel, Nifty. He don't know you. We'll let him lead us to whatever he's after, the double-crossing little skunk."

* * * * *

Stephen Talbot laid down the evening newspaper and stared thoughtfully at his feet which were on the mantelpiece. From them, his gaze wandered round the comfortably furnished sitting-room of his flat in Mayfair.

Receiving no inspiration there, he addressed his friend who was asleep in another arm-chair.

"Bored, that's what I am," he remarked. "Little did I think when I was sweating hard for a living that I'd regret Uncle Bill's legacy. What are we going to do about it, Barry?"

Stephen's companion opened one eye, and apparently being uninterested in what he saw, yawned loudly and closed it again.

"You're no help," Stephen commented sulkily. "For all you care I can get into mischief through nosing into other people's affairs. This time I'm heading straight for trouble, I'm sure. You're nothing but a selfish lout, snoring away while I'm aching for a spot of excitement to wake things up. Who said you could sleep in that chair, anyway? I've a good mind to run over to Paris again and leave you, or," he raised his voice a little, "go for a good long walk alone."

At the word "walk" his friend was galvanized into sudden activity.

"Now you're talking sense," Barry told him as plainly as a spaniel could speak. "Come on, let's go."

Stephen eyed the eager animal plaintively.

"That's all very well, my lad, but I want some fun too. I think we'll pay a surprise call on a beautiful and mysterious young lady. You might be welcome; I know I shan't be. Still, even a row is preferable to boredom."

IX. Stephen Drops In

Wednesday night, November 24th.

"A LETTER for you, Naomi. Paris postmark." The two girls were in the kitchen, clearing away after their evening meal.

"It's from Vanda Quayne. She arrives at the house about five o'clock to-morrow," Naomi said a few moments later. "It's quite short. Read it if you like."

Phil shook her head.

"I'm dying to, but I won't let my ugly curiosity get the better of me. We'll start as we must go on, so long as you're her secretary."

"Miss Quayne says I'm to wear a smart dress and have cocktails ready. Her manager, Mr. Ferrari, who acts as her press agent, and Nicola, her dancing partner, will be there."

"Have you met either of 'em?" Phil demanded.

"Not yet. I'd better try on my new afternoon frock to see if it's all right. Hello, that's the telephone bell. I'll answer it."

Going into the hall, Naomi lifted the receiver.

Her expression hardened as she listened to the brief message. Then, the call ended, she went to her room and dressed with deliberate care, trying to forget the orders she had just received.

She was calm when Phil appeared to see the effect of the dress.

"It's lovely, Naomi. You look like a tall Madonna lily. Who rang up?"

Naomi adjusted a wave of hair.

"The caller didn't give his name or address," she said. "He suggested in a few pithy words and an East End accent that if I didn't give up my job with Vanda it would be the worse for me."

"The gent seems to have common sense and be kindly disposed towards you, anyway," Phil observed dryly.

"The threat that garnished his remarks rather does away with that theory. It makes no difference to my intentions, of course."

"It wouldn't," Phil said in terse tones. She listened for a moment. "Somebody's in the sitting-room, Naomi. I thought I heard our front door open a moment ago. I must have left the latch up again. See who it is while I make the coffee."

"Surely it can't be Bob Deane!" Naomi exclaimed. "He would never dare to come here after his article in to-night's *Record*."

It was Bob Deane, however, she found; quite unrepentant and very much at his ease, lying on the couch by the fire.

"You two seem to have dug yourselves in pretty comfortably," he remarked with kindly patronage. "For an attic flat, it's really creditable."

Naomi's chin tilted.

"I wish I approved of your efforts as much as you do of ours," she said icily. "Are you making a lengthy stay to our poor home?"

The young man helped himself to a cigarette.

"As long as possible, most gracious hostess. I'm tired and cold: a nap will freshen my great brain for further literary labours."

"You must need sleep badly," Naomi retorted.

"Lovely one, your taste begins and ends with interior decoration." Deane turned his head languidly and scanned the girl's green gown with its swinging gold girdle. "That's a gorgeous affair. Going to a party or is this only a dress rehearsal? The latter, I fancy, as you are wearing outdoor shoes. Perhaps Vanda is giving an arrival 'do' to-morrow," he added shrewdly.

"Didn't you say that the great brain needed sleep?"

"Never when it smells a story, beautiful. What time does Vanda come?"

Annoyance gleamed in Naomi'.s blue eyes. "I have nothing to tell you about Miss Quayne, Bob."

"Don't worry: I'll find out. Enjoy your trip to Paris? No answer, as before. However, I'll try to bear up. Skinny Gibbs, when expensively oiled, has been and still might be a mine of information."

"You will feel a proud man if you cost him his job," Naomi observed.

She looked up with relief as Phil came into the room carrying a tray.

"You here again!" the latter remarked as she saw the reporter.

"No, I sailed for New York yesterday," he replied. "Three lumps and lots of cream."

"One lump and no cream," Phil snapped, as she poured the coffee.

"Let me see, Phil. You're great at arranging flowers, aren't you? I'll bet Naomi has roped you in to make Vanda Quayne's rooms a bower of roses to-morrow," Bob said. "Like to take me along to help? I've a delightful touch at that sort of thing. Once I made a wreath for a pet cat's grave."

"I'd make a beauty for yours," Phil rapped back. Her glance flashed from the complacent impudence of Deane's face to Naomi's strained expression. "I dislike committing murders after six pip emma, but I'm almost willing to in this case, Bob. If you kept to your own job instead—"

She broke off as the bell rang and went to answer it in no amiable frame of mind.

Outside the door was a tall young man in a wet mackintosh, accompanied by a spaniel.

"We've called uninvited to see Miss Naomi Marsh," the visitor stated, when Phil looked hard at him. His grey eyes crinkled with amusement as he added with engaging confidence, "I shan't be greeted as the prodigal son, I'm afraid. The name is Talbot, Stephen Talbot. May we come in—that is if you don't object to dogs?"

"At the present moment, I prefer dogs to human beings," Phil said bluntly. "As for you, well, you can't be worse than what we've got here already. Come in, both of you. I'm Naomi's friend, Phil Ingram. What's your dog called?"

"Barry." Stephen's brows lifted in a puzzled manner as she stooped to pat the animal's soft muzzle. "Haven't we met before?"

"No. That's rather a stereotyped opening for a travelled man, isn't it?" Phil's tone was curt.

"Do travelled people act differently from other folk?" he inquired mildly.

"They ought at least to be experienced enough to avoid clichés that fall from the lips of an errand boy," she said with rising temper.

"A mere trip to Paris surely doesn't make one travelled or experienced," he argued lightly. "Or does it?" he rapped with sharpness.

"How do I know, Mr. Talbot? I'm the stay-at-home type."

"I see." He nodded. "Let's call it a blank then: we haven't met before. Is Miss Marsh as cross as you are?"

Phil seemed relieved by the change of topic.

"She has every reason to be. Naomi has had a trying evening. Do what you like to our precious guest, but go gently with her."

Stephen hesitated.

"It's rough luck for her to have two unwelcome visitors. Maybe I'd better fade out."

"Maybe you won't be so unwelcome as the reptile of a reporter who is inside. I suppose you couldn't chuck him out."

"Why not?"

"Why indeed." A broad smile spread over Phil's face. "Naomi told me about your—shall we say—persistence.

She was terribly angry, which I've heard is a sure sign of interest."

Stephen felt that that theory was without foundation as he received Naomi's frigid greeting. The spaniel, however, gave her such a demonstration of affection that a smile flickered on her lips.

"Your dog seems to be more tactful than you are, Mr. Talbot," she murmured.

Bob Deane eyed the newcomer with bristling indignation.

"Are you Naomi's boy friend?" he demanded.

"No," Talbot said blandly. "Are you?"

Both girls laughed as the reporter flushed to his temples.

"Perhaps you're Vanda Quayne's latest sweetie," he suggested.

"Perhaps," Talbot agreed.

"What's your job?" questioned the reporter.

"I've had several," was Talbot's smooth reply. "Shall I ask questions now or would you rather I guessed the answers?"

Deane sneered.

"You imagine you're head of Scotland Yard, I suppose."

"Give him the works. Mr. Talbot." Phil urged softly.

"My dear young friend, a simple copper could tell that you were a reporter, hard up for news, and here seeking a story from Miss Marsh concerning Vanda Quayne."

"I'll get it too." Deane was obviously roused to anger.

"Not to-night," Talbot said quietly. "And, if you're wise, not any other night either."

"Who's going to atop me?"

"I am, if necessary."

Naomi stepped into the breach. "Why should you trouble on my account, Mr. Talbot?" she inquired.

Talbot swung round to her.

"I might be doing it for Miss Quayne," he suggested with a grin.

The reporter slung himself off the couch and with a sulky nod to the girls, went to the door.

"I'll see you again, Mr. Talbot," he said darkly.

"With shirt-sleeves rolled up, Mr. Deane," the, other man promised, "if your ideas on journalism become unruly."

Naomi's lips were twitching as Deane made a noisy exit.

"Thank you," she said to Talbot. "Are you going through life delivering me from undesirable persons?"

"I don't know. I hope not if you act sensibly," was his answer.

"What about a drink?" Phil put in practically. "We've half a bottle of vile cooking sherry and some tepid coffee."

"Coffee, please. Perhaps Miss Marsh would be kind and reheat it for me." His fingers caught Phil's sleeve as he spoke.

Naomi noticed his gesture. Taking the tray she went into the kitchen.

Phil's brow crinkled in surprise when she was alone with Talbot.

"You're certainly not overpowered by my beauty," she said. "Why did you do that?"

"Listen to me," he said urgently. "Can you persuade Naomi to give up this post with Vanda Quayne?"

"No, I can't. Anyhow, why should I?"

"Never mind; there's no time to go into that. You seem to have horse sense, and she's as obstinate as a mule. What kind of a suitcase did she take to Paris? I mean, was it valuable?"

"No, it was an old one of mine." Phil's eyes gleamed with humour. "And I rather fancy you damaged the lock when you opened it to steal that packet. You're a poor thief."

"I need training." agreed Stephen. "About your bag which Naomi took to Paris. The handle broke and it fell into the sea as the French porter was carrying it on to the boat. Do you understand?"

Phil looked at him squarely.

"Enough to teach Naomi that sentence."

"Good girl. It's a pity your friend isn't as cool brained and sane as you. Now, if Vanda asks for the packet, Naomi must say what I've told you."

"I'll remember." Phil's face was grave.

"And burn Naomi's white gloves—the pair that she wore in Paris."

"Why?" The question came from Naomi who stood in the doorway with the coffee pot in her hand.

"Because," said Stephen imperturbably, "nice girls shouldn't let the world know that they've soiled their pretty fingers." He glanced at Phil as he hurriedly drank some coffee. "You won't forget?"

"I won't forget," Phil repeated softly.

"Then Barry and I will be getting along," he said. "Good night, Phil."

"Good night, Stephen," she responded promptly. Naomi looked from her friend to the man.

"I suppose I ought to express my gratitude to you for clearing Bob Deane out," she said with reluctance.

"Certainly not," Stephen Talbot replied. "Gratitude means that one feels under an irritating obligation to someone. Good night, Miss Marsh," he said formally.

Phil followed Stephen into the hall.

"I wonder if that bit of fiction about Naomi's suitcase falling overboard really matters."

"Forget it if you prefer." His tone was detached.

"No. I shall tell her." Phil bit her lip and turned away from the quizzical expression in his grey eyes. "I can't make up my mind whether you're laughing at Naomi and me or whether you're deadly serious."

"I shall be most interested to know your decision. May I call again to hear it?"

"It will give you an excuse to do so, won't it?" she said. "Are you trying to pique Naomi by showing coldness to her and attention to me? If so, you'll fail both ways. I'm not vain and she's not a fool."

"Isn't she?" Stephen's glance was alight with mischief. "I'm delighted to hear it."

"How did you know where Naomi lived? She didn't give you her address."

"An oversight on her part that the telephone book rectified."

Phil pursed her lips.

"Very adroit," she commented. "But the telephone happens to be in my name because my employer pays for it. And Naomi only spoke of me as her friend when you were in Paris."

Stephen stroked his chin.

"H'm, that does make things awkward for me. Call it my gift of second sight and let it go at that."

"Call it your passion for snooping," Phil retorted. "I can do a bit that way myself. I think I'll visit your place when you're out and have a look round."

The man chuckled.

"I'm not in the telephone book yet, Phil Ingram."

"Who needs that when a wise law insists that every dog should wear a collar, engraved with his owner's name and address? Good night, Stephen Talbot. I like you, if only because of your pretty work with that news hound, but I don't trust your reasons for calling here."

Stephen eyed her speculatively.

"Quite right," he agreed. "It's rarely safe to judge people by appearances, is it? By the way, if ever you fancy we have met before, come along and let's have a chat about old times. Good night."

X. VANDA'S ENTOURAGE

Thursday morning, November 25th.

"YOU acted with great presence of mind, mademoiselle," said the French doctor as Vanda Quayne paid his bill. They were in her room at the Convent Hospital in Paris. "I fear it was a considerable shock to you to learn about the poor girl."

"A great shock," Vanda agreed. "Henriette was an excellent maid. I'm only sorry that indirectly I caused the trouble by sending her on that errand. Has she recovered consciousness?"

The medical man evaded the question by assuring Vanda that she was not to blame.

"The steps were wet and slippery," he added. "In the darkness, one presumes that she fell backwards and crashed her skull against the rockery stones at the bottom."

"I suppose so. It was good of you, doctor, to spare me from any publicity."

"My dear lady, you were still under my care. Your explanation to the sergeant of police here was most exact. You had asked Henriette to get you a bottle of cognac and most generously lent her your magnificent fur coat. She came back, gave you the wrap and offered to open the bottle in the kitchen for you. Running down the steps from this verandah, she slipped and fell. You heard the crash and rang for help." He paused and taking a cigarette from his case, lighted it with deliberation. "*Eh bien*, to-day you travel to London to give your delightful dances."

Vanda nodded.

"Yes, I am leaving for the train presently."

"Oh, by the way, you heard no cry or scream when the maid fell?"

"None."

"You were alone?"

"I was alone," Vanda stated calmly. "My new secretary had been with me, but she had gone before the accident happened."

"Ah, yes, I remember you told me so. You should be a great success in London, mademoiselle." The doctor bowed impressively over her hand. *"Au revoir."*

With a petulant gesture Vanda flung a cloak round her shoulders and went into the adjoining room. There, her personal maid, who had arrived early that morning to pack, was locking a dressing-case.

"Ready, Osmond?" Vanda's tone was tense with suppressed irritation.

"Yes, madame." The woman stood up and held out a bunch of keys.

"Keep them." Again there was an edge in Vanda's voice. Almost it was as if she hoped to find reason for complaint. "The rest of the luggage?" she demanded.

"It has already been sent to the station and will be registered to London as you ordered."

"Have you told anyone when or where we are going?"

"Until you telephoned to me this morning I did not know when you were leaving Paris, madame, and I have no idea where you intend to stay."

Osmond's face was as void of expression as an automaton. Her dark hair was drawn back smoothly into a thick coil at the neck. High cheek-bones, a well-cut nose and deep-set dark eyes suggested the Slav type. The fine colourless skin, void of line or wrinkle, seemed too taut for even a smile to break the effect of a mask.

Although both women had black hair and eyes, there was a great contrast between them. The maid, austere and emotionless; the mistress, volatile and capricious. A statue, cold and aloof, disdainful of artifice, against a gipsy, without restraint or inhibitions, seeking every aid to underline her charm.

Vanda pirouetted slowly.

"How do I look after being in retreat all these days?"

The maid gave a brief professional glance.

"In excellent health and, as always, perfectly dressed, madame." The impersonal tone squashed any hint of flattery.

"You don't like me, do you, Osmond?" Vanda was piqued to ask. "Oh, you're always deadly polite and most efficient," she added grudgingly.

"Has personal feeling anything to do with one's duty, madame?"

"Perhaps not, but, being honest, I own to liking admiration and affection."

"I, too, am honest," Osmond replied quietly. "If madame is ready, I will have these suitcases taken to the taxi."

On the platform of the Gare du Nord, two men holding bouquets came forward to meet them. Vanda accepted the flowers with a vague smile. "Your compartment is reserved," the elder man, her manager, informed her.

"Thanks. You must come in with me, Ferrari. I want to talk to you about several things en route."

Her eyes swept searchingly over the other man, who was her new dancing partner; a fair-haired Russian of magnificent physique.

"Did you get that costume, Nicola?"

His head bent in a graceful bow. "Of course. Madame looks radiant after her illness," he murmured. She will be a *furore* in London."

"That partly depends on your work, remember. Not too much vodka, please, and no late parties."

"I promise. When do we rehearse?"

"To-morrow at ten o'clock. There is a large studio in the house I have taken. Don't be late. Ferrari will give you the address. You'd better travel with Osmond, my maid."

Again Nicola bowed in acquiescence.

"I shall see you again to-day?" he asked with a subtle inflexion that indicated homage and devotion. His hazel eyes held hers audaciously as he waited for her answer.

"Very well," she agreed, warmed by any conquest. "Ferrari can bring you along for a cocktail when we arrive."

Nicola pressed his lips to her fingers. Still holding them, he asked softly, "What am I permitted to call my beautiful partner?"

"I suppose I must let you call me Vanda." Her glance fell on Osmond. Was there a gleam of derision or contempt in the maid's cold eyes? "Take Monsieur Nicola to your carriage, Osmond," she ordered peremptorily. "I'll send when I need you."

The maid moved away with Nicola in her wake. When they were out of earshot Osmond spoke to him.

"All goes well?"

"Excellently, and with speed," he replied.

"Be careful," warned Osmond. She is vain, but very shrewd."

Nicola nodded

"I will not forget." He helped Osmond into the compartment and arranged a rug round her. "You look tired, beloved."

A tender light illumined the woman's face, and her lips parted in a smile that revealed perfect teeth

"Looks! What do they matter? My heart is no longer tired now that you are here, my Nicola. Tell me, did you have any difficulty with Ferrari?"

"None. When you wrote to me that Vanda's dancing partner had killed himself, I applied to Ferrari and sent my press notices. He made an appointment. Vanda and I tried several dances, together and she was satisfied with my work. That very day she was taken ill and went to the hospital, so we have not met since, until a few minutes ago."

Osmond flung back her head proudly.

"That you who were trained for the Royal Russian ballet should descend to play second fiddle to that posturing creature!" she exclaimed.

Nicola shrugged his shoulders

"What does it matter? You must regard it as merely the means to a desired end. Besides, Vanda is an interesting type to study."

"She is also brave when danger threatens, and clever enough to save herself," his companion said in warning tones. "I do not trust her."

"Is that your English father speaking or your Russian mother, my Tania?" he asked laughingly. "Don't be anxious about me."

On their arrival at Dover, Osmond joined her mistress and helped to take the smaller luggage to the train.

Vanda sent her away when she saw her manager approaching with some newspapers.

Ferrari looked annoyed as he opened a copy of the previous evening's *Record*.

"Someone has spilt the beans, Miss Quayne," he said irritably. "Your absurd wish for secrecy concerning your address is answerable for this piece of work! Why you would not stay at the Ritz and let me boost your arrival beats me."

"I had my reasons." Vanda glanced through the article. "Since this information has leaked out, you might as well telephone to some people and bring them to my house for cocktails this evening."

Ferrari was pleased at the suggestion.

"I'll ring them directly we reach Victoria. Let me see. We'll invite—" He reeled off a few names that included the owner of the cabaret where the dancer was to appear.

Vanda's brows met in a sharp frown.

"Casinier!" she repeated. "Does the Regis belong to him?"

"Yes. He has his finger in a good many pies, from mineral mines to beauty parlours, and theatres to shipping. Have you met him?"

"I'm not sure." Vanda's tone expressed reserve. "I knew someone by that name many years ago."

"I'll bet it's the same man. He wasn't keen on booking you but his cabaret manager pressed the point and Casinier gave in."

At Victoria Ferrari saw Vanda into one taxi and her maid and luggage into another.

"Nicola says that you've invited him, Miss Quayne. Shall I bring him along later?"

Vanda gave a slow provocative glance at the handsome Russian who was standing near them.

"No. Nicola can come now—with me," she replied.

Ferrari put his head through the cab window.

"Better go easy, Miss Quayne," he said in an undertone. "Your last partner shot himself. If you vamp this one, he might shoot you."

XI. MURDER DRAWS NEARER

Thursday evening, November 25th.

BRIAR LODGE was ready to receive its new tenant. A little tired with the strenuous work she had packed into the past two days, Naomi went into the hall.

"They should arrive in a few minutes, Anderson," she told the placid-faced Scottish housemaid who was waiting there.

The telephone bell tinkled. Lifting the receiver, Naomi heard someone—a man—ask for Miss Marsh. It was Ferrari.

"This is Miss Quayne's manager speaking. She is on her way," he stated. "There may be a dozen or more guests for cocktails presently. How are you off for supplies? I can bring along anything you need."

"I can manage, thank you," Naomi replied. She hesitated for a moment. "I thought Miss Quayne wished no one to know this address."

"So she did, for some obscure reason," Ferrari laughed. "Probably a whim of hers. However, the column in the *Evening Record* finished that nonsense, hence Vanda's decision to throw a party."

"She is not annoyed—I mean, about the *Record* article?" Naomi's tone showed nervousness.

"I saw no signs of irritation," Ferrari assured her. "The lady likes the limelight, and possibly was thankful that her plans for seclusion were blown up. I expect reporters and camera men are about. See you presently, Miss Marsh."

After giving instructions to the maid about the expected guests, Naomi slipped a wrap over her thin frock, and walking down the short drive, looked up and down the road. It was very dark between the lamps, but she could see that the few passers-by were not loitering and seemed uninterested in Briar Lodge.

Almost opposite the house, a light gleamed in her own flat, showing that Phil was home. Naomi pictured the cheerful fire in their living-room and felt unaccountably homesick for its peaceful comfort.

Resolutely she turned her back on it and studied the Victorian exterior of Briar Lodge, with its unimaginative double-fronted structure and stolid stone porch in the centre.

Chinks of light showed through the curtained windows, yet to her mind they had no look of welcome. She had a queer fancy that those gleams resembled the eyes of grim, critical old women peering out inquisitively to see what was going on. Such old women would certainly not have approved of Vanda as a tenant!

For the first time, Naomi wondered whether she had acted impulsively in taking this house. Would the dancer find its high privet hedge depressing?

Naomi walked up the, gravel path and opened the heavy front door. It had the massive locks and bolts one might have expected; also a Yale lock as a concession to modernity.

Solid furniture of oak or walnut, with comfortable couches were in the rooms on either side of the square hall. The room on the left had folding doors leading into the large studio which some artist had built.

The studio had an independent exit to the garden by means of a narrow path at the side of the house, and could be entered without approaching the front door.

Naomi stood surveying the studio and decided that after all she was right. It would make an ideal practice room. The polished floor had only one good Persian rug to hide its smooth perfection, which was again reflected by long mirrors. Right-angled couches fitted into two of its corners, a huge fire glowed in the open hearth, and flowers were banked everywhere except on the small dais at one end which was occupied by a grand piano and gramophone. At the opposite end was a buffet table, laden with cocktails and delicacies.

An hour ago she had paid a surprise visit to the kitchen and blamed Skinny Gibbs, spotless in his chef's cap and coat, for cutting such mounds of sandwiches.

"Only three or four people will be here," she had said reprovingly. Caviare is very expensive."

"Pooh! what's a quid or two to Vanda Quayne?" he had, replied. "The stuff will be eaten. You're sure to get a lot of hungry reporters in."

She was glad now of his preparation.

The sound of taxi-wheels grating on gravel made her hurry to the hall.

A man, blond and hatless, got out and with a grave bow helped Vanda to alight. With a veiled smile at him, the dancer swept up the steps and greeted Naomi.

"This is Nicola, my dancing partner," she introduced briefly. "Miss Marsh, my secretary."

The man's light eyes rested for a second in bold challenge on the slim, fair-haired girl. Naomi gave him a cool impersonal nod and directed her attention to Vanda.

"Everything is prepared, Miss Quayne. Shall I take you to your room?"

"Show me the house first. Then I must change quickly. My maid, Osmond, is in the second taxi with the luggage. Tell her where to take it."

Nicola stepped forward.

"I will carry the suitcases," he offered, and ignoring her refusal, approached the other cab where Osmond was standing on the path.

Naomi saw him exchange a warning glance with the white-faced woman in black before she led Vanda through the various rooms.

Within a few minutes Naomi discovered that the dancer had an alert and practical side to her nature. She asked intelligent questions concerning the staff, household arrangements and dinner menu, throwing a curt word of approval to Naomi for her efforts.

"Get my bath ready, Osmond," she ordered when they reached the bedroom.

"Will madame wear the green velvet robe?" the maid questioned.

"How stupid you are. Of course not. Lay out my purple chiffon, gold slippers, diamond waist-belt, bracelets and necklace to match."

Vanda turned to Naomi again.

"Ask Ferrari to tell you when everyone has arrived. Then send a maid up to let me know, and see that all the studio lights are switched on. I want Nicola to receive me at the door." So Vanda intended to make a theatrical entrance! Apparently the maid realized that too, for Naomi noticed a shade of contempt on Osmond's chiselled profile.

An odd thought came to her that if they exchanged clothes, the maid would look younger and certainly more distinguished than the mistress. Osmond's calm and aloof manner, as though her dignity could not be assailed by her mistress's impatient irritability, had impressed itself strongly upon Naomi.

Downstairs there was an air of bustle. Ferrari had come and other people were arriving. Quickly he made himself known to Naomi, presented the guests informally, and praised her preparations.

A little pulse of excitement tingled in the girl's veins: this was better than the static job Phil had begged her to take.

Already the episode in Paris, with its varying degrees of unpleasantness, was fading into unreality. Inside these solid walls, embellished though they were with the dancer's exotic atmosphere, nothing could happen. Indeed, Vanda's fantastic personality might even take on a mellower tone. As for the threatened danger to her life, it seemed absurd to think of it.

Under Ferrari's guidance, the guests were assembling in the drawing-room; apparently he intended to usher them into the studio just before Vanda's appearance.

Naomi noticed that a curtain was swaying at the far end, behind the raised dais. A maid must have opened the door which led to the garden. She walked across the parquet floor to close it.

On the music rest of the piano, her eye caught a gleam of white paper. It was an envelope, addressed in block letters—"Vanda Quayne." Wondering a little who had placed it there, she took the note and went to the window.

Footsteps sounded on the gravel as if someone were trying to make a quiet retreat.

Naomi slipped noiselessly into the garden, but although she could still hear the steps, it was too dark to distinguish anything.

Returning hurriedly, she sought Vanda's manager. "Mr. Ferrari, please see who that is wandering round the garden," she requested.

"It's probably some reporter."

He pulled open the front door and ran down the drive.

"There was a small shabby looking fellow just outside the gate," he informed her a minute later. "He might merely have been passing by."

"Was he wearing a longish overcoat?" Naomi inquired breathlessly.

"Possibly. A white-faced, furtive-eyed individual. Don't worry, Miss Marsh. He looked insignificant and harmless." Ferrari scanned the guests swiftly. "I'll shepherd this crowd into the studio if you'll send a maid to fetch Miss Quayne"

"I will go to her," announced Nicola imperiously.

Ferrari grasped his arm.

"You'll do nothing of the sort, my lad. Your job is to stand inside the studio doors and make the low bow that's your strong suit."

With a nod over his shoulder at Naomi, Ferrari led the Russian away.

"And where do I stand?" asked a man's mocking voice behind her.

In the hall was Stephen Talbot, his grey eyes looking as amused and audacious as ever.

"Tell Miss Quayne that everyone is here," Naomi instructed the housemaid before turning to Stephen.

A wave of anger rose in her as she saw him calmly throw his overcoat and hat on to the hall seat.

"How dare you attempt to gate-crash in here?" she demanded furiously. "Please leave the house at once, Mr. Talbot."

"Well, well, if it isn't my old enemy, Miss Naomi Marsh," he tormented. "I could have sworn that you lived in a flat across the road with a delightful friend called Phil Ingram. Phil is a really charming person, so kind and frank."

"Will you go?" Naomi said in tense tones.

"Certainly, if this is your house. Perhaps you've come into money. I ought to have guessed it when I saw your faithful trailer outside the gate. You remember, the man I rescued you from in Paris. He's still wearing that ghastly brown overcoat."

Naomi put her hand to her throat.

"If—if, he's there, I'm sure you two are in collusion." Upstairs at door opened and she heard Vanda's voice. "Take your hat and coat quickly."

"Isn't this Briar Lodge?"

"You know it is. I shall have you turned out by the servants if you won't leave at once."

Ignoring her, Stephen strolled to the foot of the stairs and smiled up at the woman who, was descending.

"You're just in time to save me from being thrown out on my ear," he remarked. Vanda's eyes widened in surprise. Then she hurried down to meet him, her face radiant.

"Stephen!" she exclaimed. "How adorable of you to come. I thought you'd forgotten all about me. My dear, it seems long years since I saw you." One jewelled arm went round his neck, and drawing his face to hers, she kissed him on both cheeks.

"Come in and meet my guests," she said. "Oh, this is my new secretary, Miss Marsh."

Stephen bowed with an ironical smile to Naomi. "Secretary, eh! I thought she was a professional chucker-out."

"Really?" Vanda gave a ripple of laughter. "Mr. Talbot is a very, very great friend, Miss Marsh," she explained. "I am always at home to him, remember."

Naomi swallowed the retort she longed to make. "I won't forget, Miss Quayne." At the top of the stairs she saw Osmond's still face and quiet, watchful eyes. The sight helped her to control her own raging feelings. Holding out the note that she had found on the piano, she added: "Shall I put this with your letters for you to deal with later?"

Vanda tore open the envelope, and glanced idly at the enclosure.

Naomi noticed a queer tension grip the dancer as though she were frozen mentally and physically. With stiff precision Vanda folded the paper and gave it to Naomi.

"This may interest you, Miss Marsh," she said calmly, "even if it does not entirely convince you."

As she moved away with Stephen, Naomi read the communication, which was written in large block letters.

TO-DAY IS THURSDAY. BEFORE TUESDAY YOU WILL DIE

A stab of real fear—perhaps the first she had ever experienced in her life—made Naomi's fingers tremble. Was the man in the brown overcoat responsible for this, or was he merely the agent of Stephen Talbot, whom Vanda had greeted as an old friend?

XII. ECHOES OF THE PAST

Thursday evening, November 25th.

THE chatter of conversation in the studio was hushed abruptly as Vanda appeared in the wide doorway, one hand resting lightly on Stephen Talbot's arm.

Diamonds flashing with theatrical effect at neck, wrists and waist, were thrown into relief by the sombre purple of her chiffon gown. The skirt, cunningly pleated, clung to the curved hips, whence it billowed out, revealing gold slippers.

Fully aware of the striking picture she made, Vanda stood poised, gazing from one to another of her guests with a look that was a mixture of arrogance, amusement and triumph.

Stephen broke up the tableau by carelessly removing her arm and walking towards the buffet table.

If Vanda were piqued, she gave no outward sign of it. Making a low curtsey, she extended her hand to Nicola with a smile, and announced him as her new partner.

From the dais at the far end came the sound of a gramophone record: Ferrari had timed its opening notes correctly.

Without a word, the Russian swept Vanda into his arms and they glided off in a dance that was a revelation of grace and rhythm.

The music quickened, and the swaying grace that resembled a delicate breeze became a tornado of fiery speed. Nicola whirled his partner around, flung her from him at arm's length only to gather her closely as the music trailed to a languorous end.

The dancers bowed conventionally to the guests who applauded loudly, and to each other.

"A remarkable pair," exclaimed one man.

"They will be the rage of London in a few days. You're a lucky dog, Casinier, to have booked them. They'll pack your cabaret."

Julian Casinier, a stockily built man in the early fifties, with cynical eyes that seemed to hold an age-old knowledge of human nature, acknowledged the compliment with a nod, and strolled towards the purple-clad figure of the woman dancer.

She drew away from the other guests as he approached, and gazed at him with beseeching eyes.

"Well?" he demanded in a gruff tone, either ignoring or not observing the depth of feeling in her expression.

Vanda's glance changed to one of hard defiance. "Well?" she echoed challengingly.

"Your dancing is as admirable as your nerve is daring, Vanda. I never imagined you would come."

"But as I have, you have had the foresight to rope me in for your show, my dear Julian."

He spread his hands. "Why not? My business is to give my clients what they want. Nevertheless, I think you are—" Again he made the same gesture.

"Finish your sentence," she ordered.

"Shall we say—a trifle unwise? Don't forget that your bitterest enemies were English; they are probably in London."

A ripple of contemptuous laughter answered his question.

"You're becoming cautious in your old age, Julian."

His face flushed.

"Beware lest you never reach that unfortunate time."

"There may be more in that warning than you think."

Casinier glanced significantly in the direction of Nicola and then back to the woman.

"Aside from risks here, you love the dangerous joy of flirting with adventure, don't you?"

"Nicola?" She smiled confidently. "There's no danger there. He's only a hard-up temperamental Russian who knows how to use his feet. Are you paying me the compliment of being jealous of my new partner, or merely giving me a friendly, warning about him?"

"Neither; I've merely a business eye on the future when you and Nicola will be dancing in my cabaret." Casinier paused. "Maybe also I've a keen memory of the past."

"When I was extremely useful as decoy for your gambling den in Rio."

"Must I remind you, Vanda, that I took over that place and you with it, when your parents were killed in a brawl? You weren't famous or sophisticated then; merely a pretty child whom I guarded from worse evils than gambling until I sold the place back to you for a song."

"Yes, I'll admit that you played the heavy father while you were there." The woman lowered her voice. "Perhaps what has embittered my whole life would never have happened if you had kept that place and," she caught her breath, "cared for me."

Casinier shook his head.

"No power of mine could have changed your passion for jewels, or your determination to possess them, honestly or otherwise. Well," he spread his hands, "you wanted them, you stole them, and you paid the price. Better forget it. You probably still have the bracelet."

Vanda gave a mirthless, laugh.

"I helped to steal many things and got away with them. There was queer irony about the theft for which I served nearly two years' imprisonment. The bracelet had been seen in my possession. But it was stolen from me before I was arrested, by someone who meant me to suffer," she declared. "Had I been able to return it to the original owner all would have been well. Two years out of my life!" Her voice had a note of anguish. "Every hour of them shall be paid for."

"Hush! calm yourself," he warned. "Other people suffered too. Who has the bracelet now?" Vanda's eyes gleamed with anger.

"That's what I mean to find out. When I do, I'll punish him, if I hang for it. I know someone who can help me. Did you ever meet Filmer in Rio?"

"Yes; a weak, harmless kind of fool. He isn't much better now; runs a restaurant somewhere off Oxford Street but can't make it pay. A month or so ago he called and asked me to advance some money. I didn't let him have it."

The woman nodded with satisfaction.

"Good. I shall—in return for information. Filmer was one of our happy band years ago."

Casinier eyed her uneasily.

"I advise you to forget personal revenge," he said. "You're in a law-abiding country now."

"That won't stop me."

"In which case, I shall not allow you to appear at the Regis. I'm a well-known and respected citizen, and I can't afford to have any violent hysterical artistes who are threatening to create a breach of the peace."

Vanda threw her head up with an impatient gesture "Nonsense. Where's your business head? The cabaret would be packed: people love a sensation." The man caught her arm.

"I will not have you in the Regis unless you swear to give up this absurd melodramatic idea of revenge. No public scandal of any kind shall be connected with my name. Remember that."

"Very proud of your honour!" she sneered. "I wonder why."

"You wouldn't understand if I told you," was Casinier's cold retort. For a moment he was silent. Then in hard, decisive tones he added, "It will be wiser for me to cancel your engagement. If you make a claim for compensation through your business manager, I'll deal with it. I'll also back up any reasonable excuse you care to offer the public for your non-appearance at my cabaret. That's final."

He was moving away when she stopped him.

"You win, Julian Casinier," she said in a low crushed voice. "I can't afford to wreck my future for the sake of the past."

"All right. That's a promise you must keep." He changed the subject. "I saw you embracing Stephen Talbot in the hall before you danced—as if he were your long-lost brother."

"I don't waste affection on a brother, Julian. Up to now, Stephen has been nothing more than a friend—unfortunately." She smiled slowly. "But, as I've always called him my second-best, and I still retain my charm, who knows what might happen?"

"Who indeed!" Casinier remarked grimly. "What do you imagine that Talbot does in London?"

"I'm never interested in what men do."

"Quite." Casinier nodded. "Only in what they have." He glanced across at Stephen who was talking to Naomi Marsh. "When did he meet your new secretary? They appear to be old friends."

"They met here half an hour ago. She nearly turned him out for gate-crashing!"

"Apparently, he has forgiven her," observed Casinier dryly, and was quick to notice the sharp look Vanda turned on the pair.

Making an excuse, she left him and claimed Stephen's attention.

A while later when the guests were dispersing, Casinier had a word with Naomi alone.

"Have you told Miss Quayne that you were once in my City office?" he asked.

"No, there was no occasion to do so. I gave her several later references," Naomi told him.

"Good. Then it's just as well she doesn't know, or she may think I had an axe to grind and recommended you for this post. Vanda has had a hard life and very little reason to trust people, Miss Marsh. Good-bye."

In response to an imperious signal, Naomi hurried to her employer's side.

"There will be three guests for dinner, Miss Marsh," Vanda told her. "I have asked Ferrari, Nicola and Mr. Talbot to stay."

"Very well, Miss Quayne. I'll tell chef. Do you want me again this evening?"

Vanda frowned.

"Of course. You must dine here. Oh, by the way, we're a girl short. Can you get the friend who shares your flat to come? I don't know her name."

"Phil Ingram," Naomi said with reluctance

"Well, ask her when you go home to change"

"Phil may have an engagement."

"Then make her put it off." Vanda spoke with the assured manner of one accustomed to her own way. "She can amuse Nicola, and Ferrari will want to talk to you on business."

"Leaving you free for Stephen Talbot," Naomi reflected to herself.

The parlourmaid's anxious face caught her eye, and she went into the hall.

"What is it, Anderson?"

"There's a young gentleman insists upon seeing the mistress alone," the maid told her in broad Scottish accents " He says he was no' invited for the cocktail party, but he was so importunate I thought the matter might be airgent. He's in the dining-room, and I'll be glad to be rid of him and get on with my table laying!"

"I'll see what he wants," Naomi said.

Convinced that the visitor was Bob Deane, intent on copy for his paper, she opened the door prepared for battle.

A pale young man rose, obviously in a high state of nervous agitation.

"Can I—I must see Miss Quayne, please," he began.

"She is occupied just now. I am her secretary. Is it anything I can do?"

"Oh no: it's a private matter."

This youth looked desperate enough for anything. Naomi's thoughts flew to the attack on Vanda in Paris.

"Tell me your name and I'll ask Miss Quayne if she can see you."

"If!" The young man gave a hoarse laugh. "She must—you understand—must. I won't be put off any longer. I've written and she won't answer my letters. Say it's Cyril Wyburn and that she met me in Berlin. She knows all about it."

Outside the dining-room Naomi found the dancer in the hall.

"I want to rest before dinner," Vanda informed her. "The men are going home to dress."

"One moment, Miss Quayne." In an undertone Naomi explained about the caller.

"Cyril Wyburn!" Vanda deliberately raised her voice "Tell him I never knew anyone by that name and don't wish to."

Her words reached the ears of the agitated visitor. Rushing out, he confronted the dancer and caught her by the wrist.

"You shan't evade me with that excuse," he shouted, his haggard eyes now wild with anger. "I must have the money for that pendant."

Vanda wrenched her arm from his grasp.

"Go away before I send for the police," she said insolently, and mounted the stairs.

A hand was laid on his arm.

"Better, come along," Stephen Talbot warned kindly. "You'll do yourself no good by making a scene."

The young man swung round at Stephen's quiet tones.

"But I must see her. You don't understand," he began pleadingly.

"Ferrari, throw him out," came Vanda's order from the staircase.

Stephen took the youth by the elbow and piloted him to the front door swiftly.

"There are seven days in a week, and three hundred and sixty odd of 'em in a year, my lad," he said when they were outside. "Choose any one but to-day for settling your business with Vanda Quayne. She's only just arrived and is feeling a bit temperamental. Hop into my car and I'll give you a lift."

XIII. A Price For Information

Thursday, November 25th.

"WE needn't be at Briar Lodge for an hour, Phil. As I'm ready, I shall write two or three letters first." Vanda's dinner invitation having been eagerly accepted by Phil, she and Naomi were dressing in their flat.

"That suits me. I'll have a walk and come back for you if ever I can get this blasted thing to meet," Phil groaned, emerging from her room. "Getting fat, that's what l am. Compare the bulges in my chassis with your heavenly stream-line effect!"

"You're nicely upholstered, not fat," Naomi pronounced as she adjusted the hooks on her friend's gown. "There! It's all right now."

"Thank you. By the way, did Vanda ask for the packet she gave you in Paris?"

"No. I forestalled her question by saying, as you urged, that my bag fell into Boulogne harbour. I fancy she was relieved. Phil, do you think the French maid, Henriette, was injured last Sunday?"

Phil gave her friend a sharp look.

"Forget it." She changed the subject. "Will that odd youth with a grievance against Vanda—I forget his name—turn up again to-night?"

"I shouldn't imagine so. He's called Cyril Wyburn. Mr. Talbot took him off before there was trouble."

"Stephen's a good egg," commented Phil, powdering her nose thickly. "A lad after my own heart, or is he after yours? Do you mind my calling him Stephen?"

"My dear girl, call Mr. Talbot what you like. He means nothing to me—for an excellent reason of my own."

Phil gazed at her friend thoughtfully.

"I wonder how much he means to Vanda," she remarked. "That was an odd business. I mean about his being an old friend of hers."

Naomi's lips set lightly.

"There are a whole lot of equally odd things about Stephen Talbot."

"And several very nice ones," Phil put in "I'm in such a dither that I'll probably eat my fish with a spoon and disgrace you. Can I vamp Stephen this evening?"

"No. He's reserved for Vanda. You can make eyes at Nicola if you feel inclined. You may regret it. I'm sure he has jungle habits and will paw you if you give him the ghost of a chance."

Phil raised her arm and felt the muscles.

"Watch me if he does. You'll see some real fun," she promised. "I do wish young Wyburn hadn't called on Vanda this afternoon. It would have jollied up the dinner party no end if he'd waited until tonight."

"There was nothing jolly about the affair. I felt sorry for the poor youth. He looked desperate enough to do something—"

"With a leaden weight in a glove?" Phil cut in.

"I hadn't thought of that." Naomi looked puzzled. "How did you know that was the weapon? I don't remember telling you."

"Of course you did," Phil assured her. "How else could I have known?" She pulled on her hat and coat. "I'll be back in good time to fetch you."

Outside the house, Phil hailed a taxi and gave the man Stephen Talbot's address.

"There's something I want to explain," she began a little breathlessly when Stephen opened the door clad in dressing-gown and trousers. "Perhaps we have met before, but I want no one to know it."

"Come into the lounge. I make no extra charge and it's more comfortable than the doormat," he said in his easy manner. "Have a cigarette and talk to my dog while I finish dressing. My man is about to become a proud father so I've given him the day off, hence my answering the bell in this informal outfit."

Phil paced the room restlessly while she was waiting. Occasionally she paused and fondled the spaniel's ears in an abstracted fashion, her mind absorbed with her own problems.

Presently the front-door bell rang.

"Do you mind seeing who it is?" Stephen called out. "I'll be there in a minute."

"How can I tell if it's friend or foe?" Phil called back.

"Take Barry with you," was Stephen's request. "He'll sort 'em out. He growls if he hasn't been introduced by me."

There was no doubt that the tall, well-built man in a heavy ulster who stood outside was a stranger, for the spaniel growled ominously.

"Hold that animal," ordered the visitor, stepping uninvited into the hall. "Where's Mr. Talbot?"

Phil caught Barry by the collar, and glanced suspiciously at the man. She could see little but his eyes. He had not removed his soft felt hat which was pulled down over his face, and his upturned coat-collar hid his mouth and jaw.

"Go into that room," the man commanded, "and don't release the dog if you value its life."

"I do; so hold on Phil," came Stephen's voice. He walked in and moved close to the girl. "What's the meaning of this extraordinary intrusion?" he asked the stranger coolly.

The man drew a revolver from his pocket and pointed it in Stephen's direction.

"I've a little private business to settle with you, Mr. Talbot," he said, "peaceably or not, as you will. What about this girl?"

Stephen shook his head and grinned.

"Oh, my red-haired confederate won't talk."

The man shot a swift look at Phil, and addressed her in a language she thought was Spanish, although she did not know what he said.

"I don't understand," she told him in English. The man seemed satisfied.

"Good," he replied. Turning to Stephen, he spoke rapidly in the same foreign tongue for a moment.

"So that's why you're here," Stephen commented in English. "And supposing I refuse?"

"In that case," the man told him, "I shall have to rely on this," he jerked his head towards the weapon he held, "to induce you to change your decision. If you're wise—"

"All right," Stephen interrupted. "Keep, your finger off that trigger while I unlock a drawer. You needn't worry. I rarely carry a gun when I'm wearing a dinner jacket: it makes the pockets sag."

The stranger waited silently while the drawer was being opened.

"Here it is," Stephen said, holding out a small black box. "Take it and get out."

With his left hand, the man raised the lid, and peered at the contents.

"Thanks," he said briefly, and placed the box in an inner pocket. "You probably won't believe me when I say that this is going back to its rightful owner."

Stephen chuckled.

"And you certainly won't believe me when I say that so far as I'm concerned you can swallow it." He put his head on one side, striving to see the strange visitor's face—"Have we met before?" he asked impishly, and swung round facing Phil so that the question embraced her also.

"Maybe," said the man, and moved towards the door.

"Yes," Phil said. "That's why I called on you."

She listened until the sound of the outer door closing assured her, that the visitor had gone.

Then, "Yes," she repeated. "We have met. Only I didn't want anyone to know it." Her voice dropped. "I'd still rather no one knew. Will you promise not to tell?"

"Very well," Stephen agreed.' "Providing there's no vital reason why I should."

"How could there be?" Phil flared at him. Stephen shrugged his shoulders.

"Surely that is for you to tell me! It seems unnecessarily mysterious, though."

"Was it any more mysterious than the queer scene I've just witnessed?" she demanded astutely.

"Perhaps not." His tone was indifferent.

"Right. You hold your tongue about my business and I'll be equally silent about yours."

"It seems a fair bargain," Stephen observed casually. "Although I don't care a row of beans if you tell anyone what occurred here, and I'm consumed with curiosity to know why our previous meeting must be kept a dark secret."

Phil gave a sigh of relief.

"Don't be absurd. The reason is because Naomi would be furious if she knew, and I only wanted to protect her." She held out her hand. "Is it a pact?

"Have it your own way, sister." Stephen glanced at the clock. "My hat, we must hurry. I'll drop you in Warne Road and give you and Naomi time to get to Vanda's house first."

Naomi was ready when Phil entered the flat. "Enjoyed your walk?" she asked.

Together they strolled across to Briar Lodge. Inside the gate, they heard men's voices, talking in hurried undertones. The sound was fairly close but darkness and thick shrubs hid the speakers

"Two men are coming up the side path," Naomi whispered anxiously. "Let's watch and see who they are."

"Ugh! What's that?" breathed Phil in her ear as a thin white form stood outlined against the trees.

"I tell you, Mr. Deane, I daren't do it. Miss Marsh warned me that I'd be fired if I told you any more," came from the shadows in a man's quavering tones.

"Bilge!" exclaimed his companion. "You're chucking away a fiver, Skinny. I can handle Miss Marsh."

Naomi went to meet the pair as they emerged into the lighted drive.

"Go back to the kitchen, Gibbs," she ordered the white-clad form who was already slinking away at her appearance. She turned to the reporter: "As for you, Bob Deane, if you attempt to get information again from the chef, you'll cost him his job. I mean it."

Bob Deane touched his hat in assumed humility.

"Lady, I'll lay off your menial if you'll give me the real dope," he whined. "All about Vanda's party and the scene afterwards."

"Tell him something to keep him quiet, Naomi," Phil advised softly.

"There was no party and no scene, Bob," Naomi told him. "Miss Quayne merely had a few friends here to greet her."

Bob whipped out a notebook.

"List of the guests, please."

Naomi mentioned a few names.

"And now clear off, Bob," she added.

The reporter shook his head.

"Not on your sweet life, girlie. You're holding out on me. I want to know who the wild man of Borneo was and why he wanted to see Vanda so badly."

"You're crazy, Bob," Phil put in tersely. "Go home and put some ice on your head."

"Keep out of this," the reporter snapped. "Now then, Naomi, quit stalling or Vanda Quayne will wish you had talked to me. Skinny Gibbs said an angry young man came here, and Vanda pretended she didn't know him. In the middle of the row, a man whom Skinny thinks is called Talbot, ran the caller out of the house."

"History is going to repeat itself, Mr. Deane," remarked a man who had just walked up the drive. "My name's Talbot, and off you go."

He gripped Deane's elbows and marched him sharply to the gate.

"Any more annoyance from you to Miss Marsh or Miss Quayne," he said, "and I'll tell the police."

Deane flicked his hat to a jaunty angle.

"Meanwhile, I'll tell the world. So long, dear Mr. Talbot. Glad to have met you again. Boy! what a story."

Stephen shut the gate and returned to the girls.

"My role in life seems to be that of rescuing you from awkward situations, Miss Marsh," he remarked.

"I hate the frequent necessity for your efforts as much as the sense of gratitude it involves," Naomi said icily.

"The latter state hasn't been noticeable in you. In any, case, I too hate gratitude—coming or going." Stephen took Phil's arm. "You look plump and pleasant, Phil: two things I admire in a girl."

"Miss Quayne would not be overjoyed to hear you say that," Naomi observed.

Stephen grinned.

"At last I know you're human," he told her. "I never thought I could get under your skin so success fully."

"You've no idea how sensitive Naomi is," Phil put in.

"She's given me no opportunity," Stephen retorted. "Frigid obstinacy is her outstanding feature so far. Here come Ferrari and Nicola. Let's behave prettily. "

Inside the house, their hostess, in an exquisite gown of amber satin, met them.

"Welcome," she exclaimed as if they had not previously seen her. "Stephen, at last I can have a talk in peace with you. Tell me what you've been doing all these years."

Dinner was nearly over when Vanda asked him to drink to her health.

"Wish me fame and long life," she requested. Stephen rose and raised the glass. "Success and long life, Vanda," he said obediently.

"Success and long life," echoed her guests obediently, and drank.

"Long life!" An ironic smile curved Vanda's lips. "What is it?" she demanded with curt impatience of the parlourmaid who touched her arm.

"A gentleman is on the telephone and wishes to speak to you. He says it is vairy airgent," the maid said.

"Shall I answer the call, Miss Quayne?" Naomi inquired, thinking it might be Cyril Wyburn.

"The gentleman wants no one but Miss Quayne, miss. Vairy reluctantly he gave me his name. It is a Mr. Filmer."

The dancer's eyes held an extraordinary glow of triumph as she rose from the table.

"I'll speak to him," she told the maid.

With fingers that trembled, Vanda held the receiver to her ear.

"This is Vanda Quayne speaking. Have you any news for me?"

"All that you need," was Filmer's reply. "I know who has the bracelet. His valet told me."

Vanda repressed an exclamation.

"Who is he?" she demanded.

"Not so fast, my lady. What do I get for my trouble?"

"You're a sweet soul, Filmer: not changed at all." Vanda's voice expressed contempt. "Well, how much?"

"I'll see you alone and discuss terms," Filmer said cautiously.

"Name your price and give me the name and address. Quickly. I've guests waiting for me."

A cackle of hoarse laughter came over the wire.

"Still acting as if you were an empress. In a hurry because you've got guests! I like that, Miss Quayne, when I may get it in the neck. No, we'll meet and you'll hand over the money before I tell you anything—that's if I live long enough. I rather fancy I'm being watched."

"Not because of this affair, Filmer. Probably you've double-crossed the gang you work with."

"They deserved to be nabbed for not splitting fair with me. Corney swears he'll get me," Filmer replied.

"Possibly you're in a panic for nothing. I've never heard of Corney and care nothing for your private affairs. Who could guess that you're coming to see me? No one knows that we've ever met."

"All right. I'll take a chance and come to your house at eight o'clock to-morrow night. You can get two hundred quid ready in pound notes. Yes or No?"

"Yes," rapped Vanda and ended the call.

XIV: NAOMI'S DECISION

Thursday, November 25th.

NICOLA sat on the edge of a couch in the studio feeling, very disgruntled. Three exceptionally pretty girls were here and not one of them seemed to notice his existence. Worse, they clustered round that lean, grey-eyed Englishman and listened eagerly to his conversation. Nicola decided that he didn't like Stephen Talbot.

Even Ferrari appeared to be interested, and ordinarily his life centred only on boosting Vanda for big money of which he received a high commission.

Nicola looked at them sulkily, comparing the fair proud elegance of Naomi Marsh with the auburn hair and lively personality of her friend, Phil Ingram

He had had no success with either of them during and since dinner. Naomi had pretended not to hear his whispered remarks on her beauty, and Phil, although she was his partner, had flatly advised him to keep his hands in his pockets after she had twice removed them—with some force—from her arm.

As for Vanda, any fool could see that she was crazy for Talbot. Whether Talbot was crazy for Vanda or merely leading her up the garden for some unknown purpose, Nicola was not sure.

The Russian was not broken-hearted. Only Vanda happened to be his employer, and astute to see her weakness for flattery, he was more than ready to play up to it for his own ends. She loved conquests, and it wouldn't disturb Nicola if she imagined that he was one, while it might add materially to his advantage.

Bored with being out of the picture, he advanced towards his hostess.

"If you will excuse me," he murmured, "I will leave now and retire early. Being of an artistic temperament, I rarely sleep well in—"

Vanda cut his explanation short.

"Good night, Nicola. Ten o'clock sharp tomorrow, mind," she ordered abruptly.

With a hurt expression in his tawny eyes, Nicola bowed and left the party.

"Wounded to the quick!" commented Stephen with a grin. "Vanda, you're a heartless wretch."

"Not to everyone," Vanda replied softly.

A while later Ferrari looked at his watch and pleading business, made his exit.

"I must clear out too and let you get some beauty sleep," Stephen said to his hostess.

"Do I appear to need it so badly?" Vanda asked. "Stay a little longer." She glanced at Phil and Naomi.

"Perhaps your friend would like to see over the house, Miss Marsh," she suggested.

Phil took the invitation as a hint.

"I'd love to," she agreed, and led Naomi away.

"Young man Talbot seems rather fickle, my lass," she remarked dryly. "First you, then me, and now Vanda."

Naomi's chin tilted. "Mr. Talbot was and is nothing but an inquisitive nuisance so far as I'm concerned," she stated. "You and Vanda can toss up for his favours if you like."

"With you out of the running, I might stand a chance," Phil said complacently. "Let's go upstairs. I'm dying to see my rival's stables."

Naomi stalked ahead in injured silence.

"This is Miss Quayne's bedroom," she said coldly, flinging open a door.

Phil inspected everything from the gold-stoppered bottles to the pale green negligee and satin pyjamas.

"Finished?" Naomi's voice from the landing was curt.

"Almost." Phil gently turned the handle of a second door near the wardrobe and opening it a few inches, peeped through. Then she closed it again and joined her friend.

"Do you want to see Miss Quayne's boudoir?" Naomi asked.

"If it's the room that has a second door to her bedroom, I've seen it—and its contents, thanks." Phil's tone was significant.

"You're absurdly mysterious."

Phil drew her friend away.

"Listen to me, Naomi. You're an obstinate mule; you determined to get this job, and you're determined to stick to it. Queer things have happened to Vanda already, and queerer things will happen in which you may be unpleasantly involved."

"You're looking for trouble, Phil. I suppose you fancied you saw something odd in Miss Quayne's boudoir."

"There's no fancy about it: my eyesight is excellent. What do you make of Vanda's maid?"

"Osmond is a cold, reserved type of creature."

"Cold, eh?" Phil grunted. "How long has she known the dancing tiger?"

"If you mean Nicola, Miss Quayne told me that she introduced them to-day on the journey from Paris. That must be true, for Osmond asked me his name!"

Phil laughed.

"Then she's a faster worker than her mistress! I heard low voices and looked inside the boudoir. Osmond and Nicola were searching some attaché case, with their backs to me. Nicola said something in Russian, closed the lid and pulled Osmond into his arms. For the cold reserved type who'd only met him to-day, she thawed quite well. I left 'em still kissing. Maybe Nicola is Vanda's Enemy Number One."

An unhappy, expression crossed Naomi's face.

"I wish—" she began wretchedly, and murmured the rest of the sentence to herself.

"What did you say?" Phil demanded.

"I said 'I wish I knew.'" Naomi replied quickly.

"Oh" Phil did not argue the point although she was certain in her heart that Naomi had said "I wish it were true." In which case a whole lot of things called for explanation. Why did Naomi wish that Nicola was Vanda's unknown enemy? Was it because she feared that Stephen Talbot occupied that position?

Stephen was bidding his hostess good night when they reached the hall.

"Wait a minute, Stephen," Phil called to him. "Naomi and I are just going."

"If Miss Quayne doesn't need me again," Naomi replied, more in courtesy than necessity, for her duties were obviously ended at this late hour.

Apparently her employer thought otherwise.

"I want you for two or three things, Miss Marsh," Vanda said bluntly.

Naomi immediately complied by following the dancer back to the studio.

"That woman means to get her pound of flesh," Phil commented to Stephen as they walked down the drive. "Or maybe," she added with a sharp glance at her companion, "Vanda has another reason for requiring overtime from her secretary. Are you too modest to guess what it is?"

"Call it indifference," answered the man. "Would you like to invite us up to your flat for a little while?"

"All right. We always make tea at this hour. But what do you mean by 'us'?"

Stephen walked across to a small shed just inside the gate of Briar Lodge and unfastened the door. Joyous whimperings greeted him and a squirming excited dog rushed up to Phil.

"You're the most patient and ill-used animal in the world," she said, caressing its silky head "Your heartless master doesn't deserve one-half of your affection, leaving you out in that cold shed while he gorged an expensive dinner."

"Don't put ideas into Barry's head, please," Stephen told her. "He would rather be near me than shut up in my flat alone. Besides—unknown to my hostess—I took him out an equally gorgeous dinner, which I scrounged from the kitchen."

"Although Barry only saw me once before, he knew me again," Phil observed as they crossed the road.

"He's very intelligent. I told you he never forgets anyone whom he has once met or seen me talking to." Stephen's voice held the usual pride of the dog-lover.

Phil's eyes watched the animal speculatively.

"Does it ever greet strangers with affection?" she asked.

"Never." Stephen's tone was almost indignant.

He followed her upstairs to her flat, expounding on Barry's merits, while Phil, absorbed in thought, prepared the tea.

Soon after it was ready, Naomi arrived, looking tired and depressed.

"Who do you think I saw outside the—" she began, and broke off when she noticed Stephen Talbot.

"A policeman," he suggested lightly.

"Sit down, Naomi, and don't let his chatter bother you," Phil rapped. "If this is a sample of Vanda as an employer, I'll say that she's a slave-driver."

"She pays a good salary." Naomi replied.

"You'll earn it, my girl. Drink your tea. Shall I turn this young man out?"

A faint smile flickered on Naomi's pale face.

"It seems rather harsh; the dog's quite nice."

"If I'm not," Stephen finished. He rose in a few minutes. "Good night, Miss Marsh. Don't bother, Phil. I'll let myself out."

"G'night," she said curtly. When he had gone she turned to her friend.

"Whom did you see outside this house just now, Naomi?"

"That horrid fellow in the brown overcoat who trailed me to Paris. Phil, what does it mean?"

A scowl darkened Phil's good-humoured countenance.

"I can't tell you. All I know is that Stephen Talbot's dog ran up to the man and greeted him as an old friend. Stephen didn't see that: I did. There are a whole lot of things that that young man has to explain before I'll trust him."

Naomi's lips quivered. She pressed her fingers against them.

"Are you going to give up Vanda Quayne's job now you realize that Stephen Talbot is crooked?" demanded Phil.

"No," said Naomi.

"Threatening letters, attacks on Vanda, this wretched little trailer, the sly business with Osmond and Nicola, plus Stephen's treachery!" Phil enumerated in rising tones. "What more do you want?"

"Another cup of tea and bed," Naomi replied. "Drop the subject, please, Phil. Whatever happens, I stay with Vanda Quayne."

XV. Midnight Visitors

Thursday, November 25th.

AT the end of Warne Road Stephen paused, wondering if he would take a taxi or bus. The sight of his dog's hopeful face and eagerly wagging tail settled the point.

"Very good, old lad," he said. "We'll walk until you're tired, but you won't find rabbits and you mustn't hunt cats." His eye caught the figure of a man in a shabby brown overcoat who had slouched up to him. "What is it?" he demanded sternly "You had my orders."

"Yes, sir. But this is urgent. Can I have a few words with you?" whined the man, known to his intimates as the Weazel.

"No," Stephen rapped, and strode on at a good pace that outdistanced the other.

Followed by the dog, he walked smartly until a sudden storm of rain forced him to take a taxi.

It was midnight when, opening the door of his flat, he heard Barry give a low growl that was usually the preliminary to loud barking.

"Quiet, boy," his master admonished. "Folks have gone to bed; we must behave ourselves."

The growling increased to an angry rumble as Stephen entered the sitting-room and switched on the light.

A warning bark from Barry told him that something was wrong Even before he saw the heavy window curtain sway.

"Come out of it," he called sharply, and advanced nearer.

The curtain was flung aside. A hulking fellow stepped out and faced him aggressively. With a rush, Barry darted forward and sprang at the intruder.

"Knock this brute on the head, Corney." the man called out in alarm.

Stephen caught the dog, and turning round, saw a second man who had evidently been hiding behind the door. This individual who had been addressed as Corney locked the door and stood leaning against it, while his mate handled a large spanner suggestively.

"Hold on to that dog, mister," he said, "if you want him to stay healthy."

Stephen sat down on the arm of a chair and grasping Barry's collar, looked from one to another of his visitors with an amused smile.

"It's nice of you to call," he observed, "even if your mode of entry was a trifle unorthodox. I presume—as you are evidently burglars—that you know quite a lot about the penalty for such efforts. The pity is that you may suffer rather unjustly, since I have so little here worth stealing."

"We ain't burglars," retorted Corney contemptuously. "Quit stalling."

"Quit stalling!" echoed Stephen."That   makes   it perfect. I was waiting for you to say that. Now I know that this is a gangster film rehearsal. Please introduce your pal, Corney."

"Give him one on the napper," urged the nameless one with the spanner. "He'll stop wisecrackin' then. We got no time to waste."

"You'll waste more if you do," Stephen told him. "If you're not burglars, you must have dropped in for a chat, and if I'm knocked out, you'll have to wait until I come round for me to talk, won't you? Why not sit down comfortably and start the conversation?"

The intruders stared at each other, weighing up the suggestion in case there was a snag in it.

"Park yourself, Josh," Corney ordered, and pulled up a chair for himself.

"Now we can be more matey," remarked their host. He pushed a box of cigarettes along the table. "Smoke? Don't be afraid to take your eyes off me. I've no arms except those attached to my body."

"And one of them had better be used to grab your dog tight," warned Corney. "Light up, Josh. The gent's a bit queer in the head but we'll get it across to him somehow."

Stephen summed up his chances of escape. Wiry and fit as he was, he would be no match for these two burly creatures, even with Barry's help. Besides, he valued his dog's life and Josh, although seated and smoking, showed no inclination to be parted from the spanner.

"Bolt the outside door, Josh," Corney said, "and stay in the passage."

"My manservant may fetch the caretaker if he can't get in." Stephen wanted to test their knowledge of his habits.

"Do as I say," Corney growled. "You needn't try them tricks on me, Mr. Stephen Talbot. We had a look round before you come. There's only one small bed in the whole flat, and I s'pose your valet don't sleep with you or in the bath."

"He certainly don't!" Stephen echoed with fervour, recalling the portly figure who came daily to attend to his needs. "You score, Corney. Get on with the next. I like you more every minute."

"I'll put up with that if you don't try to kiss me," retorted Corney. "Now—"

"Quit stalling," suggested Stephen helpfully.

"Yep. Quit stalling. What d'you want with the Weazel?"

Stephen laughed outright.

"Good heavens, man, you must be queer in the head too! I hate every kind of vermin and have never even seen a weazel?"

"Oh yes, you have. A smallish ferret-eyed chap, with a sickly face; he mostly wears a brown overcoat. We call him the Weazel."

"You must bring him along next time," Stephen said easily. Throughout his light badinage with these men, mentally he had been standing aside in order to sense the atmosphere and be ready to meet any situation that might arise. Up to now he had been able to parry with words, but this question concerning the Weazel had forced him into an awkward corner from which he must extricate himself with delicacy. "There's whisky on that side table. What about a drink?"

"What about a plain answer to my question?" demanded Corney pertinently, although his eye went to the decanter.

Stephen observed the glance and decided to play for time.

"I've a widish circle of acquaintances. Get me a drink while I rake 'em over and think which one is the Weazel. If I move, my dog may get tiresome again. She's a fussy snob about new friends and doesn't appreciate you as I do."

"Ugh!" Corney grunted as he went to get the whisky. This bloke's chatter was getting on his nerves. "Now perhaps you'll talk sense," he said as he banged a tumbler down before his host, and took a long draught from his own.

"Here's to our next merry meeting." Stephen raised his glass. "Drink up and have another."

Corney obeyed and helped himself generously. "Going to talk?" His tone had menace. Stephen shook his head.

"I don't think so. No one of the name of Weazel is on my visiting list. You won't believe me, so talking seems a waste of time, doesn't it?

"Then I'll do a bit for a change, mister. Are you after Vanda Quayne's sparklers?"

"What gave you the impression that jewel snatching was in my line?" Stephen fenced.

"You employed the Weazel to watch her movements and report to you, didn't you?"

Further evasion being impossible, Stephen tried a new line.

"Now I know the funny little fellow you mean," he declared. "Weazel is a good name for him. But he seems to have misled you." He assumed a confidential manner. "I wanted to keep a watch on Vanda's secretary."

"That blonde bit called Naomi Mirsh," Corney supplemented. "Your yarn won't wash, mister. The Weazel never could keep his trap shut. You're planning to get Vanda's jewels through the Marsh girl."

Stephen smiled.

"If you knew this, why come here and ask questions?"

"Just to tell you that the Weazel is our dirty bit of work; part of our outfit, so to speak. Me and my pal outside will lend you a hand if you guarantees to split even."

"That seems very fair. The only snag is that I'm not likely to have anything to split, Corney."

"You will if we help. Josh and me know our job and we can do our part when you give us the tip. It ought to be easy seeing how you went to Miss Quayne's party to-night. But—lay off letting the Weazel in on your ideas. He ain't to be trusted for anything big. And keep away from a dirty little fence called Filmer who runs a resterong. He sent two of our chaps up for a stretch, we're going to arrange it pretty for him so that he won't be healthy enough to join in our plans, see? Who's that?" he demanded suspiciously as a bell rang.

"Who indeed?" thought Stephen anxiously as he heard Josh's voice in the hall.

"Mr. Talbot don't want to see nobody," he was saying.

The new visitor, evidently, meant to come in and test the truth of that statement. .

"Put that spanner away, you fool," came from the hall in a voice that Stephen felt was familiar although he couldn't, in that moment of tension, remember to whom it belonged.

There was a scuffle and a moment later the sitting-room door was flung open by Bob Deane. He gave Stephen a mock salute and glanced with raised eyebrows at Corney.

"Entertaining company, I see," he remarked. Stephen chuckled.

"Not so far as I'm concerned. Corney, do the honours and give the gentleman a drink."

The reporter stared at Corney's sullen face. "I rather fancy we've met before," he said slowly.

"Never," Corney assured him.

"Oh yes. We weren't exactly introduced, but shortly after you went away for quite a long holiday. Somewhere on the moors, I think. I hope it improved your health."

"If you don't stow that, yours won't be improved," snarled Corney. He turned to Stephen. "Me and my mate must be getting along, mister. We'll see you another time."

Stephen followed him into the hall where Josh was waiting.

"Which of you two has a key to my front door?" he asked.

Corney gave a snort of derision.

"Very raw at the game, ain't you? Me and Josh can manage most locks without any, key, but," he lowered his voice, "the Weazel can't. Let us in on your job and we'll play ball with you."

"And if I prefer to do my job—whatever it is—alone?" questioned Stephen.

"Then we'll put the brainy one of our bunch on to your little idea. He don't like competition, least of all from amatoors."

Stephen's eyes flashed with amusement.

"More and more like a gangster film! So you've a brainy boss, have you? I'd love to meet him. Of course you call him 'Chief.'"

"What we call him is our affair, and what he'll call you mister, if ever you meet, is nobody's business but his," growled the exasperated Corney. "Now, you let us in on your little racket or it'll be the worse—"

"For me," finished Stephen.

"Not for you, but for that yellow-haired Marsh girl. That'll make you think, perhaps, before you turn us down or tell tales to that reporter bloke who's just come."

Stephen closed the door on them with the inward reflection that it certainly would make him think.

"Old friends of yours?" questioned Bob Deane artfully when Stephen joined him.

"Never saw them before in my life," his host told him with truth. "They called to ask my help about a job."

Deane pondered the statement for a moment and decided that in the main it was accurate, if a trifle reserved.

"I thought they were trying a spot of blackmail. Look here, Talbot, those fellows are up to no good. The one with the spanner is merely a thug. His pal Corney is the danger. He has a pretty touch with locks and safes, and they've both done stretches in jail."

"Thanks for the tip. I'm glad you dropped in."

The reporter looked awkward.

"I owed you a kind of apology for worrying those girls for news. That's one reason why I came here to-night."

"And the other?" asked Stephen.

A naïve smile broadened on Deane's face.

"I thought you might thaw and give me a bright slant on your friendship with Vanda."

Stephen appeared to be amused by the confession.

"Sorry, lad; the facts are extremely dull," he said. "As hundreds of other men did, I met Vanda Quayne years ago, and seeing the announcement of her arrival in your paper, I called to-night at her new home. She remembered me, and asked me to stay to dinner."

"And that's the works!" The reporter was obviously crestfallen. "Ah well," he said hopefully, pulling on his overcoat, "maybe a real good crime will bob up soon and give me a break I'm sick of this gossip stuff about Vanda Quayne's past."

"So; I imagine, must be her secretary and Phil Ingram," Stephen commented. "Be a sportsman, Deane, and don't hound those girls. Phil can't know much, and if Naomi Marsh does, she would jeopardize her post by revealing it"

"I see your point." Deane's tone was non-committal. "Good night."

Was Talbot being merely gallant to the two girls, the reporter reflected, was he in love with Naomi, or was he protecting Vanda Quayne whom he admitted was an old friend?

XVI. The Man Outside

Friday, November 26th.

"WHAT time are you going across to Briar Lodge?" demanded Phil when she and her friend had finished breakfast.

"At nine o'clock."

"Nonsense. That's the hour for 'woiking goils.' like me, not for highly paid secretaries of film stars. I'll bet the exotic Vanda won't risk daylight until noon."

"She has an appointment for a rehearsal with Nicola at ten o'clock," Naomi replied

"Bet you fifty cigarettes she won't keep it."

"I don't know the lady's habits yet, but she seems serious about her work. I'll take the bet."

"Good. It's a cert for me. Bring the cigarettes along to the beauty parlour this morning. It will be a bright spot in a dull day. I'm weary of seeing a bunch of vain old women eager to be 'made over' to look young." 'Phil glanced at the clock. "Here's where a young woman must dash off for her bus. Good-bye."

To Naomi's surprise, the dancer was already in the studio, practising steps alone to the gramophone.

"Good morning, Miss Marsh," she greeted her secretary briskly "Give chef his orders before you see to the mail, please. No luncheon. Tell him to prepare for a dozen or so people for cocktails at six o'clock; and a light dinner—for ourselves only. I'm going to the Regis this evening as a guest, to see what it is like. Nicola and I appear there to-night. Have you a couple of reasonably smart evening gowns?"

"I think so, if they are needed."

"They will be. I shall take you with me both evenings."

Naomi flushed with pleasure. "Thank you so much."

"You needn't thank me at all. It's merely good publicity," Vanda stated with blunt honesty. "One woman with a party of men looks '*déclassée*.' We might have Phil Ingram too; she's a good contrast to both of us. By the way, I need a shampoo and set; make an appointment for me at noon at her shop. You must come with me. I hate being alone."

"Are you sure you would prefer that place?" Naomi did not want Phil to be worried if the dancer proved exacting.

Vanda laughed.

"Julian Casinier owns the place; his motto has always been 'The best is good enough for me.' That probably is the secret of Casinier's success in everything."

Naomi was typing replies to a pile of letters when Nicola arrived, a few minutes late.

Vanda rebuked him sharply, but an hour afterwards the Russian seemed to have regained her favour.

"It is wonderful to dance with you," he declared. "You have such fire, such inspiration in your work." His eyes rested on her caressingly.

"I think we shall be a big success," Vanda told him. "Be here to-night at nine o'clock. Correct evening dress, mind; no fancy ties or foreign innovations."

Nicola bowed in assent.

"It is so long until nine o'clock. May I not see you before?" he asked in a pleading tone.

A gratified smile lighted the dancer's face.

"Silly boy," she murmured softly. "You may lunch here with me if you like. Go for a walk and come back at half-past one." She called to her secretary. "Miss Marsh, I've changed my plans. Order luncheon for two with caviare. It can be served in the studio, which will leave the dining-room undisturbed for your typing."

In the kitchen Naomi delivered her employer's message to the chef.

Skinny Gibbs grunted.

"Trust a woman to know her mind for two minutes, least of all a furriner." His voice dropped and he jerked a thumb over his shoulder. "Must I have 'er messing about?"

Osmond lifted her eyes from the garment she was pressing.

"I am sorry to intrude here, Miss Marsh," she explained coldly, "but madame needed this and my electric iron is out of order."

"Give it to me and I'll mend it," Skinny volunteered with alacrity. He turned to Naomi. "So madame wants caviare for lunch, eh? That means the Russian bloke will be here to eat it. If you ask me, miss—"

Naomi noticed the colour flash suddenly to Osmond's pale cheeks.

"Do your work without discussion, please, Gibbs," she ordered shortly.

Through the kitchen window she noticed a man sweeping the garden path.

"Who is that?" she demanded.

"A poor chap who came to the back door and asked if I could give him a job," Gibbs told her. "I said he could clear up the dead leaves and I'd let him have a bob out of me own pocket. It went against my nature to turn him away. I got a kind heart, miss."

"In future, Gibbs, use it elsewhere. I engage the staff here, temporary or otherwise." Naomi's tone was definite.

Peering at the stranger outside, she saw a big, broad-shouldered individual, quite unlike the smallish man in the brown overcoat who had followed: her.

"What type of man is he? I can't see his face," she said anxiously.

"What's wrong, miss? Surely you haven't got the jumps because a poor beggar's doing a bit o' work here! He ain't no burglar."

"Perhaps not, but I'm responsible in this house, Gibbs, remember."

Reassured, Naomi was moving from the window when she caught sight of the temporary gardener's feet. For one who was out of work, he possessed remarkably good pair of shoes, muddy though they were. Shoes that were not in keeping with his ragged coat and trousers.

A nameless, and she felt, probably groundless fear nagged at her heart as she waited in the hall for Vanda.

Beside her a grandfather clock ticked solemnly. Other than that, the house was singularly quiet. So quiet that her ears caught a faint sound, as of a chair being scraped on a parquet floor.

It seemed to come from the studio. Perhaps the housemaid was replenishing the fire. The sound was repeated. This time she knew it to be too stealthy to be normal.

Cautiously she went through the drawing-room and pulled aside a fold of the curtains that divided it from the studio. Curled up on a corner divan, apparently asleep, was Nicola!

Naomi smiled inwardly at her stupid nervousness. If the Russian was too lazy to go for the walk Vanda had ordered, what did it matter? He was an invited guest and had a right to remain in the studio.

Outside the windows at the far end, a bent form appeared, using a broom assiduously. As Naomi watched, the man glanced over his shoulder and, approaching the window, tried to look inside

The slightly foggy morning had evidently darkened the studio so that he could not discern much, for he turned to his task with the dead leaves. But not before Naomi had seen his profile. For a moment she stared incredulously, her heart thumping in hard, terrified beats.

"Are you ready, Miss Marsh?" came Vanda's voice impatiently from the hall.

With an effort at control, Naomi joined her, hoping that her agitation would pass unnoticed.

"Shall I telephone for a taxi?" she inquired. Vanda laughed, and opened the front door.

"Film stars can't afford to ride in taxis! My manager has hired a Rolls for me. Here it is—complete with chauffeur."

Her eyes swept critically from the cream and silver car to the uniformed driver who stood, rug on arm waiting to assist his new mistress.

"H'm. Ferrari has done his job well," she said to her secretary as they glided along. "His services cost me a lot, but he's worth it. Incidentally," her lip curled, "he is one of the few people I know to whom I am worth more alive than dead."

Naomi caught her breath.

"Am I not also excepted?" she asked.

"I'll decide that point later," was Vanda's cryptic reply. "You don't look like an active assailant. Probably you are merely indifferent to my fate. I've no vain illusions about loyalty from my employees, or love from so-called friends. Most of them have an axe to grind."

They were silent until the car stopped outside the beauty parlour.

"Shall I wait here?" Naomi offered.

"No. Come in and have a manicure or something. Charge it to me."

Vanda's mood of bitterness had changed to one of warm generosity, and her greeting to Phil had no hint of patronage.

"I shall be delighted if you will come to the Regis to-night and to-morrow, Miss Ingram," she said.

"Not so delighted as I shall be," accepted Phil promptly. "Thank you."

She handed her client over to an assistant and returned to Naomi.

"I'll be getting too big for my boots if this high life goes on. Your Vanda's a queer egg; she's almost human at times. Is she like this with you?"

"I've not been overwhelmed by her affection yet." Naomi's tone was dry. "You seem to be changing your opinion of her."

Phil gave her a sideways glance.

"Why not?" she asked lightly. "You still hate her, don't you?"

"Don't be idiotic, Phil. A good secretary should have no emotions whatever. Miss Quayne is nothing more to me than my employer."

Phil observed the hot colour that had flooded Naomi's face, the irritation in her voice.

"We won't analyse your feelings for Vanda any more. What about our bet? Was she up early or do I get my cigarettes?"

"She was in the studio when I arrived."

Phil groaned.

"I knew my luck would be out when I saw the new moon through my window last night."

"There are more worrying things than a moon that one can see through a window," Naomi replied with a shiver of remembrance.

XVII. A New Dance

Friday, November 26th.

VANDA was in high spirits on the way back to Briar Lodge. Like most vain people, she loved talking about herself, but unlike the generality of them, she never minded dissecting herself ruthlessly.

She drew a mirror from her handbag, and studied her face.

"That assistant at Casinier's shop does her work well," she observed. "She has made me look younger. Sometimes I shudder to see myself in the morning"

"Something has certainly made you very happy," Naomi replied.

"All women feel like that when they know they are looking their best and are on the verge of a new *affaire du coeur*. Not that I intend this one to be serious. Directly Nicola ceases to amuse me, it will end so—" Vanda brought her hands together sharply. "I wonder if he is back from his walk. He's a lazy creature. I positively pushed him outside the front door."

Naomi repressed a smile as she recalled the figure of the Russian huddled into the darkest corner of the studio.

"I'll have a few sandwiches in the dining-room and get on with my typing," she told her employer tactfully. The last thing she wished to do was to make a third at luncheon and see Vanda exercising her wiles.

Nicola was in the hall when they entered.

"You look radiant," he murmured to his hostess."

"Pour out a cocktail for me. I must give Miss Marsh a few instructions, first." She turned to Naomi. "Come to my room. We can talk while I change my dress." Once more her tone was hard and businesslike.

The easy good humour that had been shown on the drive home slid away, and was replaced by a harsh scolding manner when she addressed her maid.

"Why haven't you laid out a gown?" she demanded irritably. "I never lunch in a tailor-made suit if I have a guest."

Osmond opened a wardrobe.

"Which gown does madame wish to wear?"

After a moment's consideration Vanda pointed to one of flame colour cloth.

Without a word, Osmond slipped it from the hanger. Her mistress glared.

"Why, you fool, you've not pressed it! I told you to get all my things in order this morning. You are not paid to waste your time."

Embarrassed at being a witness of this incident, Naomi interposed.

"I was in the kitchen this morning and heard Osmond say that her electric iron was out of order, Miss Quayne."

"That is no excuse," Vanda retorted. "She could have sent a maid to buy a new one. My wardrobe comes before petty expenses, and she is aware of it." She swung round to her maid. "Thanks to your disgraceful carelessness, I have to appear in a crumpled garment."

"Would madame not select another?" Osmond inquired in even tones that Naomi admired.

"No. This suits my mood to-day."

The anger evaporated from Vanda's face as Osmond dressed her and smoothed out one or two tiny creases.

It was a severely cut garment, relieved only by a silver girdle. Never had Vanda appeared more alluring, Naomi thought.

Endeavouring to ease the situation for Osmond, she paid her employer a sincere compliment on the perfect effect.

Vanda nodded.

"You're right, Miss Marsh. The man who designed this for me was literally my slave. Men in love work

better for their idols, I find." She gave a high-pitched
laugh. "I'll go down and see what it does to Nicola. His
dancing may improve!"

There was a gleam of cold hate in the maid's eyes as
Vanda went out of the room. A second later it had
vanished, leaving her face as emotionless as usual.

"Thank you, Miss Marsh," she said in a low voice.
"That was kind of you. But do not be anxious: Miss
Quayne cannot hurt me—by her words—and she might
have turned on you fiercely."

Naomi looked straight into the woman's eyes. "Miss
Quayne cannot hurt me either, Osmond," she replied
slowly.

Going into the dining-room, she rang the bell.

"Tell chef I want to speak to him," she said to the
housemaid.

Presently Gibbs entered.

"I hope you'll overlook that little affair this morning,
miss," he said. "It's just my kind heart. I've been out of
work myself."

"It mustn't happen again, Gibbs. Miss Quayne has
valuable jewels."

The man fingered his white coat awkwardly.

"I'll feel easier in my mind if I tell you something,
miss. When that bloke had done his sweeping, I hadn't
anything less than half a crown."

"I suppose he offered to get change and never came
back," Naomi suggested.

Gibbs shook his head.

"Will you believe it, he pulled out a handful of money,
gave me one and a tanner, and said, 'Thank 'ee, mate.' He
was off before I could say what I thought of him. And he
didn't call at any of the other houses for I watched him go
down the road. D'you think I ought to tell the police?"

"It is not your place to tell the police or—" Naomi
looked at him sternly—"any reporter who may call on
you. Remember that, Gibbs. I will do all that is
necessary."

She pressed her fingers to her throbbing temples when she was alone. Might she not have been mistaken this morning? The studio was a very large room, and from where she stood, concealed by curtains, the window was surely too far away for one to identify with certainty the glimpse of a face. Fear and distorted imagination could play strange tricks.

She clenched her fists. Why, oh why had she not gone into the garden at once? If Vanda had not called her, she might have done so and ended this suspense one way or the other.

It was too late now. There was nothing to do but carry on with her task in the hope of forgetting the sword that hung over her head.

She typed furiously all the afternoon, and there was a stack of letters on the table when Vanda came in at about four o'clock.

"You've certainly not wasted your time to-day, Miss Marsh," she observed. "I hope the gramophone doesn't disturb you. Nicola and I have been working out a new dance with excellent results, I think a kind of dying swan effect at the end." She made a grimace. "I'm the 'swan' of course, and Nicola bends over me with all the tragedy that he can call up. He's really quite good. Come in and we'll let you see it."

Naomi accompanied her to the studio where the Russian was mopping his brow.

"I want Miss Marsh to see the dance." Vanda's tone was curt. "Start the record."

"Again?" groaned Nicola.

"Again and again, if necessary. Don't forget at the end to lower me to the floor gently."

From a seat near the curtains Naomi watched with interest. There was no doubt that Vanda took her art seriously. Every move and step betokened the most delicate and finished work, and the finale was a triumph of grace.

"Any criticisms?" demanded Vanda of Naomi. The girl shook her head.

"None. It is perfect."

"Then we'll make it our last number at the Regis to-morrow night. That will do, Nicola, for to-day.

He looked hurt at this brisk dismissal.

"I do not escort you to the Regis to-night?" he asked, gazing at her with eloquent eyes.

"On second thoughts, no. You will appear there for the first time when we dance. To-night is a private party for my friends. Fetch me at ten to-morrow morning: we're going to rehearse at the Regis with the orchestra."

The Russian went away, a trifle sulky, and Naomi returned to her work in the dining-room. She had barely started when Vanda opened the door

"I'm going to rest until cocktail time. Keep any early guests amused until I come down, please, Miss Marsh."

"I fancied I heard the front-door bell when you were dancing, but no one has appeared."

"It's early yet." Vanda yawned. "Don't work too hard or you won't stay the course." Her manner changed to one of less assurance. "Would you mind answering the door at eight o'clock to-night? I am expecting a caller on private business. Please take him straight up to my boudoir and then come and tell me. Will you promise to do this and mention it to no one?"

"Of course, Miss Quayne. But," Naomi puckered her brow quizzically, "how can I be sure of the right person if I don't know the name? There may be more than one visitor at that hour."

Vanda bit her lip.

"His name is Filmer," she said reluctantly.

XVIII. CASINIER'S WIFE

Friday, November 26th.

A FEW minutes after Vanda had gone upstairs, the parlourmaid disturbed Naomi.

"You're wanted on the telephone, miss, by a gentleman who says he is the King of Siam," she announced in rather an awed tone. "Should I have called him 'Your Majesty'?"

Naomi suppressed a smile as she rose.

"Possibly he has exaggerated his rank, Anderson. I'm sure you were sufficiently polite."

"What do you want?" Naomi demanded over the wire.

"Come, come, my girl, that's no way to address royalty," came the reply in a familiar voice.

"It's almost too good a way to address you, Bob Deane. I'm busy, I've no news for you, and if you bribe any of this staff I shall give them notice. Is that plain?"

"Hideously plain and most uncalled for," he replied pathetically. "I rang up to tell you that I'd decided to lead a better life and stop hounding you and Phil for snippets of news."

"It sounds too good to be true, Bob. Is there a snag in it?"

"Nope; just my sweet nature coming to the surface. Maybe too I've better fish to fry."

"Whatever the reason is for your reformation, I'm grateful to you," Naomi told him.

"Of course I mustn't take all the praise," Bob replied. "The idea was put into my head by your friend, Stephen Talbot. Noble chap, Talbot. I called on him latish last night. We had quite a jolly party. He has some unusual friends. You must get him to tell you about them."

"Neither Mr. Talbot nor his friends interest me. Good-bye, Bob."

Replacing the receiver, she turned round to see the object of her last remark facing her.

"Sorry you find me so dull," he remarked.

"When did you arrive, Mr. Talbot?" Naomi regarded him with a puzzled expression.

"A short while ago. Julian Casinier's with me. His car had conked out at the far end of this road. He and I had a go at the plugs. We left his chauffeur working on it and Casinier tootled along in mine. As we were covered with grease, we went in there," Stephen indicated the cloakroom, "to have a wash first."

"If you arrived when I heard the bell, you've been here long enough to have a bath," Naomi retorted.

"It's evident that you've never had car oil on your lily-white hands," was Stephen's comment.

"Anderson ought to have informed me that you and Mr. Casinier were here."

"Casinier told her not to. We were in a filthy state."

Naomi gazed at him absently. The cloakroom was near the dining-room. Had these men overheard Vanda's request about the stranger who would call at eight o'clock? Probably not, she decided; and even if they had, it could be of little importance. Vanda was by nature an actress and prone to dramatize trivialities.

"Miss Quayne is resting," she said. "Will you and Mr. Casinier wait in the studio?"

Stephen shook his head.

"I must push off. My only reason for coming was to bring him. He can do as he pleases. There he is."

Naomi wheeled round as the older man came towards them from the drawing-room, and handed her an envelope.

"Please give this to Miss Quayne," he said in the deep commanding voice that matched his powerful face and rather massive figure. "As she is resting, I've written this note. There is no answer."

"Shall I give you a lift?" Stephen asked him

"Thanks, Talbot, but I see my chauffeur has come. We may meet at the Regis to-night. Will you be there, Miss Marsh?"

"Miss Quayne has kindly invited me and also Phil Ingram," Naomi answered.

Casinier gave her a pleasant formal bow, nodded to Stephen and left the house.

"He reminds me of the Rock of Gibraltar," Stephen remarked. "D'you think that unhurried calm is a pose?"

"No. He is always like that."

Stephen eyed her curiously.

"Always! I thought you met him yesterday for the first time."

Naomi remembered Casinier had advised her not to mention that she had been employed in his office.

"There is no reason why I should give you a timechart of my acquaintance with anyone, Mr. Talbot. Concerning Mr. Casinier, you have forgotten that my friend Phil has been employed by him for some time."

"Ah yes, of course. You've a deft touch in conversation, Naomi Marsh. I only wish you'd a little more sense, then you would have taken my advice and kept away from Vanda Quayne. However—" Stephen opened the front door and smiled at her.

"We may meet to-night. Meanwhile, think of me as the perfect altruist."

"I dislike wasting my time, Mr. Talbot," was Naomi's answering shot as she returned to her work.

It was perhaps a quarter of an hour later when Osmond came into the room.

"Madame wishes to see you immediately, Miss Marsh." She spoke in low controlled tones, yet Naomi sensed that there had been a scene between mistress and maid.

"I'll go at once," she replied.

Vanda was pacing up and down her bedroom, evidently the prey of some strong emotion.

"Where is Julian Casinier?" she demanded of Naomi. "How dare you keep him chattering in the hall?"

Naomi steeled herself to explain calmly.

"He left this note," she added.

Vanda tore the envelope open with nervous impatient fingers, and scanned the brief message.

"Order a taxi, and tell anyone who calls that I am out on urgent business," she said.

"Including Mr. Filmer?" inquired Naomi.

"No. I shall be back in time to see him." Clad in a dark fur coat and little black hat with a veil partially shading her eyes, Vanda looked entirely different from the stormy-eyed woman of a few minutes earlier. The change was not to her advantage, since hers was a beauty and personality that required brilliant colours and vivacity. Subdued and in quiet garments, she lost much of her charm.

Even her step seemed different as she walked down the path. Giving the driver an address off Park Lane, she sank into the corner of the taxi.

Before the vehicle could move away, the door was suddenly opened and a letter was tossed on to her lap. She only saw a hand, and caught the sound of running feet as the taxi started.

Tearing the envelope open she read:
LEAVE ENGLAND OR YOU DIE BEFORE TUESDAY.

That, in printed capitals, was the message.

A scornful smile flickered on her lips, and she lighted a cigarette with cool, steady fingers.

On arrival at her destination she asked the butler if Mr. Casinier was in.

"He is engaged just now, madam. Will you wait?" As Vanda followed the manservant along a spacious hall an audacious idea occurred to her.

"If your mistress is at home, I will see her," she said imperiously; adding, as the butler hesitated, "Tell her it is Miss Vanda Quayne."

So this was Julian Casinier's wife, she thought, when a frail, slender woman rose to greet her, and in cultured tones invited the visitor to sit down.

For once, Vanda's self-assurance deserted her. Here was a type of which she knew nothing: a gracious easy dignity against which her own charms appeared garish and florid. Casinier had evidently married someone who was his social superior, which accounted for the fact that no one of Vanda's circle had ever met her.

The dancer's lips tightened: Casinier had bluntly refused her two requests and he could take the consequences. Maybe the wife he held too highly to introduce to his old friends might learn a thing or two that would surprise her concerning his past.

Anger welled in Vanda's heart as her gaze roved from the woman who sat, serene and secure, to the exquisite furnishings of the room that might have been chosen to suit her personality.

"I'm afraid I did not hear your name when you were announced," Mrs. Casinier said.

The dancer flung back her head haughtily.

"I am Vanda Quayne."

She was annoyed to see that this conveyed little.

"You wish to see me?" prompted Mrs. Casinier, with a faintly puzzled expression.

"Don't you ever go to movies, or revues, or—the Regis?" Vanda demanded.

"Very rarely, I'm afraid. Many years ago I had an accident while hunting, and my husband still takes very great care of me. Occasionally I take my ten year-old son to a matinée when he is home for the holidays. Are you an actress, Miss Quayne?"

The simple question cost Vanda her last remnant of control.

"I am considered a world-famous dancer," she retorted, "and to-morrow night I appear at the Regis. I requested your husband to bring you to my supper party on that occasion. You don't seem to be much in his confidence or he would have told you about me and my invitation."

Mrs. Casinier was unmoved by the impertinence. "I accept practically no social engagements because of my health," the older woman replied. "And my husband has so many business interests that there is little time for him to bring them into his family life."

Vanda leaned forward, a gleam of triumph in her eyes.

"I am not altogether a 'business interest,'" she stated. "Julian knew me when I was a young girl in Rio. You must get him to tell you of the jolly times we had together."

Mrs. Casinier pressed the bell beside her.

"My husband will tell me anything that I wish to hear, Miss Quayne," she said evenly, and turned to the butler who had entered. "Tell your master that Miss Vanda Quayne wishes to see him on business."

"I suppose you think I've lost my temper," Vanda snapped as the butler went out.

"No; merely that you have mistaken your audience, Miss Quayne." A tender smile swept across her face when she saw her husband open the door. "Julian, this lady is waiting. I'll leave you."

Casinier closed the door behind his wife and confronted the dancer.

"Why did you come here? This is my home, not an office."

Vanda peered at him through half-closed lids. "So I'm not good enough to meet your lady wife, eh?"

"If you want plain truth, no, you are not. You are in different worlds. You've lived your life as you wanted— without fear, I grant, but with a total disregard for certain conventions that I have learnt to respect."

"You'd go far to protect your home, Julian, wouldn't you?." There was an ominous note in Vanda's voice.

"Farther than you could guess," he told her grimly.

"I told you to bring your wife to my party, and I asked you to let me have two hundred pounds in advance of my salary by five o'clock to-day. You wrote me a curt refusal to both requests, saying that your cheque would go to Ferrari, my manager, in due course."

"Well, what of it?" demanded Casinier. "I've not changed my mind on either point."

"No, but I've changed mine, dear Julian. I now want five hundred pounds, having an altruistic desire to pay off an old debt to a foolish lad I once met in Berlin."

"Your demand favours of blackmail; it's a risky game, even though it misses fire in this case."

"Strangely enough, I've never had that sin on my conscience before. I'm only asking for my salary in advance. What is more, I intend to have it as firmly as I promise to earn it—if I live long enough."

Casinier gave her a sharp glance.

"I should like to know the worst if I refuse."

"Your wife, even if she knows your past, might not like to have it made public."

Her words caused Casinier to bite his lip.

"Or," she went on, "let me have the money and I won't see your wife again. Anyhow, she bores me."

For a second the man stood silent. Then he came to an abrupt decision.

"Come into the library, Vanda. I must give you a cheque for the three hundred; the rest you can have in notes." He paused and searched her face closely. "I wonder why you want it so urgently to-night."

"I told you that the cheque is to pay an old debt. The rest," Vanda laughed harshly, "is for useful information which I hope to receive. You unconsciously gave me the idea where I could obtain it!"

"Still hankering after revenge despite your promise to behave yourself! Well, take care, Vanda, that someone doesn't spike your guns."

XIX. A MAN CALLED FILMER

Friday, November 26th.

VANDA returned to Briar Lodge with the exalted spirit of a conqueror. She had stormed the secret citadel of Casinier's life and emerged from the fight unscarred.

True, there was stern warning in his last words, but she refused to believe that anything could hinder her plans now. Filmer wanted money and she wanted his information: a simple exchange that no one could interfere with.

"Any visitors, Miss Marsh?" she inquired.

"Reporters, cameramen and a few callers who were told you were out. Also that young man, Cyril Wyburn, who wished to see you yesterday. I had great difficulty in persuading him to go away. He was sure that you were at home. I'm afraid he is in a very angry frame of mind."

Vanda seemed amused.

"The young idiot should have left his address." She took out Casinier's cheque and endorsing it, placed it in an envelope. "Give him this next time he calls. It's twenty minutes to eight. Mr. Filmer should be here soon. Bring him to me at once."

The next hour tried Naomi's patience sorely. Filmer did not come, and each time the bell rang Vanda appeared at the head of the stairs in a frenzy of excited irritability.

At a quarter to nine she came into the dining-room where Naomi had been waiting.

"I'm sorry to have kept you in vain all this time, Miss Marsh," she said in a quiet, reasonable manner. "Go to your flat and have a rest before you change for the Regis.

I have ordered the car to be here at ten o'clock. Bring Miss Ingram across and she can come with us."

Naomi was about to pull the cover over her typewriter when her employer stopped her.

"Leave everything as it is. You work far too hard. Indeed, I can't think why you put up with my caprices and ill-humour." Vanda hesitated a moment. "I've had another letter this evening reminding me of the date. I'm beginning to think they mean it. To-morrow I'm going to be business-like and with your help make a list of my known enemies. Perhaps I might call at Scotland Yard and see if they can suggest any plan." She patted Naomi's arm kindly. "There, run along, child. You're white as a ghost. Put an extra touch of colour on your cheeks."

Naomi left Briar Lodge and slowly climbing the stairs to her flat, opened the front door.

Crossing the hall with a tray of glasses was Phil, already dressed for the Regis.

You poor tired creature," she exclaimed as she saw Naomi's weary face. "Bed is the proper place for you."

"I'll be all right presently, Phil. A hot bath will freshen me up."

"Let me get rid of this tray and I'll 'maid' you."

"There are some odds and ends in there," Phil indicated the sitting-room, "and a little of Mrs. Gibbs's home-brewed muck may keep 'em quiet."

A little later when Phil was applying a few deft touches to her friend's toilette, Naomi looked at her strangely.

"You took me very much on trust, Phil, when we first met."

"Nothing of the kind. I'm too hard-boiled." Naomi sighed.

"Oh yes, you did," she went on. "You thought we met by chance in that restaurant two years ago. I maneuvered it, because I knew you would be useful to me. I wanted a job in Casinier's office, and you helped me to get it."

"A pity you didn't keep it. Casinier doesn't work his staff until nine o'clock at night. Hold your head still if you must reminisce: I nearly put the rouge on your nose."

"And you were right when you said that I had schemed to get the post with Vanda Quayne. If only I could back out now, but I can't—I've got to see it through. You see, there's a terrible reason. It is—"

Phil placed her hand over Naomi's mouth.

"Be quiet," she ordered. "You're far too worked up to realize what you are saying. Women in an overwrought state reveal secrets that they'd give their eyes to take back next day when they're normal. If you had wanted me to know, you'd have told me before. I'm not going to take advantage of you now. We've all got our private skeletons and secrets. Lean forward. I'm going to powder your back."

Presently Naomi stood up, once more calm and poised.

"Thanks, Phil," she said. "You're as bracing as a cold shower. We must leave here in twenty minutes. Who is in the sifting-room?"

"The queerest trio imaginable. Bob Deane, very subdued and modest, and far too polite to be true. It may be a pose; I dunno. Then there's Vanda's pal, Stephen Talbot; a bit off colour is Stephen. And will you believe it, Nicola turned up, complete with deferential bow. I can't think why."

Naomi wrinkled her brow.

"How odd. Let's go and see them."

Bob Deane certainly seemed the shadow of his usual impudent self, and Stephen had an abstracted air. The Russian was dissecting his soul thoroughly, and without doubt enjoying the process very much, even though his audience were not following him.

Nicola continued to talk with animation until the girls had to go, when he took his leave and promised to visit them again.

"Well, what do you know about that?" demanded Phil.

Bob Deane roused with a start from a scrutiny of Stephen, and mumbling some excuse about his work, made a hurried exit.

"Miss Quayne has invited me to go with her," Talbot told the girls as they went downstairs.

A man was entering the gate of Briar Lodge when they crossed the road.

"If that's not Nicola, I'll eat my best hat," remarked Phil. "Look, he's dodging up the side path to the studio."

"Perhaps he wants to practise a few dance steps during Vanda's absence," Stephen suggested lightly. "He said she had not invited him to the Regis tonight."

"Please say nothing about him," Naomi urged. "Miss Quayne has had a worrying day. Here is the car."

It was a few minutes before Vanda appeared, beautifully gowned. Her maid draped a fur cloak around the dancer's shoulders.

"You needn't wait up, Osmond. I shan't want you again to-night," Vanda told her.

Stephen helped the girls into the car and told the chauffeur to drive to the Regis.

They had reached the end of Warne Road where there was a pillar-box when Vanda tapped on the glass for the man to stop. Gathering her dress up, she got out, posted a letter, and gave the chauffeur some instructions. Then she resumed her place in the car and talked cheerfully to her companions.

"Hello!" Stephen exclaimed as the car turned a corner. "This isn't the way to the Regis."

Vanda's lips curved to a cryptic smile.

"The chauffeur is obeying my orders," she said. "I hope you don't mind a short detour, Stephen."

"Phil and Miss Marsh may be hungry," he replied. "I certainly am not. After a two-hour bout of bridge at the club, I had a very stolid dinner."

"Where is your club?" Phil inquired.

"In Pall Mall." Stephen seemed a little surprised at the question. He was still more surprised when the car drew up outside the gate of Briar Lodge and Vanda alighted.

"Wait here," she told the chauffeur. Walking up to the front door, she opened it with her key.

Naomi leaned out and spoke to the man.

"Why didn't you go up the drive?"

"Madam particularly ordered me to stop outside the gate," he replied.

In a very few minutes Vanda returned and the car moved off again. But not before they had seen Nicola hurry away from the house.

"Nothing wrong?" Stephen questioned.

Vanda gave him a brilliant smile.

"Nothing at all. It always exhilarates me to prove to people that I'm not such a fool as they think I am."

"Who imagined that you were?"

"Nicola and Osmond They were upstairs in my boudoir. She was weeping with her head on his knees when I opened the door! The wretched creature was trying to entrap the best dancing partner I've ever had. Nicola and I can go far in our work together. I have now forbidden him to enter the house unless I am there, Miss Marsh."

Naomi drew in her breath.

"What about your maid?" she asked.

Vanda laughed contemptuously.

"Oh, Osmond! I've discharged her, of course. She will leave on Monday. Fortunately my old French maid has written asking me to take her back at once."

The Regis was a blaze of light when they arrived. The elaborately uniformed porter left them in the hands of the manager, who with obsequious pride led them to their reserved table.

The head-waiter reverently removed Vanda's mink cloak. He remained still and admiring, while she stood gazing from one table to the other, collecting the attention of the guests with quizzical, languid eyes

For a moment they stared at the beautiful woman, clad in white cloth-of-gold, and gleaming with diamonds. Suddenly they recognized her and broke into a storm of applause.

Vanda smiled delightedly, waving a white-gloved hand. Then with a gesture of dismissal to them, she sat down by Stephen and looked at him with almost a wistfully tender expression.

"Well?" she asked softly.

"Very well. As an actress, you're superb, Vanda."

"And as a woman?" There was more pathos than audacity in her tone.

"Be content with my remark and let the other millions of women have a chance," he parried "How, about supper? The girls must be starving."

Vanda's manager joined them presently, in evening clothes that almost but rivalled those of the headwaiter.

"Where's Julian Casinier?" Vanda demanded sharply.

Ferrari frowned and looked round the restaurant

"He ought to be here, it's good publicity for you both. You made a grand entrance: I watched from the balcony." He turned to the others at the table with the air of a true showman. "Miss Quayne always has the exact touch with an audience. This place will be packed to-morrow night."

The head-waiter approached and spoke to Ferrari in an undertone.

With a word of excuse to Vanda, her manager left the restaurant.

"What is it?" she asked when he came back. Some reporter who wants to know what I'm wearing?"

Ferrari's face was grim.

"It's a reporter all right," he said, also a police inspector. "A man was found shot in a taxi this evening, and has been taken to a hospital."

"It's very sad, but I don't see why on earth you were sent for," Vanda remarked. Is he a friend of yours?"

Ferrari shook his head.

"No, and I am only concerned in so far as I am your manager. What fresh idiocy have you been up to?" he demanded savagely.

Vanda raised her hands.

"A strange man has been killed or injured and you blame me!" she exclaimed. "Are you mad? What possible connection can there be?"

"The man kept a small café, I hear, near Oxford Street. Before he left his shop, he wrote down the address to which he was going, and gave it to his waiter 'in case there's an accident,' he said. Queer phrase, that."

Vanda's face was as void of expression as a mask. "Go on," she ordered.

"Your name and address was on the paper that he left with the waiter," Ferrari told her. "The man's name was Filmer."

"Filmer!" Vanda repeated and fixed her eyes on the blanched face of Naomi. "Has anyone of that name ever called at Briar Lodge, Miss Marsh?" she asked in a crisp tone.

"No," Naomi replied, and was conscious of the other woman's relief

"It's probably some crazy individual who wanted money and thought he'd apply to me," Vanda told her manager. "I get hundreds of begging letters."

"Let's hope that is so," was Ferrari's gloomy reply. "If there's any hint of a scandal, I'm sure Julian Casinier will back out of your engagement. He's a very cautious man where his reputation is concerned, and I believe he's half sorry that you are appearing here."

A flame of anger, rushed over Vanda.

"His reputation! It doesn't matter about mine, I suppose." A cunning look crept into her eyes. "Why, I've remembered now. Casinier mentioned a man called Filmer who had been bothering him for money. Perhaps Filmer was blackmailing him! Julian Casinier wasn't always the whited sepulchre of respectability that he likes to think he is."

XX. Naomi Is Afraid

Saturday, November 27th.

NEXT morning the telephone beside Vanda's bed jangled at nine o'clock while she was talking to Naomi. She stretched out a listless hand and put the receiver to her ear.

"Oh, it's you, Ferrari," she said irritably "No, I'm not up yet. That stupid scene last night upset my sleep. Miss Marsh is with me, no one else. Don't be so mysterious."

"I've had an interview with the police that has exhausted all my ingenuity," Ferrari rapped back over the wire. "I'm convinced that there is some link between you and Filmner. All that flow of spite against Julian Casinier was eye-wash. It didn't fool me for a minute."

"Did you tell the police that Casinier knew the dead man?" Vanda demanded

"No. That was not my business. The man is not dead yet, though he is unconscious and badly injured."

"In which hospital is he?" There was veiled eagerness in Vanda's question.

"That can't interest you if you don't know him," Ferrari told her. "If the police call on you—and they probably will—say as little as possible, and don't drag in Casinier's name or you may regret it. He is a powerful person."

Vanda gave a gurgle of laughter.

"I happen to know that he has a vulnerable spot."

"So have you," Ferrari reminded her. "Your cash value for future engagements will be considerably diminished if your name is any way attached to the Filmer episode. I advise you to tell the police that you have never heard of the man."

"All right, I'll be cautious."

She replaced the receiver and turned to Naomi.

"That conversation was about Filmer who was found shot in a taxi last night," she said. "He was a fool to leave my address with the waiter in his café."

Naomi held up a warning finger and indicated the open door which led into the boudoir.

"Osmond might hear you."

"That sulky fool is too engrossed with herself to do me any harm. By the way, Miss Marsh, what are you going to say if the police ask you any questions?"

"That I have never seen Filmer, nor any correspondence from anyone of that name, which is the exact truth."

"And about my request that you should personally bring Filmer to my room when he called last night?"

"I have forgotten any such request." Naomi's tone was cold and reserved. "There is no necessity for me to offer information, only to answer questions."

Vanda's expression softened.

"In a world of faithless souls, your loyalty to a stranger is as remarkable as it is comforting."

"Don't overrate the value of what costs me nothing," Naomi said, "I'll go down and get on with these letters."

Vanda glanced at the clock.

"I shall have to hurry. Nicola and I are going to rehearse at the Regis. I'll bring him back to lunch: he'll do better to-night if I make a I little fuss over him." Her face hardened as her maid entered from the boudoir. "Have you been in there listening?" she demanded. "Get my bath ready."

"Madame's bath is prepared." Osmond's tone held no hint of annoyance.

"Well, I hope it's the right temperature," her mistress retorted. "Yesterday I was nearly boiled alive. See that all the mending and ironing are done before you leave. I don't want Marie to come back to me and find you have left your work piled up for her."

"Everything will be finished," Osmond answered.

"If it isn't, you won't get a reference from me." Osmond looked at her mistress with steady eyes.

"I shall require no reference that madame could give me," was her reply.

All that morning Naomi worked without interruption. About half-past two the parlourmaid told her that Miss Ingram wanted to see her.

"Ask her to come in," Naomi replied.

"It's my half-day," Phil announced, "so I thought I'd bob in and see if I could lend the white slave a hand." She pushed her friend away from the typewriter and sat down in front of it. "Come on. Dictate a few letters. It will be a change for you and keep me in practice."

"You have a good post at the beauty parlour."

"I've more money perhaps, but as the cliché goes, money's not everything. One day I shall lose my sweet temper and my job at the same time by throwing something at the elderly mutton who come there eager to be made into lamb."

"Money isn't everything," Naomi agreed wearily.

"H'm. Found your senses at last, eh! Hello, there's the telephone. I'll read some of Vanda's fan mail while, you answer it."

Naomi came back so quickly that her friend looked at her in surprise.

"You soon turned him down," she remarked; "Was it one of Vanda's admirers or yours?"

"The call was for me," Naomi stated, "but I gather that the gentleman, who spoke with a real or assumed East End accent, was not exactly an admirer. He told me to get out quick if I wanted to avoid a nasty mess."

"That's the second warning you've had by telephone, Naomi." Phil rose and went towards the door. "I'm going to try to have the call traced."

"No, no." There was a note of anguish in Naomi's tone. "Leave things as they are, Phil. The man meant well, perhaps."

"If it's necessary for him to act in this furtive fashion to save you unpleasantness, he must know of something worse than unpleasantness which is shortly going to happen to Vanda."

"That is not my affair," Naomi said obstinately.

"Vanda has had attacks on her life and threatening letters. She could protect herself if she wished by calling in the police. As she refuses to do so, there is no reason why I should interfere."

"Do you watch someone walking blindfolded towards a precipice and refuse to interfere? What's the matter with you, Naomi? Your whole outlook on life seems to be altering. Or else—"

"Or else I am different from what you thought," Naomi finished. "Last night I should have blurted out certain facts but you prevented me. To-day—"

She broke off abruptly as Vanda Quayne entered the room.

"Do you mind if I help Naomi for a while?" Phil asked in her direct fashion.

"On the contrary, I'm very pleased, Miss Ingram. Your friend is almost too zealous in her work." Vanda put her hand on Naomi's shoulder with an affectionate gesture. "You were very kind this, morning. I shall not forget it."

Naomi's lips quivered but she made no reply.

"I've dealt with the police. They found me at the Regis," Vanda continued. "The matter will probably end there." She stretched her arms with a yawn. "I'm going for a walk."

"Would you like me to come?" Naomi asked with a touch of eagerness.

Vanda negatived the suggestion.

"Usually I prefer company. This afternoon I want to think out a few things alone."

"Shall I order the car? The chauffeur could drive you to the Park, and you could walk there. The roads around here are lonely, and not very interesting."

"Thank you, Miss Marsh.; but my thoughts will be interest enough for me. Be sure you give Miss Ingram some tea."

Naomi pressed her hand to her forehead when Vanda had gone.

"Scared stiff, aren't you?" Phil remarked.

"Of course not. But, as things are, it's unwise for Miss Quayne to be wandering about these deserted roads. There's a fog coming on, and it's dark already."

"Look here, Naomi. You can't have it both ways: if you think there's danger, why didn't you warn Miss Quayne of that telephone call before she went out?"

"It would be absurd to attribute so much importance to an anonymous message," parried Naomi.

"That's a fool answer. However, if you're not going to do anything about this affair, snap out of it and let's do some work. Switch on the light."

The two girls carried on steadily until the maid brought in tea.

"Would you not like me to draw the curtains, miss?" she inquired.

"I'll do it, Anderson, thank you. Has Miss Quayne returned?"

"Not yet," the maid told her.

Naomi went towards the window and pulled one of the curtains across.

"Is it raining?" Phil asked her.

Shading her eyes from the light in the room, Naomi peered through the glass.

"It's so foggy that I can't see—Ah!" She pressed her fingers to her lips to subdue a startled cry.

Outside the window, staring at her, was a man. This time there was no mistake, for the light shone on his face.

Quickly she jerked the other curtain across. Her hand shook as she lifted the teapot, and a cup clattered over.

Phil turned round from the typewriter at the sound.

"I don't want to seem fussy, but in polite circles one doesn't fill the saucers." She frowned as she saw Naomi's terrified expression. "What's up now?"

"Nothing. I was clumsy. That's all."

Phil stirred her tea thoughtfully.

"I'm glad to hear it. By the look on your face, I thought you'd seen a ghost." Phil paused as she heard a man's voice in the hall. "Pull yourself together. Company's arrived."

Naomi bent quickly over the fire and put some coal on as Anderson opened the door.

"Mr. Stephen Talbot is calling. Will you see him, miss?" she inquired.

"No," whispered Naomi to her friend.

"Yes, you idiot," Phil replied softly. Then aloud to the maid, "Show Mr. Talbot in and bring another cup, Anderson."

Stephen glanced at the girl who was stooping over the grate and sat down by Phil.

"Tea's a pleasant institution," he remarked cheerfully. "Two lumps and strong, please. So Miss Quayne's fan mail demands an extra secretary? I thought the job would be too much for Miss Marsh."

There was a tinge of emphasis in his last remark that made Phil purse her lips.

"Perhaps you feel she ought to give it up," she said sharply.

"I've told her so several times," he replied. "Can I have a piece of cake?"

Phil thrust the plate at him.

"You can have the lot so far as I'm concerned. Tell me, Mr. Stephen Talbot, have you done any telephoning this afternoon?"

"Quite a lot. This is jolly good cake: I like the orange cream filling."

"Were any of your calls made to this house?" Phil demanded impatiently.

"Probably. Dear Vanda likes her devoted swains to ring frequently." Stephen's tone was imperturbable.

"Who answered the telephone?"

"Someone who snapped my head off, so I expect it was Vanda's worthy secretary." He grinned. "I'm sure that fire is sufficiently stoked, Miss Marsh. Do turn round and take my part. Phil is putting me through a positive inquisition."

"I've finished," Phil said in a sullen tone as Naomi came back to the table.

"Good. Then I'll ask a question." Stephen looked straight at Naomi. "Do you think I ought to tell the police that there is—or was—a man in the garden peeping through this window?"

Her eyes, wide and alarmed, gazed at him as if in horror at the suggestion. Then with an effort she controlled herself and gave a laugh.

"You evidently saw our chef's protégé," she said, "an out-of-work individual whom he employed to sweep up the dead leaves."

Phil gave Stephen a scornful glance.

"Have some more cake, then you won't talk so much," she told him.

Stephen rose, and strolled to the door.

"I'll take the rest of it in a paper bag. If I'm not mistaken, Miss Quayne has come back. I must ask her what time she'd like me to escort her to the Regis to-night."

"The perfect play-boy!" Phil summed up as he went out. "Or isn't he? I'd give a lot to know."

XXI. Bob Deane At Work

Saturday, November 27th.

PHIL was preparing an early supper in the kitchen when Bob Deane walked in. Flinging his hat and coat down, he perched himself on the table.

"Thought I smelled something burning," he observed. "You'll never make a poor man's wife."

"I never intend to." Phil retorted. "I wish you wouldn't burst in here uninvited."

"The latch was up as usual. Here, I'll show you how meat should be grilled." Bob slid off the table and inspected the chops critically. "If you've another, I'll stay to supper if I'm asked."

Phil gave an exasperated sigh and fetched another chop from the larder.

"There you are. Bang goes my Sunday lunch, and a lot you care, Bob Deane."

"Reporters can't afford to, angel. You'll find copy of *the Evening Record's* last edition in my overcoat pocket"

"Thanks, I don't care for tripe in any form." Bob turned the chops deftly.

"Do as I say," he urged "Front page, last column but one. My work, and very pretty, if I may say so. A fine rush I had to get it done in time."

Phil scanned the article quickly.

It dealt with the man, Filmer, who had been found shot in a taxi the previous night. There were some details about the wounded man, who apparently was unmarried and had few friends, if any; also there was an interview with the waiter.

The last paragraphs read:

There is no change in Filmer's condition, which is critical. A police official is remaining by his bedside, in case the wounded man recovers consciousness.

Up to now no person has come forward claiming to have witnessed the attack. The taxi-driver states that he saw nobody approach the cab, neither did he hear any shot. Oxford Street was crowded at the time and the taxi was frequently held up by traffic blocks.

Miss Vanda Quayne, the dancer and film artist, called at the hospital this afternoon and made anxious inquiries concerning the injured man. She was not permitted to see him.

Filmer had left Miss Quayne's name and address in charge of his waiter, "in case of any accident." This remark points to foul play. The doctors think it is unlikely that the wound was self-inflicted, although a loaded revolver with one empty chamber was found on the floor of the cab. The bullet extracted from Filmer is of the same calibre as those remaining in the weapon. No finger-prints were found on the revolver nor upon any part of the taxi.

Miss Vanda Quayne told the police to-day that although she did not know Filmer, she fancies his name was mentioned by someone in her presence. At the moment Miss Quayne affirms that she cannot remember who this person was, but has promised to communicate with the police directly she can do so.

Phil Ingram flung the paper down in disgust.

"Snappy bit of work, wasn't it?" Bob demanded.

"I still dislike tripe—with or without a qualifying adjective. Your reformation was short-lived, my lad. I'm sorry I said you could stay to supper."

"There wouldn't have been any if I hadn't turned up: another minute and you'd have ruined a pleasant portion of travelled sheep." Bob placed the result of his culinary efforts on a dish and regarded it with pride. "I only wish Vanda Quayne had been on that grill."

"There speaks the true Bob Deane I thought the reform stunt was only a fake."

The man faced her.

"In a measure it was," he said soberly. "Ever heard of a sprat to catch a mackerel? Keep that under your hat, Phil. As to the rest—I'm a journalist who loves his job. It has its nasty phases, but first and foremost I've got to have news, even if it means offending or hurting people I like. I've tried, genuinely tried, not to be offensive with Vanda Quayne gossip for Naomi's sake. But I'm the *Evening Record* crime expert, and now this Filmer attack has cropped up, I'm forced on to it. Those are the exact facts. What are you going to do about it?"

"Eat my supper," stated Phil. "Naomi's just come in. Bring the tray and talk about roses—if you must talk. She's tired and we have to dress up and go to the Regis presently, where there'll be a lot of fancy bits and nothing solid to eat." Phil opened the kitchen door.

Bob promptly closed it again.

"What do you know about Naomi's friends and relatives?" he asked in a curiously quiet voice. "Whether you believe it or no, I'm not asking this for the sake of my paper."

"It doesn't matter whether you're asking it for the sake of the *Undertakers' Gazette* or *Our Dogs*, because I don't know the answer and don't want to know it. For one thing I haven't a prying village mind, and for another, this is the twentieth century in which decent people don't ask personal questions. Naomi and I get on very well. We like each other for what we are, go our own ways, and mind our own business."

"You mean she keeps hers to herself, Phil, while yours is an open book. Don't delude yourself. What do you know about Naomi? Your father was a banker. You told me that, when he died, your mother and sisters settled in the North of England. They welcomed Naomi there last year for a holiday."

"Yes, and they didn't play the Nosey-Parker act," snapped Phil. "One more word from you, Bob Deane, on that subject, and the third chop goes back to the larder and stays there. Now then, do you eat or don't you?"

"I eat," Bob decided. "It won't be the first time that a man has been tempted from his duty by his stomach. I'm just a modern Esau."

He kept his promise faithfully; even washing up in a sketchy fashion while the girls changed into evening dresses.

They were nearly ready when the telephone bell rang.

"I'll answer it," Bob called out.

Presently Naomi appeared.

"Who was it?" she asked.

"Anderson, the housemaid from Briar Lodge. In a broad Scottish accent she said that a young man by the name of Wyburn had forced his way in and made a scene because she wouldn't let him see Vanda. Knowing that her mistress was already in an agitated state and would be dancing to-night, Anderson made him go away. He did so, uttering 'tairrible imprections,' she says."

"I wish she had rung me up before she sent him away," Naomi said in a vexed tone. "I had a letter for Wyburn from Miss Quayne."

"What's the matter with the post?" Bob inquire.

"Nothing, only we don't know his address and his name is not in the telephone book." A frown puckered Naomi's forehead. "If Miss Quay didn't see Wyburn, why should she be in an agitated state? It's so bad for her just before her opening the Regis."

"Anderson said her mistress had had a row the foreign maid," Bob told her. "Never a dull moment when our Vanda is about!"

"I must go over to Briar Lodge at once," Naomi said anxiously. "Are you coming, Phil?"

"I certainly am," her friend declared.

"Shall I trot over with you in case there's any trouble?" Bob's face had the hopeful expression a terrier who has seen a belligerent cat in his garden.

"There'll be worse trouble if you're there," Phil retorted. She looked at him severely. "You've just taken a private telephone call; see that it doesn't become public news. That's all, Bob. Scram!"

The reporter pulled on his overcoat.

"I gather you don't want me any more. Shall I see if your funny little escort is still waiting for you?"

Phil let down the latch and closed the front door after them.

"The poor lad's crazy!" she remarked.

Naomi caught Bob's arm.

"Were you making some silly joke?"

He shook his head.

"Not exactly. There was a fellow standing near the gate of Briar Lodge when I came to this house. He was a shortish bloke with sharp cunning eyes; he's wearing a long dark overcoat. I've noticed him hovering around here before. He was still there when I looked out of your window ten minutes ago. Don't worry, Naomi," he added as he saw her strained look. "These out-of-work chaps hang about the houses of well-known people in the hope of getting a tip by fetching taxis. I'll run down and clear him off."

"That's the best idea you've had for a long while," Phil said approvingly.

"No," Naomi cut in. "It might cause some bother."

Her tone was so desperate that Bob raised his eyebrows in surprise.

"Another good intention gone west. So long, girls. Enjoy yourselves," he said lightly, and raced down the staircase.

XXII. Vanda Visits Filmer

Saturday, November 27th.

THERE was no sign of the man Bob had spoken of when the girls crossed the road. Anderson met them in the hall.

"I'm very glad you have come, miss," she said. "These disturbances are most unpleasant."

"If Mr. Wyburn calls again, fetch me at once," Naomi told her. "Did he leave any address?"

"No, miss. He was too angry to do anything so sensible as that. Nearly off his head he seemed, muttering dreadful threats about what he would do. The poor lad must have a serious grievance." Anderson drew herself up primly. "If this kind of thing is going on I would rather hand in my notice. It's no' respectable for a decent maid."

"There will be no further trouble with Mr. Wyburn when I have seen him, Anderson."

"If you can quiet him, you cannot quiet Miss Quayne. She has been raging at that foreign maid of hers for more than an hour. I've no personal complaint against Osmond, but judging by the way Mr. Nicola goes sneaking round her, I'm afraid they're plotting something."

"Try to forget it all, Anderson. I'll go up and see what I can do towards restoring peace."

The storm between mistress and maid was apparently over, Naomi found. Vanda was sitting on the edge of her bed, dressed in hat and fur coat, speaking to someone on the telephone.

Signalling to Naomi not to go away, Vanda continued her conversation.

"I am sure that I can get him to talk," she was saying. "Get the necessary permission. I will come at once."

Replacing the receiver, she turned a radiant face to Naomi.

"At last!" she exclaimed triumphantly. "Oh, you don't know what I'm talking about, do you? Filmer has recovered consciousness and has asked for me. I shall just have time to see him before I go to the Regis."

Naomi looked bewildered.

"It's most kind of you to visit the poor man. But wouldn't you be wise to leave it until to-morrow?"

"Most kind!" laughed Vanda. "It is Filmer who is going to be kind. You don't understand and there's no time to explain." She placed her hand on Naomi's shoulder. "Always remember how grateful I am for your loyalty to me. I'm foul-tempered, cruel, hard, and many worse things, but I appreciate loyalty. In case anything happens to me at the end of this month, I want you to have this now as a proof of my gratitude."

Vanda picked up a necklace composed of strings of seed pearls plaited together, and clasped it round the other girl's neck despite her embarrassed protests.

"No, you're not robbing me at all," Vanda declared. "It's one of the very few trinkets I ever bought with my own money, and not worth much. I never wear it; pearls don't suit my temperament. Now, I want you and Miss Ingram to wait here until Stephen Talbot arrives. Get him to bring you both to the Regis in the car. Ask the head-waiter for Miss Quayne's table. I shall join you before and after my dances. Don't tell anyone where I have gone."

A few minutes after Vanda had left the house, Stephen Talbot arrived.

"Am I late?" he asked. "I thought I saw Vanda in a taxi turning the corner of Warne Road."

"Miss Quayne has a call to make on the way." Naomi's tone brooked no questions.

She glanced up in surprise to see Osmond, in outdoor attire, descending the stairs. The maid's pale face was even whiter than usual, and her eyes had a tragic expression. Could she be running away, Naomi wondered, as she noticed the two large suitcases which the maid was carrying! The next moment Osmond solved that problem.

"How can I get to the Regis with madame's dresses, please?" she inquired. "Usually I travel with her, but to-night she preferred to go alone."

"We will take you in the car," Naomi told her. "I had forgotten that you would be going to dress Miss Quayne."

Osmond lowered her eyes.

"That has always been part of my duties," she said.

"Very odd of her to dash off alone," Stephen commented when they were all in the car. "Where can she have gone at this hour?"

Before Naomi could stop her, Osmond had replied.

"Miss Quayne is graciously visiting the poor man who was wounded last night. He is better and has asked for her."

Stephen cocked his eyebrows.

"Indeed. A sudden impulse, I suppose; How quixotic of her to go to-night."

"Not an impulse, sir," Osmond corrected. "My mistress has rung up the hospital several times to-day making inquiries about his condition. I have never seen her so anxious. She was extremely happy when she heard a short time ago that he had recovered consciousness and decided—"

"That will, do, Osmond," interposed Naomi. "You should not discuss your mistress's actions."

Osmond accepted the rebuke and apologized.

"I have never done so before, miss," she added, "but as Miss Quayne will not be my mistress much longer, I did not think it mattered if I spoke the truth—for once."

To ease the strained conversation, Phil changed the subject as the car stopped outside the Regis, by drawing attention to the waiting crowd.

"They'll expect Miss Quayne to be in this gorgeous Rolls. If I waggle my hips, do you think they'll mistake me for her?" she demanded.

"You might try bowing and throwing kisses right and left, and see how they react," was Stephen's suggestion as he helped the girls to alight. "I'll get the porter to take those suitcases to Miss Quayne's dressing-room, Osmond."

With a dignified bow, the maid thanked him and stood aside.

"That's Vanda—the fair girl," said someone amongst the onlookers.

"No, it isn't. It's the other," cried another voice. Suddenly Osmond spoke, and in clear tones addressed the crowd.

"Neither of these ladies is Miss Vanda Quayne," she stated. "Miss Quayne will be here later. She has gone to the hospital on an errand of mercy to visit a man whom she declares she does not know. A very gracious lady."

"Stop her, please; get her away somehow," Naomi whispered to Stephen.

With an understanding nod, he grasped Osmond's arm, and forced her into the entrance.

"Can I get to the dressing-rooms this way?" he asked a commissionaire. "I want to avoid the crowd."

"Yes, sir. Go straight. Through the restaurant," the man answered.

Telling Phil and Naomi to wait in the hall, Stephen ordered the maid to follow him.

Half-way through the restaurant, Julian Casinier, an imposing figure in evening dress, was standing.

"Hello, Talbot," he said. "Where's Vanda? She ought to be here."

Before Stephen could reply, Osmond gave the explanation that she had made to the onlookers.

A queer light burned in Casinier's eyes for a moment. "It was absurd of her: the man's unconscious."

Osmond shook her head.

"Not now. He has asked for Miss Quayne."

"How do you know?" Casinier demanded.

"I am Miss Quayne's personal maid. Madame rang up the hospital many times to-day." Osmond met his scowling eyes in an odd glance. "Do not fear, sir. Madame will not be late and she will dance well after her interview."

"I hope you're right," he remarked. "Doubtless you understand Miss Quayne's temperament better than I. Naturally I don't want the show to be spoilt."

"Everything shall be ready for madame when she arrives," Osmond assured him. "She is a quick dresser."

Casinier nodded.

"Very well. I'll take you to her room. Are you coming too, Talbot?"

"Yes. I rather like a peep behind the scenes."

Vanda's dressing-room was almost luxuriously furnished and contained several huge bouquets and baskets of flowers.

Ferrari looked up with a worried expression as the two men came in with Osmond.

"That woman will be the death of me," he exclaimed. "She goes on in three-quarters of an hour and hasn't turned up yet."

Briefly Casinier explained the situation.

"If she isn't here in five minutes I'll get her on the telephone at the hospital," Ferrari declared angrily. He waved his hand towards the floral display. "These must be presented to her after her dances. She always decides which and when and how! Woe betide me if she gets the wrong one first."

"Perhaps her maid could assist you," Casinier suggested. "She seems to know her mistress very well."

Osmond left her task of laying out the dresses and examined the cards attached to the flowers. She selected three or four bouquets, while Talbot strolled across to glance at Vanda's gowns.

"Present these after the second dance, please, Mr. Ferrari," the maid said.

Casinier glanced at a card attached to one of them.

"This Prince Heidenberg won't be here to-night," he commented.

Ferrari chuckled.

"Hush, he never has been. That card is one of Vanda's dearest treasures. It's getting a bit soiled with long usage." He turned to the maid. "These two baskets might do after the third dance. We must keep the largest and best for the finale. Pass me that bunch of red roses. Who sent them?"

The maid read the message attached. Tossing the bouquet down as if she had been stung, she went back to her unpacking.

Ferrari picked up the roses and laughed as he read the card which was pinned to the ribbon.

"Listen to this! 'To my lovely and wonderful partner from her devoted Nicola.' Why, Vanda has only known the fellow two or three days."

"Smart work," Casinier agreed with a smile.

Stephen noticed the maid's tense expression.

"Perhaps Vanda sent herself those roses as well as the 'Prince Heidenberg' lot," he remarked.

"Maybe," Ferrari agreed. "But that's not her writing on the card." He sauntered over and inspected Vanda's dancing frocks. "When does Miss Quayne wear that?" His finger indicated a garment of scarlet and gold brocade with a waist-belt composed of huge round circles of glittering stones.

"It is for the new dance," Osmond replied.

"I bet Nicola will find them uncomfortable when he lowers Vanda to the floor," Ferrari remarked. "They're bound to cut into his wrist. She isn't such a light weight as she looks."

"So that is how my worthy manager speaks about me behind my back!" The words came from Vanda who stood at the open door regarding the men. Vanda, alert and buoyant, her eyes dancing and an impish smile on her lips. "Never mind, I could forgive anything to-night." She turned to Casinier "See, Julian, I have a surprise for you.

Apparently my persuasive powers are greater than yours. My supper party would have been incomplete without this guest."

She moved aside and with a gesture invited their attention to a woman who advanced with reluctant dignity into the room.

Casinier stepped forward, startled, and aghast. "My dear," he said in low tender tones to his wife. "Why are you here?"

XXIII. THE UNWILLING GUEST

Saturday night, November 27th.

MRS. CASINIER glanced from him to the dancer who was watching them with amused eyes.

"I scarcely know why I came, Julian," she answered slowly. "Miss Quayne seemed to feel that my presence was necessary."

Beside the flamboyant figure of Vanda, she was as a delicate bird of paradise is to a peacock. Ferrari, sensing the strained atmosphere, took charge of the situation.

"Draw the curtains, Osmond," he ordered. And to Vanda, added, "You'd better go in there and dress. Time's getting on."

The maid pulled the curtains that screened one half of the room, and with a shrug, Vanda disappeared.

"Should we not go to our table?" Mrs. Casinier inquired. Every vestige of colour had drained from her cheeks, and her lips had a bluish tinge.

Before her husband could reply, she swayed and would have fallen if he had not caught her in his arms.

"Her heart is weak," Casinier explained to Ferrari as they lifted her on to the divan. He opened his wife's handbag and, taking out a case, broke a tiny phial under her nostrils. In a few moments her breathing became more regular, although her eyelids remained closed.

"Ever since her hunting accident my wife has been subject to these attacks," Casinier added. "It was monstrous of Vanda to induce her to come."

Ferrari nodded in agreement.

"You're right, but say nothing now or we'll have hysterics from that quarter," he pointed to the curtain, "as well as this to cope with. Would you like me to see if there is a doctor on the premises?"

"No I know how to manage," Casinier told him. "This, fortunately, is not serious. With an hour's rest, my wife will be sufficiently recovered for me to take her home. Can she lie here meanwhile?"

Vanda's manager pursed his lips sternly.

"If anyone disturbs Mrs. Casinier, I shall have something to say about it." He looked round the room. "Talbot might have waited to see if he could do anything. I didn't know he had gone."

"He slipped out a moment after my wife entered," Casinier explained. "I don't think she saw him. Miss Marsh and her friend were expecting him in the restaurant!"

"If I can't do anything for you or your lady, I'll scout around and see if Nicola is ready." Ferrari raised his voice from the undertone in which he and Casinier had been speaking. "Buck up, Vanda. You and Nicola are on in ten minutes."

"I shall be quite ready," she called back from behind the curtain. "Have a drink, Ferrari. You'll find a bottle of excellent liqueur brandy and glasses, on that table in the corner. Perhaps Julian and Mrs. Casinier will have some too." Her voice rippled with laughter. "How absurdly formal that sounds, Julian, but I don't know your wife's Christian name."

"Nor will you," Casinier muttered as he gently chafed the icy fingers of the woman he loved.

Ferrari placed two glasses of cognac near them, and left the room quietly. He was far too good a business man to upset his star artiste at that moment, but he promised himself the pleasure of giving her a generous piece of his mind at the earliest suitable opportunity.

In a restrained measure, he was able to give vent to his indignation when he saw Nicola seated before his mirror, spraying himself with perfume.

"Stop fooling with that disgusting stuff," Ferrari snapped irritably. "You'll make Miss Quayne sick."

Nicola raised his hands protestingly.

"How can that be when it is the same that she uses? Only to-day I—" he hesitated'—"obtained a little."

Ferrari noted the hesitation.

"Her perfume is very expensive and made specially for her. Did Miss Quayle give it to you?" he asked with suspicion. "You may as well tell me the truth for I shall ask her."

In a flash the Russian adopted a cringing tone.

"No, no, please, Monsieur Ferrari; I beg of you. To-day—or perhaps it was yesterday—I asked her maid to give me some, and she did so."

"I don't believe it. Osmond is too fine a type to take a pin from her mistress. She may have her faults, but I am sure dishonesty is not one of them."

"A little perfume—a few drops only, what is it?" whined Nicola.

"The beginning of more serious things. You've only been with her a few days and this pilfering starts." Ferrari grasped his arm. "Now then, did Osmond give it to you or did you take it?"

"I myself poured some into this small bottle when I was in—" Nicola paused awkwardly, aware that he was getting into deep waters.

"Miss Quayne is very careful of her possessions; perfume would only be in her bedroom or boudoir. You had no right of access to either."

"I admit my fault. It shall not occur again; never, never. I promise," pleaded the Russian. "I went upstairs at Briar Lodge—I forget when—to ask her maid which flowers Miss Quayne liked best. No one was there so I took the perfume," he ended glibly.

"Then the maid came and told you that red roses were her favourite flowers?" Ferrari suggested.

Deceived by his encouraging tone, Nicola seized upon this apparently helpful query.

"Yes, that was what happened. You understand, don't you?"

"I understand that you're a liar as well as a petty thief," Ferrari said grimly. "Miss Quayne hates red roses. They were given to her by her last dancing partner just before he shot himself. I'll speak to her later about this business. Get along and wait outside her dressing-room."

The call-boy tapped at the star's door as Ferrari and his charge reached it.

"Miss Quayne, please," the boy cried.

At the sound of his voice, Vanda came from behind the curtains, and with cynical eyes surveyed the woman who lay on her couch.

"Did she faint or something?" Her glance went to Casinier, who was bending over his wife.

There was a hard impertinence underlying the question that did not escape the man.

"I shall take Mrs. Casinier home as soon as it is wise to move her. Until then, I regret to say that she must remain here," was his frigid reply.

"She won't be in my way," Vanda told him indifferently. "Come, Osmond," she called to her maid, and swept from the room.

Casinier hurried into the corridor after her.

"One mornent," he said "I want an explanation of your unwarrantable action in forcing my wife, who is a fragile woman, to come here to-night. You see the result."

"Even sickly creatures have to take their medicine." Vanda's lips curled with contempt. "When proud people cross my path, I love to humble them. I wasn't good enough for your wife to know. Take care lest she feels that you also are not good enough."

"So you're just a social climber, trying to be revengeful because you have failed to reach those heights!" Casinier commented.

Vanda shook her head. "I haven't failed in anything that I wanted to do," she asserted with slow emphasis.

"Last night I wrote and posted with my own hand a letter to your wife. Why did she not receive it?"

"'By the barest chance, I sorted the letters this morning and noticed your writing on an envelope addressed to her. Knowing that you could have no good reason for communicating with her, I burnt the letter, unread."

"That was high-handed but childish," the woman remarked. "You might have guessed that I should ascertain if she had received it. This afternoon I telephoned to her and discovered that she had not had my letter. I explained its contents and ordered her to be ready to accompany me when I called tonight. I ordered her; do you hear, Julian?" Vanda gave a high-pitched laugh.

The man grasped her arm.

"What have you told her?" he demanded hoarsely.

Vanda shook his hand off and drew her jade-green draperies around her.

"Nothing—yet," she said with significance. "I merely warned her that if she did not come to-night, I could and would wreck your name and reputation."

Casinier moistened his dry lips.

"And now that you have humbled—as you put it—my wife, presumably you are satisfied. A hollow victory to drag a delicate woman here against her will, isn't it?"

"It would be hollow if I were satisfied. I am not."

"You dare not do or say anything."

"Dare not! You will see, Julian, how much I dare." Vanda beckoned to Nicola who was waiting a few yards away. "Come. There are the opening bars of our dance. Take my wrap, Osmond, and wait where I make my exit from the stage."

Ferrari bustled forward with an anxious face, urging Vanda and her partner to hurry up. Mopping his brow, he watched them go and then turned to the older man.

"Don't worry, sir," he said, observing the signs of agitation on Casinier's face and mistaking the cause.

"That she-cat will do her job all right. She always dances betters if she is in a temper. I know her."

"So do I, unfortunately." Casinier peeped inside the dressing-room and then closed the door softly. "I think my wife is asleep. Miss Quayne won't be back for twenty minute or so. I'll go and make my excuses to the guests whom I had invited."

Together he and Ferrari went into the restaurant. Ferrari selected a position where he could see Vanda's performance and watch the reactions of her audience.

Unostentatiously, Casinier threaded his way past the tables until he reached that at which Naomi Marsh and Phil were seated with Stephen Talbot and three or four other people who had joined them.

"Sorry I couldn't come along before," Casinier said in general apology.

"Mr. Talbot explained your absence very nicely," a woman of the party remarked.

Casinier looked at Stephen sharply; an unspoken question in his glance.

There was the barest flicker of reassurance in the younger man's eyes.

"I hope I didn't give the show away, Mr. Casinier," he said easily, "by saying that Miss Quayne had decided to put on a new dance at the end, and that in consequence you and she, with her manager, were arranging the time schedule."

Casinier made some tactful response. He was obviously relieved that the presence of his wife in Vanda's dressing-room had not been revealed by Talbot. "I must get back presently," he added.

One of the men poured him out a glass of champagne.

"There's no need surely while Vanda is still dancing," he urged. "Have a drink with us and watch her. Maybe you'll keep Talbot quiet. He's been as restless as an eel: in and out ever since we came."

"I was expecting a friend to turn up," was Stephen's reply.

Phil Ingram puckered her brow.

"Isn't your friend complete with a tongue to ask where you are?" she inquired bluntly. "The porter could tell him."

"Or her," suggested Naomi.

"You two girls will make me think you are jealous presently," bantered Stephen. "Let's watch Vanda. That's a marvellous effect, isn't it?" He directed their attention to the rainbow-hued limelights playing on the stage.

Casinier gazed at the dancers, his mind boding on Vanda's stormy words, ending with a threat that held deadly intent. There were still several minutes before this series of short dances would be over and she could return to her dressing-room. He utilized them by trying to think of some way to quieten her—some peaceful way.

His earlier years had been hard and there were incidents in that past which were best forgotten, not only for his own reputation, but for that of his wife and little son. If Vanda, in her present exalted fit of anger, were to strike, the damage would be irreparable. His world, both in financial and private circles, had learnt to trust and honour him. Was the good name he had built up so long and arduously by honest transactions to be shattered at the whim of a revengeful woman, blinded by vanity?

He clenched his fists. Self-protection was a primitive instinct to be used in case of desperate need as chance directed. And surely that protection should be extended—at whatever cost—to save from harm his wife who was even now not fully recovered from the attack brought on by Vanda's vindictiveness.

The memory of that fragile and loved being, lying with closed eyes, her face wan and drawn, steeled her husband to grim determination.

XXIV. Stage Door

Saturday, November 27th.

MEANWHILE in the dressing-room, things were not quite as Julian Casimer pictured. Barely a minute after the room was empty, his wife roused. With the mental courage that often goes with physical weakness in those of strong character, she forced herself to sit up and drink a little of the brandy that was by her side.

From the restaurant, subdued strains of music came to her ears. She gave asigh of relief. At least the woman who had so distressed her could not return for a while.

Staggering to her feet, she walked about the room, partly to make sure that she really was alone, partly to test her strength so that she might leave before Vanda came back from the stage.

Behind the curtains which divided the room were the dresses required for the next dance.

She started when a few moments later her ears caught a faint click. It was followed by stealthy sounds. Someone had opened the door and had entered the room. It could certainly not be her husband, who would at once have called her name upon discovering that she was, not on the couch.

Concealed by the curtains, Julian Casinier's wife remained still, not wishing to meet any of Vanda's friends. When the caller saw that no one was there, he or she would presumably go away.

The footsteps came nearer. A hand touched the curtain and drew it aside, and Mrs. Casinier looked into the white haggard face of a young man.

At once she left her retreat and went back to the couch.

"Do you want to see Miss Quayne?" she inquired.

"I mean to," came the definite reply. "Are you a friend of hers?"

Mrs. Casinier shook her head.

"No. My husband owns the Regis. I was a little faint, and Miss Quayne permitted me to rest here for a while."

The young man eyed her, uncertainly.

"That is the truth?"

Mrs. Casinier inclined her head. "Why should I lie about so simple a matter?" Despite his odd entrance, she felt sorry for this young man who seemed agitated but harmless. Sorry, but also curious as to the nature of his errand. If he were contemplating burglary, he must be an amateur to be in such a shaky condition before the deed. "Who are you?" she asked.

"Forgive me, madam. I did not mean to doubt your word, but I'm terribly upset. My name's Wyburn. My mother is ill," he blurted out. "She ought to have an operation and every care afterwards in a good nursing home. We haven't the money."

"I understand," Mrs. Casinier said kindly. "You probably know Miss Quayne and want her to help you."

"Help me!" The young man's eyes blazed with anger. "She wouldn't help her own mother. No. I only want what she owes me; what she got from me, an infatuated fool, by a trick years ago."

"Surely she will repay you when she hears of your trouble."

"She won't even see me," he said bitterly. "I've called at her house, tried letters and threats. It's no use. To-night I'm going to take what is my due, even if I have to tear the jewels from her neck."

Mrs. Casinier fingered her wrap for a moment.

"Surprising as it may seem, Mr. Wyburn, I shall not prevent you from doing so. What do you do for a living?"

"I am employed in a bank."

"Suppose I offered to lend you the money you require after I have investigated your statements."

Wyburn drew himself, up proudly.

"I would much rather not take it, thank you; although I am grateful for your consideration."

Mrs. Casinier nodded.

"I thought you would make that answer." She pulled her fur cloak around her shoulders and went towards the door. "Now listen. Miss Quayne will be back in about ten minutes. I am going to wait for my husband outside. He will take me home. Don't jeopardize your career, but remember that whatever you do in this room is no affair of mine, and I have already forgotten our interview. Do you understand?"

Her eyes held his for one significant moment, then she went out and Wyburn closed the door.

"My dearest, is this prudent?" Casinier exclaimed when he saw his wife standing in the corridor a few minutes later.

"I disliked being in that room," she told him, "and you know how quickly I always recover."

"Do you feel well enough to return home alone?" There was an anxious expression in his eyes, and his manner was restless. "There are several things here that I ought to see to."

"Of course. Put me in the car and forget all about my stupid attack." She kissed his cheek. "Don't worry about me—or anyone else, Julian. Nothing can hurt us—nothing."

Casinier wandered back to the restaurant after his wife had gone, pausing to speak to various acquaintances before he finally reached Naomi and Phil. Vanda's first dances were ended, and with Nicola, she stood flushed and triumphant, talking to a group of people.

Casinier raised his eyebrows as he saw Phil and Naomi alone at the table.

"Where is your cavalier?" he asked.

"Where, indeed!" replied Phil. "Mr. Talbot has been playing Postman's Knock all the evening. The others of our party are congratulating Vanda: they'll be back presently."

Casinier turned to Naomi.

"You have not told Miss Quayne that you were once employed by me?" he said quietly.

"No, Mr Casinier. You asked me that on Thursday."

"Of course, of course. Do you like your new post?"

Naomi smiled.

"It has its moments. No one could call it dull, anyhow."

"No one could call Vanda Quayne dull either," Phil supplemented. "She can be very generous but she can be a powerful and dangerous enemy, I think; ruthless and reckless."

"Are those your feelings also, Miss Marsh?" Casinier asked.

"Miss Quayne has been extremely kind and considerate, and I should not be afraid of her as a foe," was Naomi's calm answer.

"I don't think you would," Casinier agreed

"Here comes Stephen Talbot," Phil interposed "The next time that young man leaves us to look for his long-lost friend, I'm going to dive after him."

For fully an hour, however, Stephen showed no inclination to leave his companions Whereas earlier in the evening he had been abstracted, he now was full of gay high spirits.

"Quite, the life and soul of the party," Phil commented as he led her out to dance, "but you took a darned long time arriving at that stage."

"Was I very boring?" Stephen asked.

"Very, and also extremely fidgety. You must have forgotten all the pretty manners your mother taught you, leaving two buxom lasses—one being me—while you slipped out to see where the third was!"

"Was it ill-mannered to go and chat with Vanda in her dressing-room? She is my hostess, you know."

Phil set her lips.

"That's an evasion and an untruth, Stephen Talbot. You certainly took Osmond there before the show. Possibly you saw Vanda then, but you didn't get your chat with her when you were dodging in and out because she was dancing most of the time."

Stephen paused and gazed at her in mock admiration.

"I say, oughtn't you to be managing Scotland Yard or something? It's perfectly marvellous what a fairly intelligent girl with a natural gift for snooping can find out. Now do tell me what you've discovered about Naomi Marsh. Ouch!" he cried as Phil stamped firmly on his foot.

A little later when she and Naomi were dancing with other partners, Phil noticed Stephen hurrying out of the restaurant by the main door. With a brief excuse to her partner, Phil snatched up her cloak and followed.

Outside the entrance she proceeded cautiously, keeping Stephen in sight.

A little beyond the Regis stage door he crossed the road and moved into the shadow of a shop entrance.

It was too dark for Phil to distinguish much at first. But presently, when a car flashed past, she saw that Stephen had a companion whose figure was familiar. It was the man in the brown overcoat.

Presently two other men joined the pair.

Phil crept forward a few paces to a doorway on her side of the street where she was fairly well concealed, and watched the men intently.

"Curiouser and curiouser, eh?" whispered a voice at her elbow.

She swung round to find Bob Deane beside her.

"Make room for me," he urged, and wedged himself into her temporary shelter. "Well, what do you think of Stephen Talbot's bunch over there? Queer place to go into a huddle, isn't it?"

"Do you know any of those men?" Phil asked.

"Two of 'em—the big chaps—appear to be the brace I met in his flat a night or two ago. They looked absolute 'thugs,' and one of them definitely is."

"Why were they there?"

"Search me!" Bob exclaimed. "From appearances it didn't seem to be exactly a social call. They might have been threatening Talbot or—" He paused.

"Go on. I can stand it."

"Or arranging to do some shady bit of work for him. Keep your mouth shut about that guess of mine, Phil."

"See that you keep yours shut," she ordered tartly.

"Look! The little fellow is the trailer, who's been hanging about Warne Road lately."

"Tell me something I don't know."

Bob leaned forward as another car's headlights gleamed on the men.

"Very well, I will," he said. "The big fellows are the men who were in Talbot's flat. I got a good view of them just then." Bob rubbed his head perplexedly. "Did you hear that? Talbot has told them to clear off or he'll call the police. Keep out of sight; they're going. Perhaps they're trying to blackmail him."

Directly the men had gone, Talbot returned to the Regis and went in by the front entrance.

"The party has not been a success, I fancy," Bob surmised. "You'd better go back to the cabaret."

"Where are you going?"

"Me?" Bob laughed. "I'm staying right here; glued to the stage-door exit. And it would take dynamite to move me."

XXV. The Last Dance

Saturday, November 27th.

CYRIL WYBURN walked along the corridor from Vanda's dressing-room, At the far end, by the door into the street, he could see the back of the uniformed porter. Suppose the man wanted to know why he was there?

Pressing his hat well down on his head, Wyburn jerked up his overcoat collar and pulled a letter from his pocket.

With as bold a step as he could manage, he approached the porter.

"I've an urgent note for Mr. Casinier. Did he go round to the front entrance?" he asked.

"I think you'll find him there, sir," the man told him.

Wyburn sighed with relief when he reached the pavement and was out of sight of the stage exit. He was about to hail a taxi when a man sauntered up to him.

"Can you give me a light?" the stranger asked.

Impatient at the delay, Wyburn handed the man a box of matches.

"Here you are. Keep them," he said.

"Evidently you don't come from Aberdeen," laughed the other, and extended his cigarette case. "I can't let the generosity be all on one side. Have one?"

"Thanks," Wyburn said, accepting the offer unwillingly.

The stranger studied Wyburn's pallid face with interest as he held out a lighted match.

"Seen the show?" he asked.

"What show?" Wyburn looked puzzled.

"Why, Vanda Quayne, of course. You came out of the stage door."

"Oh no. I had to deliver a note to Mr. Casinier," Wyburn prevaricated for the second time, and noted the other man's eyes dart quickly to the envelope he still held.

"Casinier, eh! Did you see him?"

"No; not exactly." Wyburn hesitated. "I must get along."

"To find Casinier?" questioned his persecutor. "He came out of the stage door about ten minutes ago, saw his wife off, and went along to the main entrance." He took Wyburn's arm "Come on: I'll take you to him."

Wyburn wrenched himself free.

"I'm in a hurry," he declared. "The note can go by post."

"If it's the one you have in your hand Casinier will never get it. His name isn't Cyril Wyburn and he doesn't live in Kilburn. You've got a grudge against Vanda, haven't you?"

The victim faced his tormentor.

"Why are you asking me all these questions?" he demanded. "Are you a detective?"

The man laughed. "Lord no; I'd make as bad a detective as you would a criminal, Mr. Wyburn. My name's Deane. I'm a poor devil of a reporter trying to get a line for my paper on Vanda Quayne, and thought you might give me a spot of news."

"I've told you I don't know the woman," Wyburn asserted angrily. "Get your beastly information elsewhere and leave me alone."

"Keep your shirt on!" advised Bob with perfect good humour. "You don't expect me to swallow that guff about a note for Casinier addressed to yourself, which you obviously don't mean to deliver, anyhow! Why, you were going to dash off in a taxi when I asked you for a light. Be a good lad and spill the beans. You're not the type to haunt stage doors unless you've a reason. My bet is that you've a sneaking regard for the lovely Vanda and were saying it with flowers."

"Flowers!" scoffed Wyburn bitterly. "I couldn't afford to buy her a bunch of violets even if I wished—and I certainly don't." His voice rose to a higher pitch. "Send her flowers indeed, when her room's crammed with them."

Bob Deane noticed the slip but gave no sign of having done so.

"Ah well," he sighed. "There's another chance gone. I'd hoped that you could have given me a story of some kind. Incidentally my paper pays a nice packet for an exclusive yarn, and as you say you're a bit hard up—" He left the sentence unfinished to sink into his companion's mind for a moment. "An intelligent fellow like you must get hold of a few bits of gossip," he added.

The tempting bait plus flattery urged Wyburn to wily endeavour. There was that queer conversation he had overheard between Casinier and Vanda when he had been hiding further along the corridor. Possibly Deane might call that an exclusive yarn worth a packet.

"Of course there's that affair with Filmer," he began cautiously.

Deane flapped his hand down in a gesture he had copied from the films.

"Don't hand me stale news, brother. I know the Filmer stuff by heart; there's nothing in it. A crazy fool got plugged in a taxi; said he was going to call on Vanda. Why, he didn't even know the woman!"

"Didn't he!" Wyburn snapped, of his guard. "Then why did she go to see, him to-night in the hospital?"

Deane's eyes were alight with interest.

"Now you're talking. Fire ahead. What did she say to Filmer?"

"It's what he said to her," Wyburn said with emphasis. "She learnt something that put terror into at least one person's heart."

"What person or persons?" The journalist resembled a hound who has unexpectedly got the scent.

Wyburn shook his head.

"Libel actions are nasty things. It would take a good sum to make me take a chance."

"The cash value depends upon the importance of the people involved. I'd have to know who they were first."

There was reason in Deane's remark which Wyburn was forced reluctantly to recognize. Dare he risk the serious consequences that might follow if he told the journalist everything? Would any monetary consideration that Deane could offer be worth while?

He was still weighing up his decision when a young man in evening dress came out of the Regis main entrance and strolled towards them.

"The deal's off," Wyburn said quickly and raced away.

"Hello," Stephen Talbot greeted the journalist.

"Hello yourself," Deane said, staring gloomily at the retreating figure.

Stephen grinned.

"Did I butt in and disturb an important conference?"

"I had a fish practically on the hook," Bob exploded, "and you frightened him off. That's all!"

"If the fish was Wyburn, I'm glad I came. Your third-degree tactics are a bit wearing."

"So you know Wyburn."

"Slightly. Any objection?" Stephen asked airily.

"None whatever." Deane changed his tone to one of artful persuasion. "Of course you met him through Vanda, didn't you?"

"Did I?" Stephen's lips twitched.

"That's what I'm asking you."

"Go ahead. I'm not obliged to answer."

The journalist controlled an impulse to use language that would have merely made Stephen Talbot laugh.

"Where has Vanda been during the last half-hour, if that isn't too much to ask?"

"In the restaurant. After her first dances she stayed there talking to friends." Stephen glanced at his watch. "I must be getting back. It's a quarter-past eleven and she comes on for her final appearance pretty soon."

"Why so early?"

"Because the cabaret must finish by midnight. It's Saturday, I must buy you a calendar, Deane." Stephen relented. "You ought to see Vanda in her new dance. Come in with me. Naomi and Phil are at my table."

"Their joy at seeing me won't be overwhelming. Besides, I'm not rigged up," Bob admitted ruefully.

"There's such a crowd that nobody would notice if you were in a bathing-costume. The lights will be lowered too when Vanda and Nicola do their turn."

Stephen conducted the reporter to the table reserved for the dancer's party, and introduced him briefly to Casinier and Ferrari as Bob Deane, without mention, of his professional status.

Casinier accorded the visitor a friendly nod and poured him out a glass of champagne. Naomi greeted him with a faint smile and Phil a pronounced scowl.

"Behave yourself, Bob, or out you go," she muttered in his ear.

Ferrari, his brow furrowed, was too anxious about his charge to give Bob more than a glance. His attention was divided between his wrist-watch and Vanda, who was talking gaily at another table. At last he caught her eye and beckoned urgently.

Releasing herself from her admirers, Vanda strolled across to him. There was an extraordinary radiance in her manner.

"It's time you changed for your last number!" Ferrari told her.

"Nonsense. I'm the world's quickest dresser, as you know, Ferrari." She noticed Bob Deane's eager face and smiled at him. "Who's the stranger?"

"May I introduce Mr. Deane?" Naomi asked diffidently. "Miss Vanda Quayne."

"You must blame Mr. Talbot for wishing me upon your party," Bob explained. "You've no idea how proud I am to meet you, Miss Quayne."

"Stephen should have brought you along before." Vanda picked up a glass of champagne and drank it with a provocative gleam in her dark eyes. "Come back to Briar Lodge with the others after the show to-night."

"I'd love to. It will be something to remember for many a long year." Bob's ardent expression changed as Phil trod on his foot.

"You're overdoing your act," she warned.

"Will you please go and dress," Ferrari begged the dancer in worried tones.

"All right." Vanda spoke a few words in an undertone to him and then turned to Naomi. "Will you come to my dressing-room while I change, Miss Marsh? I want to talk to you about something. You can get back to your seat in time to see the dance."

The anxious perplexity did not fade from Ferrari's face when Vanda and Naomi left the table. It was so obvious, that Bob Deane felt curious and moved nearer the manager.

"Miss Quayne seems in great form," he remarked by way of an opening.

Ferrari flicked his fingers.

"It's not her work I'm bothered about; it's her dangerous mood. I know her only too well. She's liable to make a scene at any minute in this high-strung state."

Bob soaked in the information and proceeded deftly to obtain more.

"Has anything happened to annoy her?" he asked sympathetically.

"I shouldn't mind if it had: that wouldn't matter," Ferrari declared. "Something has happened—I don't know what or when—to change a normally vain and beautiful woman into a triumphant and relentless vixen, aching to show her power. If nobody stops her she might—" He broke off and turned to Casinier. "Miss Quayne wants all the restaurant lights out for this dance."

"I'll see to it," Casinier promised. "But won't it make the place too dark?"

Ferrari gave an unpleasant laugh.

"That's the way she intends to concentrate all attention on herself. She and Nicola will have strong limelights playing on them, of course. By the way, sir, I suppose you won't mind. Vanda has just told me she means to make a speech when her dance has ended."

Casinier shrugged his shoulders good humouredly. "Let the lady do as she pleases," he said. "I'll speak to the electrician."

As he walked off, Bob Deane slipped away unobtrusively. Entering the telephone box in the hall, he dialled a number.

"Is that Scotland Yard?" he asked when there was an answer. "If Inspector Reynolds is there, put me through to him at once."

His fingers tapped impatiently until he heard a familiar voice.

"Thank goodness I've found you, inspector," he said over the wire. "This is Bob Deane speaking from the Regis. I smell trouble. Can you come along? No, I don't, know what it is, but I've a hunch that something is brewing. There's been a lot of funny stuff going on here to-night."

*   *   *   *   *

A grey-eyed, well-dressed man of about forty, with a genial face that frequently deceived evildoers, was met by Bob Deane a quarter of an hour later.

Bob guided him into the darkened restaurant to the table where he had previously been sitting.

Phil was there alone, watching the figures of Vanda and Nicola, as they swayed and postured on the stage in the changing tones of the limelight.

"It's all right, inspector!" Bob whispered. "You're in time."

Their eyes watched Vanda hang limply in Nicola's arms.

"In time to see a new version of the Dying Swan?" smiled the C.I.D. man. "This woman's very good, but I saw Pavlova."

The lights shaded from rose and purple to a dim green as Nicola lowered the graceful form of Vanda Quayne to the floor and bent over her, in an attitude of assumed grief. Then slowly he rose, and extended his arms to the audience, as if mutely inviting them to witness the tragedy.

There was silence for a moment: that appreciative silence which is a rare tribute coveted by artistes.

Suddenly the applause broke out, punctuated by "Bravos." On and on it roared, while Nicola stood poised above Vanda's still form.

"Speech, speech," yelled the crowd. "Speech, Vanda."

Stooping, Nicola took her hand, and placing an arm round her waist, prepared to swing her lithely to her feet.

But she lay inert.

Nicola turned a frightened imploring look towards the stage exit where Ferrari was standing.

At once the manager hurried and explained to the audience that Miss Quayne had fainted. Then with Nicola's help, he proceeded to carry the dancer to her dressing-room.

Instantly the lights in the restaurant were switched on, and the band struck up a popular fox-trot which quietened any possible commotion by luring couples on to the floor.

Bob Deane grinned

"Sorry, inspector. A fainting woman isn't exactly a Scotland Yard job."

Phil touched his arm.

"Look! Ferrari is going from table to table. I think he's asking if a doctor is present. I don't believe that Vanda merely fainted. She's not the type, and that dance wasn't very strenuous."

The C.I.D. man regarded her thoughtfully. "You're probably right," he said. "Come along, Deane. Let's go and find out what it's all about."

XXVI. A MYSTERIOUS ILLNESS

Saturday, November 27th.

FOLLOWED by Phil, Inspector Reynolds and the journalist made their way towards the stage. The band continued to play gaily, and the floor was crowded with people.

In the corridor leading to the dressing-rooms, Bob paused.

"You shouldn't have come, Phil." His tone was unusually stern. "There will be plenty of people to look after Vanda. Go back to the restaurant."

Behind the C.I.D. man's back, Phil held up a warning finger to Bob.

"Vanda be blowed," she retorted in a whisper. "I'm worried about Naomi."

"And who is Naomi?" asked Reynolds unexpectedly.

"Naomi Marsh is Miss Quayne's secretary. We share a flat." Phil was a little startled at the inspector's sudden change from easy amiability to alertness.

"Vanda asked Miss Marsh to go to her dressing-room just before the last dance," Bob supplemented.

"A normal proceeding. Why should you be worried about your friend, Miss Ingram?"

Again Phil felt disconcerted by Reynolds's directness, and gave a vague, confused reply.

There were several people clustered round the door of Vanda's dressing-room, waiting curiously to know what had happened.

As Phil arrived with Deane and the C.I.D. man, Mrs. Casinier approached her husband.

"But, my dearest," he exclaimed, "you ought not to have come back again!"

"I was too restless," she said. "Besides, I'm quite well now. Please let me wait for you, Julian."

"As you wish." His tone was reluctant. "I'm afraid you can't go into Miss Quayne's room yet. She seems to have collapsed. Ferrari and I have been looking for a doctor. Ah, he's found one, I fancy."

The circle of people divided to admit Ferrari and the medical man who entered Vanda's room and closed the door. Perhaps the latch was insecurely fastened; perhaps Bob Deane turned the handle, for it swung open again, revealing the dancer's form lying on the couch, with the doctor and Ferrari bending over her. Osmond, still and grave, stood near them. Behind her, her face ashen, was Naomi.

Phil moved towards her friend, unconsciously drawing the others with her.

The doctor said something to Ferrari, who looked at him helplessly.

Instantly Inspector Reynolds joined them. A murmured conversation took place between him and the doctor. Osmond whispered something to the inspector.

There was a tense hush for a moment. It was broken by the medical man.

"Miss Quayne must be taken to her home at once," he pronounced in clear tones. "She is ill."

"Ill!" came in a husky, surprised whisper from someone in the room.

The inspector swung round sharply.

"Who said that?" he demanded. His eyes raked each face with stern inquiry.

"Who said that?" he repeated a moment later. Phil Ingram gave a nervous smile,

"I did," she replied. "It was stupid of me. I'm very—"

Reynolds cut short her apology by a wave of his hand.

"I'll order an ambulance," said the doctor, and hurried out, followed by Ferrari.

Bob Deane cast a glance at those who remained. Phil, Naomi and Osmond stood on his right; Mr. and Mrs. Casinier and Nicola on his left.

Bob had forced his way into the room, intent on getting every nuance of this affair. His eager eyes darted from the inanimate woman on the couch to the silent watchers. Had Vanda merely fainted? Or was there a more sinister explanation of her illness? One or more of these people might have some interesting knowledge of the subject.

Bob ran them over mentally, as though he were already interviewing each one. Vanda's maid might be a cold, hard nut to crack, but she'd certainly be worth the effort. Nicola would be easier to deal with, if less reliable. The Casiniers he dismissed: Mrs. Casinier wasn't in Vanda's class, and apparently had only just called for her husband. Julian Casinier held far too important a name in the financial world to be mixed up in any monkey tricks on Vanda's life—if such tricks had been played.

Bob pricked up his ears in astonishment as he heard Inspector Reynolds addressing the great financier's wife.

"You were here earlier this evening, I believe, Mrs. Casinier," Reynolds remarked, recalling Osmond's whispered statement.

The lady bowed.

"That is so," she agreed.

"My wife had a message for me," Casinier interposed. "She felt ill and left almost at once."

"Yet she felt well enough to return," the inspector pursued.

"Madame Casinier rested on this couch for some time." It was Osmond who spoke. "She was here alone when I accompanied Miss Quayne to the stage."

Reynolds cast a cold measuring glance upon the maid.

"You gave me that information a moment ago. I will hear any further statement presently," he said, and turned again to the Casiniers. "While you were alone, Mrs. Casinier, did anyone enter this room?"

Again the lady's husband intervened with a touch of nervous haste foreign to his usual deliberate manner of speaking.

"My wife had a slight heart-attack. She suffers frequently in that way and is barely conscious at those times."

"Perhaps you will allow your wife to tell me what her condition was this evening." Reynolds spoke with dry courtesy but definite firmness.

"I'm sorry, inspector, but it is as my husband said," the lady replied. "Perhaps, however, I might have noticed if someone had entered the room."

Bob Deane had a moment of inspiration that he considered justified him for breaking into the conversation.

"Excuse me for butting in, Mrs. Casinier," he said apologetically. "Did Cyril Wyburn give you an urgent note for your husband when he came in here?"

The lady stepped into the trap.

"No, he did not mention that he had one," she said innocently.

Bob nodded to the C.I.D. man with the satisfied air of a counsel who is passing over a foolish witness.

To Bob's surprise, Reynolds did not follow up the point. Instead, his eyes rested frowningly upon the curtains which divided the room in such a fashion that the door when open lay flush against one of them.

"Who is hiding behind there?" he asked.

Osmond grasped the curtains defensively. "No one," she replied.

Thrusting the maid aside, Reynolds went to see if she had told the truth.

No word was spoken by the others until he came back and drew the curtains close again. His face revealed nothing, and the appearance of the ambulance put an end to further questioning.

The doctor waited until the men had placed Vanda on the stretcher. His face was grave as he tested her pulse once more.

"Go very gently," he urged the bearers; adding in a lower tone to Reynolds, "I've rung up a specialist who will go to Briar Lodge at once, also a nurse is on her way. This mysterious business is more than I care to tackle alone. The symptoms are curious."

Reynolds listened attentively to the medical man.

"You are going to Briar Lodge?" he asked. The doctor nodded.

"At once. My car is waiting now."

"Should not one of us go in the ambulance with Miss Quayne?" Naomi inquired. "Mr. Ferrari or myself perhaps."

"I'm Miss Quayne's manager, inspector," Ferrari explained.

"It is my place to accompany my mistress," Osmond stated in a firm voice.

Reynolds glanced speculatively from one to the other of those assembled. Nicola, the Casiniers, Naomi, Ferrari, and the maid—all these, he knew, had been with Vanda in the dressing-room at some time that evening.

He went across to Phil—the only one who had not left the restaurant.

"Will you go with Miss Quayne?" he asked.

"Yes, inspector." Phil flushed a little and then added in a whisper, "I'm sorry, but I lied to you just now when you asked which of us had spoken. I don't know who it was."

Reynolds gave her a brisk pat on the shoulder.

"I knew you lied. Run along. Should Miss Quayne speak—either in consciousness or delirium—let me know. I shall be there soon. Remain with her until the nurse arrives."

The inspector despatched Bob Deane to ring up the Yard.

"Say I want Detective-Sergeant Jenkins, a fingerprint man and an officer here at once," he ordered.

"I think Jenkins is working late on a report. Not a word of this is for the press until I give permission."

An awed expression crept over Bob's face.

"You can rely on me, inspector," he promised. "I say, Vanda's not going to conk out, is she?"

"Do as I tell you. I'm in a hurry," was Reynolds's non-committal reply. "And send in a constable. There's one outside."

Rarely had the C.I.D. man been faced single-handed with a more perplexing situation. For all he could prove to the contrary, Miss Quayne's illness might be natural and have no serious consequences. In which case, there might be considerable inquiries at headquarters as to why he had detained and questioned these people.

On the other hand, if Vanda's life were endangered and the worst happened, there might be still more inquiries at headquarters if he were lax in dealing with these people who had been in her proximity during the last few hours. Reynolds's only justification for questioning them was based on the doctor's anxious remarks made after his hurried examination. Tact must be his long suit at the moment, Reynolds decided.

There was also the added problem of where to conduct his investigations. For many reasons, he would have preferred to stay at the Regis and see if there were any clues, to be picked up.

But, if an attempt had been made on Vanda's life, obviously he should go to Briar Lodge in case her would-be murderer tried to finish the job.

He was relieved to see a police officer arrive.

"You want me, sir?" the constable asked.

Reynolds ordered him to lock the dressing-room door and stay on guard until the Yard men arrived.

"My car is at your disposal if you need it, inspector," Casinier remarked.

"Thank you. How many will it hold?"

"Six at a push, excluding the chauffeur."

The inspector counted heads. With the maid, there were six people: the Casiniers, Nicola, Osmond, Naomi and Ferrari: each of whom possibly knew something vital concerning Vanda Quayne's mysterious illness.

"I shall be glad if you will take them all to Briar Lodge, Mr. Casinier. I will join you presently."

"Might I take my wife home first? You could see her at my home to-morrow, of course, if you think it necessary."

The inspector agreed, the more willingly because the delayed journey would prevent the party reaching Briar Lodge before he did.

Directly the Yard men arrived, Reynolds gave them their instructions.

"Also," he told Detective Sergeant Jenkins, "I want you to look up Filmer in hospital, and trace a young man called Cyril Wyburn who was in Miss Quayne's dressing-room to-night—unknown to her, I fancy. Deane says he knows Wyburn's address."

"Is Miss Quayne going to recover, sir?" Jenkins asked.

The inspector pursed his lips.

"I can't tell you. But one member of that bunch now on its way to Briar Lodge seemed surprised that she wasn't dead! Now clear out for a minute or two. I want this dressing-room to myself before I go to Miss Quayne's house."

XXVII. Suspicions

Saturday, November 27th.

THE C.I.D. man closed the door when his assistant went into the corridor.

"You can come out," he remarked. "I hope you have a satisfactory explanation of your peculiar behaviour."

The curtains were drawn aside and Stephen Talbot came into view.

"Thanks for being so sporting, inspector," he said. "My wish for seclusion was purely personal, and had nothing to do with Miss Quayne, though I can scarcely expect you to believe me."

"Your explanation might assist the process." Reynolds's tone was dry.

"That, I am afraid, I am not prepared to give you at the moment."

The inspector churned over this answer and decided there was nothing he could do about it then. It was not unnatural that the young man before him should dislike being discovered hiding in an actress's dressing-room!

"Your name and address?" he asked.

Stephen supplied the information readily.

"Thank you, Mr. Talbot. Have you known Miss Quayne long?"

"Too long!" Stephen grinned. "I renewed an old acquaintance made years ago, and am beginning to regret my folly since it landed me into this predicament."

The inspector gave him a sharp glance.

"Presumably, you dived behind the curtains to avoid being seen by the people who have just gone off with Mr. Casinier."

"Something like that," Stephen admitted. "I had a close shave when you poked your head in. If I may say so, inspector, you're a darned good actor. I only held up my finger for silence and you not only caught the idea instantly, but never gave away to the others that I was here."

Flattery usually made Reynolds suspicious. Talbot, however, had a naïve frankness that made the older man feel justified in accepting the compliment with reserve.

"We will go into your motives for concealing yourself; later, if necessary, Mr. Talbot. Have you any objection in coming to Briar Lodge with me?"

"None whatever." Stephen bit his lip. "That is where Mr. Casinier is taking the others, isn't it? Will they all be there?"

Reynolds nodded.

"All except Mrs. Casinier, who will be taken to her home first." He turned and addressed Bob Deane who entered the room. "Give Detective-Sergeant Jenkins any information that he needs."

"Yes, inspector." The journalist stared at the other man. "Hello, Talbot. I suppose you've blown in to see what's wrong. Where were you when Vanda was taken ill?"

"Inspector Reynolds will tell you," Stephen replied audaciously.

The inspector was in no mood to answer questions. Marshalling Talbot and Bob Deane out into the corridor, he locked the door and gave the key to his assistant.

"Good-night, Deane. You'd better cut along. There's nothing more for you to do here when you've spoken to Jenkins." The inspector's manner was brisk and decisive.

The journalist looked sulky.

"Can't I come with you?" he asked.

"No. Mr. Talbot and I are not going your way," Reynolds told him firmly. "You can ring me up tomorrow to know how things go."

Conversation on the journey to Briar Lodge was curiously impersonal. The C.I.D. man talked with enthusiasm of roses and Airedales, both of which were hobbies of his. Indeed, had it not been for the little episode behind the dressing-room curtains, Stephen might have felt that the inspector was almost too mild and pleasant for his job. As it was, he listened with respect.

All went smoothly until they reached Briar Lodge. Lights were on in the upper rooms, and two cars were parked in the small drive. Reynolds scrutinized the vehicles.

The specialist and the doctor appear to have arrived," he surmised, "but Mr. Casinier hasn't come yet." He stopped the taxi outside the gates and stood waiting while the driver slowly counted out the change.

Behind the cab a loafer in a long overcoat lurched towards Stephen and mumbled something in an undertone.

Stephen made an angry retort. In a few seconds the man ambled away with a staggering gait just as the taxi drove off.

"A drunken cadger?" Reynolds inquired casually as they walked up the drive.

"Yes. I suppose they find it pays to hang round a celebrity's house," Stephen replied.

Reynolds gave him an odd glance.

"They certainly must if every caller tips them as lavishly as you did, Mr. Talbot."

Stephen smiled.

"Ten bob is not my usual largesse, but I felt softhearted and had very little silver."

"You didn't sound particularly soft-hearted when you told him that you'd finished with him!" Reynolds commented. "By the way, are you colour-blind or short-sighted?"

"Neither one nor the other. Why?"

"Ten-shilling notes are printed in brown ink. You'd better remember that for future occasions. Here's Mr. Casinier's car."

Inside the hall, they found Phil Ingram.

"The doctors are with Miss Quayne," she told Reynolds. "I stayed with her until the nurse came." Her eyes flashed to Stephen as she finished speaking and then back to the C.I.D. man who gave an almost imperceptible nod of understanding.

"I shall be in the dining-room, inspector, if you want me," Phil added, and slipped quietly away as Casinier and his passengers entered the house.

Reynolds called Naomi aside.

As Miss Quayne's secretary, will you take charge of these people, Miss Marsh? I don't want them to wander around the house until the doctors have gone."

"I'll have drinks served in the studio for them," Naomi promised. Remembering that Osmond was with the party, she added, "Do you wish Miss Quayne's maid to remain down here as well?"

"By all means. Let her help you in some way."

"I'll arrange it." Naomi's face looked wan and anxious. "Have you any news about Miss Quayne?"

"Not yet," Reynolds replied.

He was about to go into the dining-room when a uniformed nurse came hurriedly down the stairs, and took a doctor's bag from the hall table.

Before she could go up again, Reynolds stopped her. "Is there any change in Miss Quayne's condition, nurse?" he inquired.

"Are you a relative of hers?" the nurse asked sharply.

"No."

"Then I must refer you to the doctors for any information you require," she replied in formal tones.

Reynolds smiled to himself as the nurse went upstairs. She had come through his test nicely, and, he fancied, could be relied upon to hold her tongue, no matter what barrage of questions was hurled at her.

He faced Phil Ingram a moment later. She too seemed to be a person of determined character.

"You allowed no one to come near Miss Quayne?" he asked.

"Only the ambulance men who carried her to her room, inspector; and, of course, the doctor." Phil's lips tightened firmly.

"Did she recover consciousness?"

"She mumbled a few incoherent words about Filmer."

"Anything else? Take your time, Miss Ingram."

Watching the girl, Reynolds noted that her eyes held a wary expression, as if she were mentally treading on ground that might prove dangerous. Experience had made him deft in the art of questioning according to the personality of a witness. That same experience had taught him the even greater art of changing the subject when persistence might induce lies or evasion.

"Tell me about yourself," he urged.

Led on by Reynolds's subtle persuasion, she drew a picture of her work first in Casinier's office and later in the beauty parlour which he owned.

"So you and Miss Marsh met while you were with Mr. Casinier," he summed up. "She must be extremely capable to have obtained this post with Miss Quayne. How did she get it?"

Phil mentioned the name of Naomi's employment agency and stopped abruptly.

Reynolds, however, showed no interest in her words; indeed, it almost seemed that he was merely making polite conversation while his thoughts were far away.

"Who introduced you to Stephen Talbot?" he asked.

"He called at our flat."

A while later, Reynolds learnt how Talbot had seemingly trailed Naomi in Paris and saved her from the man in the brown overcoat. There was a glint in the inspector's eyes when Phil spoke of the latter.

"I hope I've done no harm to my friend by telling you of these incidents, inspector," she said. "Such an objectionable little spy surely deserves anything he might get."

Reynolds made no reply; instead he asked: "Did Miss Quayne ever speak of any enemy?" The colour rushed to Phil Ingram's face.

"Not to me," she said with obvious reluctance.

"But to Miss Marsh, perhaps," Reynolds persisted.

"Listen, Miss Ingram, there is a moment when frankness is necessary. As your friend is busy just now, it will save time if you tell me what you know." Always fully appreciative of dramatic values, he paused, adding in a low, serious tone, "It might also save life."

Phil gazed at him speculatively.

"If you insist, inspector, I will tell you," she agreed, "although I am afraid that Miss Marsh will resent my doing so."

In graphic sentences she outlined what Naomi had told her of the attack on Vanda in Paris, the anonymous letters, and telephoned orders to Naomi to leave her job.

"Miss Marsh disregarded these threats and preferred to remain?" Reynolds pursued.

"Naomi is very determined," Phil assured him.

"And apparently fearless," was Reynolds's comment. After a few more questions concerning Osmond, Nicola and Ferrari, Reynolds rose. "Thank you, Miss Ingram. None of this information may be needed, but it is as well to be on the safe side. I think I hear the doctors coming downstairs. Will you go into the studio with the others, please?"

Reynolds approached the two medical men. For a few minutes he listened carefully to them, remaining engrossed in thought even after they had gone. Then he passed through the drawing-room and stood silently in the wide doorway regarding the men and women assembled in the studio.

They were all there, he noted. Phil Ingram was near Casinier; Naomi and the maid, Osmond, were passing drinks and sandwiches.

Presently, as each one became aware of Reynolds's presence, conversation ceased. Still silent, he faced the group as if deliberately keeping them in suspense.

"How is she?" It was Ferrari who put the question in harsh accents.

"The doctors agree that Miss Quayne has been suffering from the effects of a narcotic," Reynolds said in impersonal tones.

"Has been suffering! You mean she is dead!" Again it was Ferrari who spoke, but this time there was almost a note of anguish in his voice. "Poor reckless Vanda. I begged her not to come to England."

"Calm yourself, Mr. Ferrari." Reynolds addressed the manager but his eyes continued to search the faces before him. "I have the doctors' permission to assure you that Miss Quayne will probably be much better tomorrow. She is asleep now and the nurse will remain on duty to-night."

XXVIII. Tragedy

Saturday, November 27th

SOMEONE gave a nervous laugh. Cigarettes were lighted. Osmond moved about with a tray of glasses. The tension was broken.

"Apparently much ado about nothing," said Stephen Talbot. "I suppose we can all go home now." His tone expressed relief.

Reynolds nodded.

"Yes, after I have received answers to two questions. Is Miss Quayne in the habit of taking drugs in order to sleep?"

"Yes, of every kind," Ferrari replied. "I've quarrelled with her often about the danger of it."

Reynolds glanced inquiringly at Vanda's maid

"Madame has taken drugs at intervals ever since I have been with her," Osmond told him

"Did anyone see Miss Quayne take any drug tonight in her dressing-room at the Regis?" The inspector's second question was put generally to the group of people ranged before him. His eyes raked their faces one by one as if he would extract the truth by some inner force.

"Would any artiste—and Vanda certainly is that— damage her chance of success by such an action immediately before she danced?" Julian Casinier parried in slow, calm accents.

"A reasonable question, Mr. Casinier." Reynolds agreed, "but I should like an answer to mine, please."

As no one spoke he added, "I will ask you individually. Did your mistress take drugs or medicine in her dressing-room to-night, Osmond?'

The maid's calm expression took on a shade of sullenness.

"I neither gave nor saw madame take any, but she had opportunity and there were others there beside myself."

The inspector frowned.

"I am aware of that," he reproved sharply, and turned to the Russian.

"I saw nothing," Nicola said hastily.

"Can you help me, Miss Marsh?"

"I'm afraid not, inspector," Naomi replied. "Miss Quayne drank a little Burgundy, I think, while I was there."

"She always does before she dances," volunteered Ferrari, "She might have put something in the glass, but I didn't see it."

"Neither did I," added Julian Casinier.

"How long was your wife in the dressing-room?" the C.I.D. man asked him.

Casinier drew himself up stiffly, but before he could speak, Stephen Talbot broke in.

"Surely the evidence of Mrs. Casinier would be of little use, inspector, as she was suffering from a heart-attack."

Reynolds looked at the younger man thoughtfully. "That would depend on the lady's condition," he observed.

"The moment my wife had recovered sufficiently, I sent her home," Casinier interposed.

"The point has been already made clear to me." Reynolds's voice had a crisp inflexion. "I also know that Mrs. Casinier felt well enough to return to the Regis, which I understand she rarely visits."

There was a little pause, then Stephen again interrupted.

"You've forgotten to question me, inspector," he remarked cheerfully. "Am I too deeply suspected?" A smile crinkled Reynolds's lips.

"I'm afraid you've been reading detective fiction, Mr. Talbot. My job is to elicit facts, not to indulge in groundless suspicions. I have not forgotten you," his tone hardened a little, "nor your two interruptions," he added tersely. "I think that is all I need you for to-night," he said to the party. "Miss Marsh, will you see that the house is locked up when we all leave?"

"I don't sleep here, inspector, but if you wish, I can do so," Naomi offered, as they went towards the hall.

"I should like you to remain."

"I'll stay here with her, inspector," Phil volunteered. "There are two beds in that room which is opposite Miss Quayne's."

Phil waited while the inspector made two telephone calls.

The first, of short duration, was to the Regis where he learnt that his instructions had been carried out; also that no drugs of any kind had been found in Vanda's dressing-room.

The second call put him into touch with the hospital where Filmer lay.

"Ask Detective-Sergeant Jenkins to speak to me," Reynolds requested.

"What's the news?" he demanded when his assistant's voice came over the wire.

"Very little; sir." Jenkins's tone was gloomy. "Filmer had a patch of consciousness but seems unconscious again."

"Seems!"

"Well, the doctors say his condition is better and his pulse pretty good. Yet he can't or won't talk now, though Heaven knows I've tried hard enough to make him."

Reynolds chuckled.

"Don't worry him to talk against the doctors' orders."

"They think there's something mysterious about his case, sir. From what I can learn he asked for Vanda Quayne who had made frequent inquiries by telephone about him. He wouldn't speak a word until she came. Then he insisted upon seeing her alone."

"Wasn't there a constable there?"

"There was. Filmer wouldn't open his lips while the officer stayed."

"That's a pity," Reynolds exclaimed. "I'd give quite a bit to know why a man who was presumably a stranger to her wanted a heart-to-heart chat with a famous film star."

"Exactly. That's why I'm trying to make the blighter talk now. I shall stay here and hope to wring something out of him and let the constable go home."

"Give me a ring at my home if you have any luck, Jenkins. By the way Miss Quayne is all right, or will be by to-morrow."

"I've an idea, sir. How would it be if Filmer heard that she had collapsed and her life was in danger. Maybe he'd open his eyes and his mouth at that news. I could mention the fact to the nurse in his room."

"It wouldn't be fact," commented the inspector. "And I give you no official permission to act as you suggest. However, good hunting."

A minute later, he met Phil and Naomi in the hall.

"Everyone has gone," Phil told him. "Naomi has arranged for us to sleep in the room opposite Miss Quayne's."

"I fancy it was you who originated that suggestion, Miss Ingram," Reynolds observed. "I'd like to have a word with the nurse. Miss Marsh, will you show me which is Miss Quayne's room?"

Naomi led the way up the wide staircase and indicated a door.

Giving a faint tap, the inspector waited until the nurse appeared. For a few moments he spoke to her in an undertone.

"I will do as you wish," she promised, and returned to her patient.

"And now, you can lock up and go to bed," Reynolds told the girls in the hall. "I'll telephone to you in the morning, Miss Marsh." He gave Naomi a card. "Ring me at this number during the night, if necessary." He opened the front door and shrugged ruefully as he saw that a fog had turned the drive into a seemingly black tunnel.

"I'll keep the door open so that the hall light can guide you to the gate," Naomi offered.

His eyes scanned the thick shrubs which lined the path; a dozen people could hide there in safety on such a night as this, he thought.

Peering into the darkness, he listened intently. There was no sound of movement, and after a moment he walked on to the gate.

"All right, thanks," he called back to the girls, and heard them close and lock the front door before he turned up Warne Road.

The fog was less opaque out here near the lamps, and Reynolds could discern the occasional dim figure of a passer-by. The regular footsteps assured him that not one of them paused at Briar Lodge. Deciding that his uneasy fears had no real basis, he took a taxi to his home at Highgate.

Late as it was, he found a cheery fire burning in the sitting-room, a kettle on the hob, and everything prepared for a light meal.

Reynolds viewed the comfortable scene with a sigh of satisfaction as he stretched himself in an easy chair and closed his eyes. He opened them as a pleasant-faced woman with calm brown eyes and a mouth that held humour and kindness entered the room.

"You ought to be asleep at this hour, Agnes," Reynolds told her with assumed sternness.

"Yes, dear; so ought you," she replied amiably. "But as we're both up, would you like tea, coffee or whisky?"

"Tea, please. Did I wake you?"

Mrs. Reynolds shook her head.

"I was doing a cross-word puzzle. What happened, or are you too weary to talk about it?

"I'd like your advice." In clear terse phrases, Reynolds related the circumstances of his visit to the Regis and Briar Lodge that night, hoping to draw his wife's opinion on the matter. In many previous cases he had proved her common sense to be invaluable. "So you see nothing really happened," he ended. "Vanda might have taken a narcotic by accident; or, as some drugs have a cumulative effect, they might have selected to-night to overpower her. The doctor told me there were several hypodermic marks on her arm."

His wife handed him a cup of tea and held out a plate of sandwiches.

"You're worried because you're not sure if Vanda harmed herself accidentally, or was harmed by an enemy."

"Exactly that," Reynolds agreed. "At the risk of looking ridiculous, because I've no evidence that the drug was not self-administered, I questioned those people to-night. There may yet be a spot of bother for me at headquarters if they complain."

His wife ignored the latter part of his sentence.

"Vanda Quayne wouldn't have been so stupid as to damage her success to-night deliberately," she commented. "Also, don't forget, Tom, this is not the first time she has been mixed up in odd affairs. The Sureté man from Paris, who had supper with us two nights ago, remarked that Vanda was billed to appear at the Regis and said trouble always came with her."

"He told me more than that," Reynolds supplemented gloomily. "A strange story about a maid called Henriette employed at a convent hospital where Vanda was recently a patient. I'm beginning to wonder—"

"Don't begin anything at this hour," his wife broke in. "You've done all you can, and need sleep. Last night you were working on that jewel robbery and didn't get home until nearly four in the morning."

"But we caught the men, my dear. I've achieved nothing to-night. By the way, Jenkins may ring me up if he can get Filmer to talk."

Agnes Reynolds smiled.

"If Jenkins rings up, he'll learn that I can talk too, and take a message. Off you go to bed."

She was preparing breakfast next morning when the telephone bell tinkled at half-past seven. She took up the receiver and heard a woman's voice ask for Inspector Reynolds.

"Please say it is urgent. My name is Naomi Marsh. I'm speaking from Briar Lodge."

Mrs. Reynolds fetched her husband and listened to his brief questions over the wire.

"What is it?" she asked when the call was finished. Reynolds's face was grim.

"Vanda Quayne was found dead ten minutes ago."

XXIX. Behind Locked Doors

Sunday, November 28th.

BEFORE Reynolds could ring the bell at Briar Lodge, Naomi opened the door to him, clad in pyjamas and dressing-gown.

"Miss Ingram has gone across to our flat for some clothes," she explained in a flurry of nervous apology.

"You said no one must leave the house, but I thought you wouldn't mind as she'll be back in a few minutes."

"I usually mean what I say, Miss Marsh." There was reproof in Reynolds's tone. "Who found Miss Quayne?"

"Anderson, the house parlourmaid. She had a tray of tea for the nurse. As her knock was not answered, she went in. Miss Quayne was dead and the nurse was not there."

The inspector gave a puzzled frown.

"Not there!" he exclaimed. "I told her last night to lock the doors and admit no one. Why wasn't she with her patient?"

"I can't say."

"Where is the nurse now?"

"She may be in the boudoir which leads from Miss Quayne's bedroom. Directly Anderson told me the news, I telephoned to you, and on your instructions I have not entered the room, nor allowed anyone else to do so. I also rang up the doctor, as you wished. He was out, but should be here presently."

Reynolds hurried up the stairs to the dancer's room. One glance at Vanda's still form told him that the maid was right. He had looked upon death too often to be mistaken.

For a moment he gazed upon the pale face, so calm and beautiful in its last repose. Two doctors had stated last night that Miss Quayne was in no danger.

Reynolds turned his attention to the room and swiftly took in the details. Nothing appeared to be disordered in any way, and there was no hint of a struggle.

The next thing was to find out why the nurse had left her patient. His face hardened as he strode across the room to the boudoir. Probably the woman had thought her patient was well enough for her to snatch a little sleep.

Extremely conscientious himself, Reynolds was never lenient with those who neglected their duty or disobeyed orders. So it was with no gentle hand that he rapped on the door.

There was no answer. He tried the handle and found that someone had fastened the lock. No key was there. A peep through the keyhole afforded him only a glimpse of one corner of the room.

The boudoir had a second door opening on to the landing. He had just discovered that that also was locked when the doctor arrived.

The inspector waited for him to make his examination.

The medical man's face showed surprise and concern when Reynolds drew him out on to the landing.

"Miss Quayne has been dead four or five hours, inspector. I can't understand why the nurse did not call me earlier. She's a very reliable girl, who has often worked on my cases."

"When this door is unfastened, you may know the answer, doctor," Reynolds replied. "The key is inside so if I smash a panel, I can get my hand in and turn it."

There was a crash as the thin wood splintered. A moment later the two men bent over the silent uniformed figure of the nurse; as she lay on the carpet.

"She's breathing," the doctor said, with relief. Noticing that one cuff was off, and her sleeve unfastened, he bared her arm. Above the elbow was the mark of a hypodermic needle. She seems to have had a recent injection here," he added, "though I'm sure she was not a drug addict, and equally sure she would not have taken anything of the sort while on duty. Someone must have given it to her against her will. Yet why a strong healthy girl didn't scream or struggle puzzles me."

Reynolds picked up something from under the table and held it out.

"Would this explain why the nurse didn't call for help?" he asked.

The doctor looked at the object—a leaden weight inside a man's glove. Bending over the girl again, he searched for bruises on her head.

"You're right, inspector. She was probably hit from behind and rendered unconscious long enough to be given a dose by hypodermic. Morphia, by the symptoms. I'll get to work on her at once."

"I won't hinder you, doctor, but I'll be glad if you can tell me one thing. Was it morphia that killed Vanda Quayne?"

"We can't be quite sure until the autopsy," replied the medical man, busy with the unconscious nurse. "See if there's a fresh needle-prick on her forearm," he suggested as he opened his bag. "Could you send up a sensible maid? I'll need coffee and a few things. Perhaps Miss Marsh would not lose her head."

"I'll send you Anderson," Reynolds promised. "She's Scottish, eminently sane, and didn't lose her head when she discovered that her mistress was dead."

"And has no reason for wishing ill to the nurse," he added to himself as he went downstairs.

Sending Anderson to carry out the doctor's instructions, Reynolds telephoned to the Yard.

He had completed his call when he saw the housemaid go upstairs carrying a cup of black coffee. Waiting until she returned to the hall, Reynolds beckoned to her.

"How is the nurse?" he inquired.

"She has just been very sick, so the poor body canna feel comfortable," Anderson replied. "The doctor seems satisfied with her condition, however."

"Good. Did you see her last night?"

"Only for a minute when she arrived, sir. A bonny lass she looked then. I asked what food I should get for her, and she said milk and biscuits were to be left on a table outside Miss Quayne's door. I was not to knock in case it disturbed her patient."

"You acted as nurse wished?"

"Yes, sir. She must have taken it in during the night. I noticed the tray in the boudoir when I gave the coffee to the doctor a moment ago. He said I was not to take it to the kitchen."

"Had nurse drunk the glass of milk?"

"It was in a pint sealed bottle. The tumbler had been used and rather more than half the milk was gone. Only a few biscuits had been eaten. There was also a tray of tea there, which the nurse must have made herself."

"It was well after midnight when your mistress was brought home. Were you waiting up for her?"

"No, sir. I had gone to bed, but got up to answer the telephone. Hearing that Miss Quayne was ill, I dressed and came down to see if I could assist in any way. For some reason, Osmond was asked to help get drinks and sandwiches." Anderson's expression showed that her dignity was considerably offended. "So I left the milk for the nurse and went back to bed."

"You heard no cry nor sounds of people moving about the house during the night?"

"Nothing. My bedroom is at the back of the house and I sleep soundly."

"What is the staff here?"

"The chef lives across the road and goes home each night, thanks be. He's often the worse for liquor, though he's a grand cook, I'll admit. There's a daily maid—she's Scottish too—who helps him or me as needed; she prefers to sleep out. Osmond has a small room near her mistress. Miss Marsh, the secretary, has not slept here until last night."

"Thank you, Anderson. Now tell me about this morning. Did nurse last night order you to bring her early tea?"

"No, sir. She was too concerned with her patient to trouble about herself. When I got up, I thought she'd like tea. At half-past seven I took some along. The boudoir door was locked, so I went to Miss Quayne's bedroom door and tapped very quietly. There was no sound. Not wishing to disturb my mistress, I turned the handle and going in softly, laid the tray on the table. It's a mercy I did so before I noticed the poor mistress, or I might have dropped it."

"You didn't scream?"

Anderson shook her head proudly.

"I'm not afraid of death. Directly I saw what had happened, I hurried across the room to try to get into the boudoir that way and tell the nurse. That door was locked too. At once I went across the landing to the room which Miss Marsh and Miss Ingram were occupying. I knocked and went in."

"Were they asleep?"

"I think so, though they roused quickly. Miss Marsh ran downstairs immediately and rang you up. Then she returned and locked Miss Quayne's door on the outside."

"Did she or Miss Ingram go into that room at all?"

"Not to my knowledge, sir. Miss Ingram certainly had the opportunity to do so while her friend was telephoning. I think it was unlikely, though, for she came downstairs dressed a few minutes later, and told me she was going to her flat to get some suitable clothes for Miss Marsh. That seemed reasonable."

"Did Miss Marsh and her friend seem surprised or shocked by the news of Miss Quayne's death?"

"Not that I noticed, but why should they, be? They have only known her a few days and were aware that she

was ill last night. Miss Marsh took it calmly and sensibly,
I thought. 'I'll 'ring up Inspector Reynolds at once,' she
told me, and I heard Miss Ingram say that meanwhile
she'd dress—'push on some clothes,' I think were her
words."

Reynolds admired the fairness of the maid's
statement as much as he appreciated the frankness of her
answers.

"Did you find any doors or windows unfastened when
you came down this morning?" he asked.

"The back and front doors were locked and bolted, and
all the windows on the ground floor were fastened. I've
not yet had time to go into the studio. Miss Marsh told me
that she locked up the house last night at your wish."

"That is so. We'll have a look now."

Followed by the maid, he went into the drawing-room,
and passing through the curtained archway, walked down
the long studio. The room was in semidarkness, with
windows still shaded, plates, glasses and ash-trays lying
around.

Anderson drew the curtains back and stood aside for
Reynolds to examine the windows and door that led into
the garden. The latter had a Yale lock and two bolts; the
latch was down securely, but neither of the bolts was
fastened.

"Anyone who had a key could get in easily," the
inspector commented. "Who uses this door?"

"The foreign gentleman, Mr. Nicola, has a key, and
perhaps—" Anderson paused feeling she had exceeded
her duty. "Miss Marsh could tell you better than I, sir,"
she added primly.

Reynolds was aware of that, but corroboration on any
point often saved valuable time.

"I'll see Miss Marsh presently. By the way, is Osmond
about yet?"

Anderson pursed her lips.

"I've not seen her, though that's not unusual. She
never eats a Christian breakfast; nothing but toast and

black coffee which she heats on a gas-ring in her bedroom. Sometimes I don't see her until midday. Perhaps I ought not to mention it, but she and Miss Quayne had a quarrel, and Osmond is leaving in a day or two."

The inspector's face expressed none of the interest that Anderson's remark had roused in him.

"Does Osmond know that her mistress is dead?" he demanded quickly.

"I don't see how she can, sir. She waits in her room until Miss Quayne rings for her. It's still early, and she probably thinks Miss Quayne is not yet awake. Though you'd imagine she would have appeared when you broke open the boudoir door."

Reynolds left her, and hurried upstairs.

Turning the handle of Osmond's door, he walked in boldly. The small room was spotlessly neat: the bed made, wardrobe and chest of drawers empty of garments.

Some time during that tragic night, Osmond had slipped quietly away. Was it before or after Vanda Quayne's death, Reynolds speculated?

XXX, The Tangled Skein

Sunday, November 28th.

SPEEDILY obtaining all the information he could from Naomi concerning the missing woman, Reynolds put through a call to the Yard, giving a description of Osmond.

He had barely replaced the receiver when Phil Ingram approached him.

"Osmond was over-friendly with Nicola, inspector, considering their acquaintance was supposedly of only a few days," she said. "Maybe she was a fast worker, although she didn't appear to be of that type."

"Get me his address," Reynolds requested

"Miss Marsh might know it, I don't," Phil told him, and went in search of her friend.

"Where does Nicola park his body, Naomi?" she asked.

Naomi shivered.

"Don't use that expression to-day, Phil. I don't know where Nicola is staying. Ferrari fixed him up, I think."

"Well, go and tell the inspector where Ferrari hangs out," Phil urged.

"There's no need" Naomi scribbled something on a sheet of paper. "Here's Ferrari's address and telephone number. He ought to be told of Miss Quayne's death; this autocratic C.I.D. man ordered me to tell no one without his permission."

Phil eyed her friend curiously.

"You find the inspector autocratic!" she observed.

"Yes. He's been giving orders, asking questions, and testing one person's word against another in a curt, bossy manner which I dislike," Naomi said with irritation.

"Murder doesn't call for party manners in his job. I wouldn't say he was autocratic, but he's certainly decisive, and could be merciless if he suspected evasion."

Naomi grasped the other girl's arm.

"What do you mean?" she demanded.

"Just this. Neither you nor I slept very much last night: only the difference was that I kept still and you thought I was asleep, while you were—" Phil made a significant pause—"restless, and I knew you were awake."

"I see. Do you propose to tell Inspector Reynolds?"

Phil shrugged her shoulders.

"Isn't it your move? He's not yet had time to ask us if we heard anything in the night, but, believe me, that question's coming with a whale of a lot more, and going all 'high-hat' won't scare him from his theme."

"I'll cross that bridge when I come to it, Phil."

"You'd better let me know the route you choose, or I may contradict you unconsciously. Fortunately I can afford to be frank."

"You're lucky. I can't." Naomi's voice was bitter. "Give the inspector Ferrari's address: that ought to keep him busy for a while."

"Will you tell him that you saw—?"

"Leave me alone," Naomi interrupted. "If I don't think things out, I shall go mad. That nurse is likely to come round soon, I suppose."

"Probably. The inspector's keeping tabs on her condition, and you can bet he'll interview her the moment the doctor agrees. Is that going to bring you nearer the bridge you seem to fear?"

Naomi stared miserably across the room.

"So near," she whispered, "that if it were a real bridge and not a metaphorical one, I'd be thankful to jump over it and end my troubles."

"You'd better think fast; the inspector won't be stalled off for long."

Reynolds, however, was too fully occupied to deal with Naomi for the moment. She at least was in the house, and was likely to remain there.

Over the wire Reynolds broke the news of Vanda's death to Ferrari.

The latter seemed more annoyed than astonished.

"I'll have the deuce of a mess cancelling her engagements," he said. "Also bang goes my job! Those doctors must have been fools last night to say she'd be well to-day. Do you want me to come round to Briar Lodge?"

"Yes. Bring Nicola with you. If he's out, find him, and please tell him nothing of what's happened," Reynolds ordered.

"All right, inspector. I can keep my mouth shut. I'll dig him out," was Ferrari's promise.

Upstairs in Vanda's room the Yard experts were photographing. The medical officer, having examined the dead woman, made a brief report to Reynolds.

"It tallies with Dr. Hawthorn's views," commented the C.I.D. man. "He is still with the nurse?"

The Yard doctor nodded.

"Yes. I looked in a minute ago and asked if he needed any help. The girl must have had a huge dose; she roused slightly, but is now comatose again."

"I hope she's in no danger." Reynolds's anxiety was based on the fear of losing a valuable witness as much as on humanitarian grounds.

"She's pretty bad. However, Hawthorn's a good chap and is doing all that is possible. He says he won't leave her yet. She won't be able to talk for a few hours at least, if that's what you're after, inspector. I'm afraid the delay is going to hinder your inquiries in this complicated case."

Reynolds gave a wry smile.

"I'm sure it is. You see, there's little doubt that somebody tried last night to kill Miss Quayne, at the

Regis. Thanks to prompt medical attention, that attack failed. So the murderer—man or woman or both—came back during the night and finished the crime."

"Someone who knew that the earlier attack had failed," commented the Yard doctor.

"Exactly." Reynolds groaned. "It doesn't sweeten my lot to realize that it was I who supplied that information unwittingly! I had no other choice. The bunch of people who had been in Miss Quayne's dressing-room, and later returned here, were all more or less entitled to hear how she was."

"Don't blame yourself, inspector. You did all you could in the circumstances, I'm sure."

"I had an extra police officer patrolling the road during the night, and told the nurse to lock the doors of the boudoir and Miss Quayne's bedroom, and admit no one. Yet the bedroom door was unfastened this morning and the nurse, drugged and unconscious, was found locked in the boudoir. I'd give quite a bit to hear who enticed her from her patient."

"Did the police constable see anybody enter the house during the night?"

"No. The fog was bad in this district, which made visibility difficult at more than a few yards."

"I suppose suicide is impracticable as a theory, regarding Vanda," mused the doctor. "Her first dose was only enough to make her sleep heavily."

"Even if Vanda awoke and was determined to end her life, think of the complicated process." Reynolds ticked the points off on his fingers. "One, she would have had to get nurse into the boudoir. Two, stun the nurse—a healthy girl, whereas Vanda was half drugged. Three, administer a big dose of morphia into the nurse's arm. Four, lock the door between the two rooms and throw away the key. Five, unlock her bedroom door which opens on to the landing. Six, get into bed and give herself a fatal dose of morphia. Meanwhile, we've found no syringe or case of drugs."

"And, don't forget that first of all she had to procure the morphia! No easy, business."

"In England. Of course Miss Quayne was abroad a great deal. Her maid and her manager agree that she took drugs, which she kept in a small case. The very dose that killed her might have been taken from that case by the murderer."

The Yard doctor buttoned up his overcoat.

"I don't envy you the task of unravelling this knot, inspector. The ambulance has come. I'll let you know the result of the autopsy as soon as possible. I suppose the inquest will be opened about Tuesday?"

"I hope to find that maid, and get the nurse well enough to give evidence first," Reynolds replied.

By half-past ten the ambulance men had removed the body, the inspector making sure that nothing unnecessary was disturbed in Vanda's bedroom.

Keenly intuitive, he was susceptible to depression when fate played against him. With Osmond gone and the nurse ill, his hands were tied. He could battle on doggedly and conscientiously, but the flair which had made him so fortunate in tracking criminals was temporarily missing in this case.

He was therefore unusually glad when his assistant, Detective-Sergeant Jenkins arrived, even though Jenkins had had no success during his vigil at the hospital.

"Filmer still won't or can't speak, sir," he announced gloomily.

"Cheer up. We're in much the same boat here," Reynolds told him. "Listen to this." He explained the situation briefly. "You see a great deal hinges on the nurse's recovery. I can only mark time until then."

"Would you like me to snoop around the rooms here, sir, or question the two young ladies?"

The inspector grinned.

"I'd better tackle them. Your efforts favour too much of the 'third degree,' young man. You can search Miss Quayne's bedroom, although I don't think you'll find much. Then put through inquiries at taxi-ranks asking if any driver brought fares to Warne Road or near here, in the small hours of the morning."

"I'll also inquire at the houses on either side. The people who live there may have heard or seen someone."

"It's not very hopeful. These oldish houses are all enclosed in high-walled gardens. The constable on duty noticed no one enter this house. I'm going upstairs to see how the nurse is getting along."

Reynolds had no luck there, however. Dr. Hawthorn's face looked harassed and tired.

"You'll have a second murder to deal with if we're not careful, inspector," he warned. "A big dose of morphia plus a nasty crack on the head can't be put right in a couple of hours."

"As bad as that!" Reynolds said with concern. "Then count me out, doctor. I won't do anything to add to your worries. Can you manage alone?"

"I've told the housemaid to telephone for my special nurse; a reliable woman who won't touch anything in the boudoir, or talk to anyone in the house."

"If I can't help, at least I won't hinder you."

XXXI. Another Disappearance

Sunday, November 28th.

A LITTLE later, Reynolds sat in the dining-room with the two girls facing-him. He had anticipated a measure of difficulty with Naomi Marsh, having already observed signs of evasion in her manner. But he was unprepared to find something of the same attitude in Phil Ingram. "A pair of stubborn mules," he reflected, regarding them sternly.

"You told me before I left last night that all the guests had gone, Miss Marsh." His tone was sharp.

"To the best of my knowledge, that was the truth," Naomi said coldly. "I did not count heads, but all the coats and hats were taken."

"Did those people leave by the front door or by the studio?"

"I fancy that Nicola—or maybe it was Ferrari—used the studio door."

"Can't you be sure?"

"No. I was talking to Mr. Casinier in the hall. One can't see the studio from there."

Reynolds wheeled round to Phil Ingram.

"Where were you?" he demanded.

"Hovering about generally. Miss Marsh asked me to keep Osmond downstairs by your instructions."

"Did you succeed?"

"I'm unpleasantly thorough, inspector," Phil told him. "Osmond had no chance until everyone had gone, when Miss Marsh sent her to bed."

"Before the house was locked up?"

Phil nodded.

"After you and the others had gone and before we locked up," she asserted. "At least I think so. One can't be positive on every point."

"Did you or Miss Marsh draw the bolts on the studio door or merely leave it fastened by the Yale lock? This is an important question, Miss Ingram."

There was an angry flash in Phil's eyes.

"This business is so distasteful that I certainly hope you won't prolong it by asking unimportant questions," she retorted.

"Every lock in this hateful house was fastened," affirmed Naomi with signs of anger, "and every bolt was made secure. I personally saw to the studio door."

Inwardly Reynolds was amused and not at all displeased by this flare-up. Temper in a witness was all to the good; things often were blurted out in anger, whereas with cold obstinacy one was battering against a rock. His harsh tactics were drawing blood and justified their continuance, he decided.

"Was Miss Ingram with you when you locked up the studio?" he asked.

Naomi wrinkled her brow.

"I think so, but I'm not sure."

"I am," Phil butted in pertly. "I was in the hall, looking round to see if the guests had left anything behind."

"And had they?" There was blandness in Reynolds's voice which deceived the girl.

"One person had forgotten something—a white silk scarf," she told him, "though I can't see what that triviality has to do with murder."

"Neither can I at the moment," the inspector admitted. "What did you do with the scarf?"

"I left it where it was—behind the oak chest. It probably slipped off when coats were piled there."

Followed by the girl, Reynolds went into the hall and looked behind the chest. The scarf had gone.

"You are certain that you didn't move it, Miss Ingram?"

"Quite. Probably Anderson picked it up this morning when she dusted." Phil's tone was casual.

Anderson, however, when asked, said that she had had no time to touch the hall that morning, and had neither seen a scarf nor heard any inquiries about it

The inspector gave Phil an odd glance that brought a flush of annoyance to her cheeks.

"Detectives have to ask seemingly stupid questions, Miss Ingram," he remarked, "because apparent trivialities can assume grave importance. That scarf was taken by someone—probably the owner—after the house was locked up."

The girls stared at him.

"You mean that that person was the murderer!" Naomi whispered.

"That remains to be proved. All we know definitely is that the person retrieved the article at a time when he—or she—had no right to be here." Reynolds's easy manner changed swiftly. "Who owned that scarf?" he demanded.

The flush still remained on Phil's face and she Moved restlessly.

"Who was wearing it?" Reynolds asked again.

Naomi moistened her dry lips.

"There were four men in evening dress," she said in slow, brittle accents.

"Ferrari, Casinier, Nicola and Stephen Talbot," the inspector enumerated. "To which of them did it belong?"

"I can't say," Naomi replied. "It might have been a woman's scarf."

"Or yours, inspector," Phil thrust in. "You were here, remember. Also there were two doctors in the house."

"I have not forgotten, Miss Ingram. I was not wearing a scarf, and the doctors—both strangers—certainly had no key to the studio door."

Reynolds led the way to the dining-room.

"And now," he began in low, serious tones, "we will go back to what happened after you had locked up last night. I should like you to tell me first, Miss Marsh."

"We went to bed," Naomi said with composure, as if the matter ended there.

"Was your window open?"

"Yes."

"You slept well?"

"Fairly well. I heard nothing, if that is what you want to know."

"Only fairly well, Miss Marsh." Reynolds's tone was grim. "Yet apparently someone opened the studio door, came upstairs and induced the nurse to unlock her patient's door. You tell me that although your door was opposite Miss Quayne's room, you heard no sounds of a struggle, or a crash when the nurse fell. You heard no footsteps on the stairs as the murderer went down, no click of the latch when he closed the studio door behind him, and walked on a gritty gravel path round the house to the front gate. You heard nothing of all this, though your open window was immediately above the studio door."

"I heard nothing," Naomi said doggedly. The inspector turned to the other girl.

"What have you to say, Miss Ingram?"

"I go to bed to sleep, and I always sleep soundly. I did so last night," she said with defiance. "Does that satisfy you?"

"It will have to, I'm afraid," Reynolds said evenly. He paused and then added, "until I hear what the nurse has to say."

There was panic in Naomi's eyes as she glanced helplessly at her friend. It was evident to Reynolds that they had forgotten the nurse's existence, or at least her potentialities as a witness, for they were obviously disconcerted by his last remark.

"I understood that the nurse had concussion as well as an overdose of morphia," Phil said with an attempt at boldness. "She might be ill for weeks and unfit to talk."

"Where did you get that impression?" Reynolds asked.

"I heard Anderson telephoning for a nurse on Dr. Hawthorn's instructions."

"Quite so. Anderson was probably describing what had occurred. She could not possibly know the present condition of the patient." He spoke with deliberate cheerfulness.

Watching the faces of the two girls, he saw that his tone had convinced them. He also saw that, although they were uneasy, if not frightened, obstinacy still predominated, and that further persistence on his part would only lead to evasion.

"How many keys are there to the studio door, and who has them?" he inquired, deftly shifting the point.

"I handed two to Miss Quayne on the day that she came here," Naomi replied at once. "One I know she gave to Nicola; the other is probably still in her handbag. Shall I get it for you?"

"No, thank you." Reynolds saw by Naomi's answer how the house could have been entered last night. Osmond, if she were not the murderer, probably unfastened the bolts of the studio door and made her escape that way, leaving the way clear for Nicola, or whoever had a key, to enter.

More and more was he anxious to have a heart-to-heart talk with that young man. Why on earth didn't Ferrari bring him along? He listened eagerly as the front-door bell rang, and a man's agitated voice became audible.

"Mr. Ferrari wishes to see you, sir," announced Anderson. "Another young gentleman is with him. Is he to come in too?"

Nicola at last, Reynolds thought with relief as he hastened to meet the welcome visitors. To his disgust, the "young gentleman" was Bob Deane, who with mock humility touched his forehead and went to greet Phil and Naomi.

Reynolds turned to Vanda's manager.

"Where is Nicola?" he demanded.

Ferrari flung up his hands with a despairing gesture.

"Gone," he replied.

XXXII, Deane On The Trail

Sunday, November 28th.

REYNOLDS drew Vanda's manager into the studio. "Where do you think Nicola can have gone?" he inquired.

"I don't know. I've raked every possible place to find him," was Ferrari's answer. "He's not at his address. It's a small house where the landlady takes one or two 'pros'— theatrical people, you know. At the moment, Nicola was the only boarder."

"Did you ask where he was?"

"Did I ask!" Ferrari said indignantly. "The house is shut up and the people have gone off for the day, the next-door neighbours told me. They hadn't seen Nicola. After that I tried pubs and restaurants in the district, with no result. My bet is that Nicola murdered Vanda and then bolted with the maid. Osmond had a Russian mother and an English father, I believe."

"You've done your best, Mr. Ferrari, but this is pretty bad news for me."

"Vanda's death is pretty bad news for me, inspector. Heaven knows what it's going to cost me one way and another. She was always running up bills in my name, and borrowing cash from me. How do I know I shall ever get my money back? I'm nearly distracted. By the way, Casinier rang me up for news of Vanda's health and I had to tell him the truth. After all, he owns the Regis and will have to make arrangements to replace her."

"That was reasonable. Why didn't he ring here and get news direct?"

"Don't ask me. I'll be in a padded cell if things don't straighten out," Ferrari groaned.

"Perhaps they will. Did you lose a white silk evening scarf last night?" Reynolds asked.

The manager ran his hands through his hair.

"Ye gods! Does it matter what I lost last night? All I can think of is what I've lost to-day through Vanda's death. Poor woman, it seems brutal to talk like this, but after all, I'm out of a job now, and am facing no end of worry and expense."

Reynolds looked at him sympathetically.

"I appreciate your difficulties, Mr. Ferrari. Meanwhile, I've a tidy few of my own. Try to help me, will you?"

"All right. Go ahead, inspector."

"Then we'll begin again. Did you lose a scarf? It happens to matter quite a lot."

Ferrari thought for a moment.

"No, I'm almost sure I didn't, though when I get back to my hotel I'll make certain. What else?"

"Is it at all significant that Nicola's landlord and his family have gone away?"

"They usually go for a binge every Sunday in a ramshackle car, so the neighbours said."

"What made you fix Nicola up in that house?" Reynolds asked.

"Because lodgings were cheap there, and he said he hadn't much money. Also because ordinary landladies would object to the very late hours which his work at the Regis entailed."

"You are called Alberto Ferrari, I understand. Are you Italian by birth?"

The manager laid a forefinger on the side of his nose and chuckled.

"My name is George Albert Farrar, and I was born in Walworth," he declared. "I'm not ashamed of name or birthplace, but neither of 'em's any good in my job. Ferrari is my trading title, and a jolly fine choice it has been—up to now," he added bitterly. "Anything more, inspector?"

"Not now, thanks."

"Then I'll ask Miss Marsh about Vanda's bills, if you don't mind."

Waiting in the hall was Detective-Sergeant Jenkins.

"I've combed the houses in this road, sir. Nobody heard anything unusual during the night. Have you had any news?"

"The worst possible," Reynolds assured him. "Nicola's bolted now!" He related what Ferrari had told him. "I'd like you to pick up what you can about Nicola. His landlord apparently has an old car. Try the garages in the neighbourhood. That landlord, if you can find him, might know where his lodger has gone."

"Off with Osmond, I'll bet," Jenkins surmised. "They probably robbed Vanda after they'd murdered her. If I catch either of them, they'll have to answer a few pithy questions."

"If you catch either of them," Reynolds said tartly, "you'll hand them over to me to do the questioning."

Jenkins accepted the rebuke in good spirit, adding, with obvious disappointment:

"I had hoped you'd let me look round the murdered woman's room and the rest of the house, sir."

"Very well," agreed his superior officer. "I've had enough of Briar Lodge for a while. There are two young women here who won't talk, and another—the nurse— who can't. You snoop round, and I'll see about finding Nicola. I must also see Mr. Casinier and Stephen Talbot. There may be time for me to make those inquiries before I'm allowed to see the nurse."

"You've not forgotten that man Filmer," Jenkins reminded him. "He's another of 'em who won't talk."

"I've not forgotten him. If my other interviews don't take too long, I shall slip round to the hospital and see him."

"That reporter from the *Evening Record* is with Miss Marsh and her friend. Has he your permission to be here?" Jenkins inquired.

"On a social visit to them, yes, but not as a reporter
with the run of the house."

"Can't you hoof him out, sir?" pleaded Jenkins, who
had no affection for this particular member of the press.
"He says he doesn't remember Wyburn's address but I
know Bob Deane!"

Reynolds's eyes flickered with amusement.

"So do I, my lad, but Deane has his moments. It was
he who called me to the Regis last night before Vanda's
queer attack. He's an old friend of Naomi Marsh and Phil
Ingram. In these circumstances, I couldn't refuse to let
him see them."

"As he's paid his social call, couldn't you entice him
away with you, sir?" Jenkins asked with feeling. "He'll
come poking after me and be in my way."

"Two of a kind, eh! I'm afraid Deane will be still more
in my way, so you'll have to bear up," Reynolds observed
dryly. "If he asks where I am, say I've gone to have lunch.
By the way, Ferrari and Deane can leave the house, but
I'd rather the girls didn't, though I've no authority to
prevent them from doing so."

"I'll do my best to keep Miss Marsh and, Miss Ingram
here," Jenkins promised. "How's the nurse now? I wish
you could get a few words with her."

Reynolds shook his head.

"We can't go against medical orders. I'll get the latest
bulletin from the doctor before I go."

The report was not cheering.

"The crack on her head is causing trouble," Dr.
Hawthorn said. "If she doesn't improve when the effects
of the drug have worn off, I must get her to hospital and
have an X-ray. I'd rather not move her until her pulse is
stronger. We'll see how she is later this afternoon,
inspector. She's in the care of a special nurse, and
between us we're doing all we can."

"I'm convinced of that," Reynolds assured him.

Going down to the hall, he put on his overcoat, and prepared to slip out of the house without Bob Deane's knowledge.

That enterprising young journalist was on the watch, however.

"Leaving us for the wide, open spaces, inspector?" he inquired, with the hopeful air of a dog who sees his master unhang the leash.

"Yes," agreed Reynolds, adding with emphasis, "Alone."

There was an obstinate look on Deane's face. "Little Bobbie might get into mischief here if you don't take him nice walkies," he warned.

"You don't go with me," Reynolds said firmly.

"And should you try to get into mischief, Detective-Sergeant Jenkins is in charge here and has my permission to throw, you out on your ear. So now you know, Deane."

"So now I know," the younger man repeated sorrowfully. "There's gratitude for calling you in to this sensational case last night! Where would Scotland Yard be if it weren't for me? Very well, my great brain shall keep its useful secrets."

"I don't believe you know a thing," retorted Reynolds. "But in case you do, need I remind you that concealment of information concerning a murder is a punishable offence?"

The journalist churned over that point without noticeable pleasure.

"All right. I'll tell you what I've found out: Naomi and Phil are hiding something," he said.

"I know that. They'll talk soon. Is that all your mighty brain has discovered?"

Deane glowered at the C.I.D. man.

"No, it isn't," he snapped. "You remember I saw a fellow called Cyril Wyburn acting in a suspicious fashion outside the Regis stage door last night?"

"I do. Jenkins asked you for his address. Why did you say you'd forgotten it?"

"Maybe I'll interview Wyburn before I tell you where he lives," Deane taunted. "Anyhow, here's a bit of news that will make you open your eyes. Vanda owed him a lot of money and wouldn't pay up or see him. Then she repented, and not knowing Wyburn's address, left a packet of notes with Naomi Marsh to give to Wyburn if he called."

"Has he received the money?" Reynolds asked with interest.

"No. He didn't see Vanda last evening before she went to the Regis, and could not know therefore that the money was waiting for him. But he went to the Regis. Out of revenge, he possibly tried to kill Vanda. This theory puts another suspect on your list, inspector."

"It does if we can prove that Wyburn got into Briar Lodge during the night. That's going to be difficult. I'll go and see him."

Deane shook his head to and fro slowly.

"Not till I've seen him first, sweetheart! When I've got Wyburn's story for my paper, you shall have his address. This time finding is keeping, even if I go to gaol for it. I didn't notice you rushing to the telephone to give me news that Vanda was murdered and her nurse was knocked out this morning!" He raised his hand in salute. "Hope you'll have a nice round of visits. Bye-bye. Me, I'm going to lunch on the house here. Murder don't spoil my appetite."

XXXIII. A CIRCLE OF ENEMIES

Sunday, November 28th.

IT was with a quiet smile of satisfaction that Jenkins watched the inspector leave Briar Lodge.

His admiration for Reynolds amounted almost to slavish devotion, and he would willingly work for him on tasks that involved long hours of drudgery.

But primarily Jenkins's tastes lay in methods which led him by speedy and often unorthodox paths to useful knowledge. Frequently the inspector had told him that if he had not been a detective he would certainly have been a burglar! There were few locks that Jenkins could not—and given opportunity would not—pick!

Therefore, to be given the run of Briar Lodge, with the exception of the boudoir, and in addition to be able to limit the activities of Bob Deane, whom he heartily disliked, brought joy to Jenkins's heart.

His first move to ensure at least a peaceful hour by keeping Deane otherwise employed, was an errand to the kitchen where his old acquaintance, Skinny Gibbs, was chef.

"Morning, Skinny," he said blithely. "Hope you've got a nice luncheon ready. What's the menu?"

Skinny's cadaverous face grew solemn.

"Well, Mr. Jenkins, in the circumstances I thought of sending up a little something cold with cheese to follow. There's only the young ladies, you see."

"That's where you're mistaken. We have a distinguished journalist here as guest. One Bob Deane, whom you already know, I think."

Skinny nodded.

"I know Mr. Deane too well," he observed feelingly. "Plenty of trouble he's got me in by giving me liquor to tell him things. Artful, that's what he is, and how he loves his stummick! Serve him right to give him nothing but cold ham."

"That's where you're wrong, Skinny. Mr. Deane undoubtedly loves his stummick as you so aptly put it, and as giving him plenty to eat is the only way to prevent him from following me about, eat he shall. Send in a hot and delicious meal of several courses with a nice bit of delay between them. Do you get me?"

Skinny drooped an eyelid, and the travesty of a smile crept over his thin cheeks.

"You leave it to me, Mr. Jenkins. Once you got me out of a scrape and I haven't forgotten it. What about your meal?"

Jenkins sighed regretfully.

"A hunk of bread and cheese is all I can spare time for, worse luck. I hope Deane chokes."

"I might manage that if I put a few fish bones in!" Skinny said cheerfully. "Lunch will be ready in a few minutes. Mr. Deane shall have the works. I've only got to hot up the soup."

Jenkins chatted amiably with Bob Deane and the girls, until the gong sounded and they trooped into the dining-room.

"Aren't you going to join the festive board?" Bob asked him, noticing that only three places were laid.

"I'll have a bite in the kitchen and write up my report," was Jenkins's reply. "The chef is going to do you proud from what I saw just now."

For a moment the reporter eyed him suspiciously. Then the aroma of ox-tail soup wafted beguilingly to his nostrils, and he sat down, consigning journalism to the nether regions.

Assured of non-interruption from Deane's quarter, Jenkins went upstairs and entered the room of the dead woman.

A meticulous inspection of her personal belongings revealed very little. He plodded on, searching handbags, pockets and even coat linings.

Surely, he thought, there must be some clue here concerning the film dancer's enemy.

With painstaking care, he decided to go through everything again. Once more he went over suitcases and trunks, examining them in the hope of finding some secret hiding-place.

Again he unlocked a large jewel-case and lifting out the tray, emptied its valuable contents.

His eyes brightened as he turned the tray upside down. Its base consisted of a thin layer of wood attached by tiny screws.

A few minutes later the screws lay on the table, and the piece of wood was removed. Inside that shallow recess was a collection of papers. Most of them, he was disappointed to find, were press cuttings. There was only one thing of interest: an old photograph of a group of men. They appeared to be English, although the tropical vegetation shown in the picture indicated a foreign country. On it was, written: To Vanda Quayne, with warning from her circle of enemies.

Placing the photograph in his pocket, Jenkins refixed the base of the tray and left the jewel-case as it was before.

He had barely finished when the door-handle was softly turned.

Bob Deane, he surmised, unlocking the door and flinging it open.

Outside stood the auburn-haired girl with brown eyes whom he knew to be Phil Ingram.

Neither hair nor eyes affected him. Jenkins had his susceptible moods, but this was not one of them.

"What do you want?" he asked bluntly.

"I don't want anything," she retorted, "but it's nearly two o'clock, and strange as it may seem, most folks feed their face round about this time. By the appearance of yours, it could do with a spot of nourishment. Bob Deane has had more than his share, and is still busy."

"Thanks, Miss Ingram, but I was going to have a snack in the kitchen." Jenkins was distinctly mollified at the knowledge that she had thought of his comfort.

"It won't take you any longer to eat it in the dining-room, and if you're quick, Bob won't have polished off all the ham omelette. Come along. One detective is worth ten reporters."

Phil laid her hand on his arm and drew him towards the stairs. Perhaps hunger played its part, perhaps also vanity had a share in Jenkins's acceptance.

He smiled pleasantly as he sat down at the table and saw Bob Deane scowl. The reporter had every reason to scowl, but fortunately he didn't know it. Deane would certainly have gambled a fiver of his editor's money for a peep at what Jenkins had found in Vanda's room.

Phil went to the sideboard and served him, talking gaily all the while, and badgering Bob Deane mercilessly on any subject he raised.

Yes, Jenkins decided, this was a very enjoyable interlude, and one that he had earned by his ingenuity with the jewel-case.

Suddenly he glanced round with a frown. Why was Phil Ingram acting as hostess? She had nothing to do with Briar Lodge, whereas Naomi Marsh was or had been Vanda's secretary.

"Where's Miss Marsh?" he demanded.

Bob Deane looked facetiously under the table, and raising the lid of an entrée dish, scanned the interior.

"Now where can our platinum blonde be?" he inquired. "Surely she can't have imitated Osmond and Nicola and done another vanishing trick!"

"Stop fooling," snapped the exasperated detective. "Why isn't Miss Marsh here?"

Phil raised her eyebrows.

"Why should she be here?" was the calm reply. "Miss Marsh finished her lunch and went to write a letter. She thoughtfully sent me to fetch you. Why make a song and dance about it? I'm waiting on you very nicely. How do you like your coffee? White and two lumps?"

"Black and no sugar, thank you," Jenkins replied mechanically.

Phil Ingram's airy words were plausible enough, yet amongst them was a phrase which impinged on his brain disturbingly. He could not link up the connection although he repeated the sentence to himself: "Miss Marsh . . . went to write a letter." Try as he would, he couldn't understand why he was worried.

Suddenly his mind worked backwards: one wrote letters with a pen. That was it: a pen! He had found a jade green fountain pen under the lace cover on the table beside Vanda's bed. Apparently it had rolled out of sight after the dead woman had last used it. Though he couldn't see why she should trouble to write letters when she had a secretary. Perhaps she lay in bed and dictated them to Miss Marsh, in which case the pen probably belonged to Naomi.

Sipping his coffee, he reflected that the last letter must have been written or dictated before Vanda went to the Regis the previous evening. Not since, for she had been brought home ill, attended by doctors and guarded by a nurse in a locked room.

A locked room! The words brought Jenkins to his feet. He had no recollection of locking Vanda's room when Phil Ingram fetched him for lunch.

With a murmured apology, he dashed upstairs. As he feared, Vanda's door was not fastened.

Entering the room, he cast his eye round it. Nothing seemed to have been touched.

But the green fountain pen was no longer on the table by the bed.

XXXIV, An Emerald Pendant

Sunday, November 28th.

JENKINS locked the bedroom door and stood on the landing in a puzzled state of mind. If that pen had belonged to Vanda Quayne, why should Naomi trouble to take it surreptitiously?

If she herself were the owner and had used it normally some time yesterday, why hadn't she asked Inspector Reynolds to see if she had left it in Vanda's room?

In that case, Jenkins reflected, there would have been no need for her friend to entice him out of the room; no need for Naomi to snatch at that chance to retrieve her pen unseen.

Supposing, however, that Naomi owned the pen, had used it during the night, and left it there accidentally. Then indeed, she might employ every cunning device to get hold of it without Reynolds's knowledge! Jenkins felt assured that he was on the right track.

Below him in the hall, he heard the two girls talking to Deane, who was apparently going. Jenkins remained out of sight, listening.

"If I had my way, I'd charge you for the huge luncheon you've eaten," Phil grumbled.

"The great brain needed it, my girl," was Bob's reply. "It has big things to do; enough to warrant a special edition coming out early to-morrow. The inspector will chew his cud when he sees my work. It will be a wow!"

"I've heard your bluff before to-day, Bob," Naomi said. "What story have you got from here to-day? Nothing!"

"Ah ha, it's what I'm going to get now, my girl. Anything I can do for you two poor prisoners? Want any letters posted to friends outside?"

"No, thanks," said Naomi.

"I wouldn't trust them to you in any case," Phil added.

That proved it, Jenkins reflected. Naomi had not written a letter; she had left the dining-room only to find the pen, which might have been incriminating evidence against her.

He waited until Bob Deane had gone and the two girls had returned to the dining-room before letting himself out of the house quietly. At all costs he must try to follow Deane, whom he could see walking up Warne Road. Jenkins hurried after him.

By luck, he picked up a taxi which was crawling through the road in search of a fare.

"Follow that man," Jenkins instructed the driver, indicating the figure of Bob Deane ahead. "Keep out of his sight if you can."

"What's the gime, guv'ner?" asked the driver with a grin. "Goin' to snatch his wallet or somefink?"

"No. Call it curiosity," Jenkins replied. "I'm a detective from New Scotland Yard."

"Blimy," said the driver. "I read lots of them 'thrillers,' but I never thought I'd be 'untin' a real criminal. Hop in, sir."

It was a remark that amused Jenkins as he watched his old enemy, Deane, dive into a taxi, unaware that he was being followed.

The trail was a long and expensive one before it ended half-way down a road of small houses in Kilburn.

Jenkins's driver pulled up at the corner.

"There y'are, sir. Goin' to arrest him?" he inquired hopefully.

"No. I only wanted to see where he went. If I duck down out of sight, will you tell me what happens?"

"Right-o. I'll tinker with my engine and keep my eyes open," the driver promised.

In a minute or, so he opened the taxi door.

"All clear, sir," he informed Jenkins. "Your man has just driven off down the road. I might be able to catch him if we're sharp."

Jenkins made a swift decision to call at the house which Deane had left.

Paying off his taxi man, he walked along the road and rang the bell.

A grey-haired, fragile woman answered it.

Is Mr. Jackson here, madam?" Jenkins asked respectfully.

"No. My son and I live here alone. Our name is Wyburn."

Jenkins was overjoyed. The inspector had told him about the Cyril Wyburn incident and had stated his wish to find that young man.

"If your son is in, I'd like to see him," he said. Again he was careful to speak with the utmost courtesy.

"He will be back at any minute," Mrs. Wyburn told him. "Would you like to come in and wait?"

There was nothing that Jenkins would have liked more at that moment, he thought as he followed the lady into a shabby but comfortable little sitting room. He could not understand why Bob Deane had gone away.

Mrs. Wyburn unconsciously enlightened him.

"I wonder if the Mr. Jackson you were inquiring for was the young man who called here a few minutes ago. He was so uncouth in his manner in demanding to see my son, that I'm afraid I told him an untruth and said Cyril would not be back until late tonight."

"You were justified, madam." Jenkins was delighted to hear that for once Deane's forceful way had cost him the quarry he was seeking. He evaded discussion of the mythical "Jackson" by sympathetic words on the subject of bad manners.

"Yes," agreed Mrs. Wyburn. "I'm old-fashioned and like my son to mix with refined people. Cyril is a good lad, but he is weak and easily led. That failing has caused grievous trouble more than once. In fact I am afraid—"

She broke off and eyed Jenkins sharply. "Are you employed at the bank where my son works?"

"No, madam."

"Will you tell me why you wish to see Cyril?" Her voice shook a little.

"I would rather discuss the matter with your son first," Jenkins said diffidently.

Mrs. Wyburn gazed into the fire for a while as if trying to make a decision.

"Is your visit here concerned with a Miss Vanda Quayne?" she asked.

Jenkins felt startled by the calmness of her question. To-day was Sunday. Vanda's death had not been discovered until half-past seven this morning, and the news could not be published in the press until to-morrow. Mrs. Wyburn could only have known of the murder from her son. Had he had a hand in it?

Feeling his way very carefully, Jenkins fenced with a non-committal question.

"What makes you ask that?"

"Because I know that Miss Quayne owes my son money that belongs to me," Mrs. Wyburn replied simply.

Jenkins noted her use of the present tense, which implied that she had not heard of Vanda's death.

"Yes, my visit concerns Miss Quayne."

"Cyril has not told me, and I have never pried into his affairs, yet," she went on; "mothers often have intuitive sense where their children are concerned. I have seen him reading paragraphs about her in the paper, and observed his anger. He was in Berlin a few years ago when she was there. In his letters to me he used to rave about her, but since his return he has never mentioned her name."

Mrs. Wyburn gave a sigh.

"However, you are of course not interested in that," she continued. "If Miss Quayne has employed you to deal with the financial end of it, I want you to tell her that I would far rather lose the money than have my son distress himself any longer. He made a foolish mistake and it is more dignified for us to forget the episode. Are you a lawyer acting for Miss Quayne?"

Jenkins shook his head pityingly. There were times in a detective's life when he detested the task that lay before him. This was one of them.

"Was your son at home last evening and during the night?" he asked gently.

"He goes out every evening as most young men do. I go to bed early, and do not know at what time he returns." Fear suddenly rose in Mrs. Wyburn's sad eyes. "Why do you ask this?"

Jenkins bit his lip.

"I am afraid, madam, that you must prepare for a shock. Miss Quayne was found dead in her room this morning. She had been murdered during the night."

Mrs. Wyburn gazed at him in horror, but no sound came from her ashen lips for a while.

"Murdered!" she whispered at last. And then, with the courage of a lioness defending her young, she said boldly, "My son could not be suspected of that. He has not seen her since he left Berlin."

"Your son has called at Briar Lodge, but Miss Quayne refused to see him. Also we believe that he visited her dressing-room at the Regis last night."

"What do you mean by 'we believe'?" asked the distracted woman. "Who are you?"

"Detective-Sergeant Jenkins from New Scotland Yard, Mrs. Wyburn. You are not obliged to answer my questions—here, but it will help very much if you do so."

"And the man, Jackson, whom I sent away by an untruth, was he a detective also? If so, I have probably caused trouble for my boy by that deception."

"Don't worry, madam. His name isn't Jackson, and he is only a reporter. You acted wisely." Jenkins was glad to be able to comfort her on this point. "You are certain that your son will be in shortly?" he asked in an uneasy tone.

"Quite certain, Mr. Jenkins." Mrs. Wyburn rose. "He said he was going for a walk and would be back to tea. If you will excuse me, I will see about preparing it. My daily maid does not come on Sundays."

Jenkins watched her go along to the kitchen at the end of the passage and close the door. Standing in the narrow hall, he longed to look round the place, but had to content himself with making a mental plan of the little house. It had obviously only one storey: two or three bedrooms upstairs, with two sitting-rooms and kitchen on the ground floor. He and Mrs. Wyburn had been talking in the front room.

With a cautious eye on the kitchen department, he turned the handle of the back room and peeped inside.

To his surprise it was furnished as a bedroom; and judging by the garments and shaving tackle, evidently a man occupied it. This must be where Cyril Wyburn slept.

Jenkins noted the French windows which led into the tiny garden, a back door in the opposite wall. All very handy, he summed up, for a young man who wished to make exits and entrances unknown to his mother. With swift practised fingers he tried the drawers and wardrobe. They were unlocked and contained only wearing apparel, arranged neatly.

The room was spotless, except for a few muddy footsteps on the polished boards that surrounded the square of thin carpet Jenkins flicked on his pocket torch and traced them from the French window to the side of the wardrobe. There, curiously enough, they ended.

He found another trace of mud on the leather seat of a chair, which was near.

Instantly it came to him that Cyril Wyburn had used that chair to stand on, presumably to place something on the top of the wardrobe—a popular hiding-place, as he knew from experience.

Jenkins stepped on to the chair and, flashing his light along the top of the wardrobe, saw a coloured silk handkerchief. Rolled inside it was an emerald pendant which was certainly of considerable value.

Replacing it, the detective slipped out of the room and strolled, along to the kitchen where Mrs. Wyburn was cutting bread and butter.

"I'll make the tea and you'd better have a cup with me, Mr. Jenkins," she said. "Cyril is sure to be here in a minute. I'll leave you to talk to him alone when he comes."

Her hands trembled as she tried to lift the tray. "Let me carry that," Jenkins offered. "I'm sorry to have had to distress you."

"It's not only your visit," she told him honestly. "I've been ill for some time and have to go into hospital for an operation. At least it was going to be a hospital, but only this morning my son told me that he had unexpectedly won some money on a horse. He insists therefore on my going to a good nursing home. I don't approve of gambling, though it shows his kind thought for me, doesn't it?"

Jenkins was spared reply by a ring on the bell.

"That must be Cyril," Mrs. Wyburn said. "Please let him have his tea before you talk to him. He is not very strong."

She opened the front door and Jenkins, listening eagerly, heard a boy's voice.

"Please, ma'am, Cyril sent me along to tell you not to wait tea as he and my brother George are going to a movie and won't be back till about ten."

Jenkins came forward and spoke to the youngster.

"Which cinema are they going to?" he asked.

"They didn't say, sir. They hopped on a Piccadilly bus and gave me a tanner to come here with the message. I'd rather have gone with them. Those big movies have a fine organ and sometimes there's a variety turn as well."

The hope that had flared high faded. There was no sense in wasting time in the Wyburn home. The best thing now would be to get into touch with the inspector and ask his advice on this new development.

After all, Jenkins soliloquized, he had had a fair run of luck here. He had discovered that Cyril could get in and out of the house without his mother's knowledge, and had told her of money he expected from a lucky bet. Also the young man had concealed a valuable piece of jewellery in his bedroom.

XXXV, CONCERNING MRS. CASINIER

Sunday, November 28th.

MEANWHILE, Inspector Reynolds's luck had been distinctly patchy.

His first interview took place under chequered conditions at the Regis. There he found Julian Casinier, looking very worried, surrounded by a group of artistes who, hurriedly telephoned for, hoped to benefit by Vanda's death.

A piano was being played while a couple of the aspirants performed before Casinier and the manager of the cabaret.

"Ghastly!" groaned the former. "Clear 'em off. And try two fresh ones."

Reynolds waited discreetly in the background for a propitious moment. One could not expect Casinier to answer questions amiably in the midst of this confusion.

More artistes arrived, however, and realizing that the rehearsal might go on interminably, Reynolds approached the distracted owner of the Regis.

"Sorry to disturb you, Mr. Casinier, but I should like to speak to you."

Casinier looked up with a frown.

"What the—" he began angrily. "Oh, it's you, inspector. You couldn't have come at a worse time. I must choose someone to fill Vanda's place. However, get on with it. What do you want to know?"

"Have you a key to the studio at Briar Lodge?" Reynolds inquired.

"No. Why should I want one when there's a front-door bell?"

"After you left Miss Quayne's house last night, did you return there?"

"I did not go to her house again," Casinier declared. "Thinking she was all right, I went home. Ferrari rang me up this morning and told me the tragic news. A nice mess it's put me in. Vanda Quayne was no angel to deal with, but the woman could and did dance. Where to find someone as good, I don't know." He rubbed his head. "Still, that's my funeral. I can't expect Scotland Yard to stop business because of that. Is that the works as far as you're concerned with me?"

"You have certainly much to lose by Miss Quayne's death: you must understand that my questions are purely formal," Reynolds said in a conciliatory manner. "Your wife, of course, can confirm the fact that you did not leave your home during the night," he added in an assumed casual manner.

Instantly anger gleamed in Casiniet's eyes.

"My wife!" he almost shouted. "She has nothing whatever to do with this horrible affair. She only met the murdered woman for a few moments. I must insist that you do not worry her in any way. Her health won't stand the strain."

The C.I.D. man was not perturbed by this outburst.

"You can rely upon my tact and discretion, Mr. Casinier, but I must do what I think is necessary. Good afternoon."

Fully anticipating that Casinier would ring up his wife and warn her of the impending visit, the inspector decided to call on the lady at once.

Hailing a taxi, he drove to the house with no definite plan in his mind. Why, was Casinier so angry because his wife might be asked to confirm his words? Was it merely the attitude of a devoted husband anxious to protect a delicate woman? Or was he afraid that she might admit something to his disadvantage?

Casinier's normal personality was that of a calm, suave and successful man. To-day, certainly, he was considerably worked up by the upheaval to his cabaret programme.

Making due allowance for this, Reynolds reflected that the anger aroused when Mrs. Casinier's name was mentioned was significant. Did the gentleman protest unduly that his wife scarcely knew Vanda Quayne?

Suppose that she was better acquainted with the dead woman than Casinier knew or admitted! The inspector had proved from long experience that the most violent protestations usually issued from the most guilty lips.

Reynolds had no reason for such assumption in this instance, but at least it opened up a new line of thought.

He rang the bell of the imposing mansion, and asked the butler if Mrs. Casinier was at home.

"Madam is resting, sir," the man replied, and prepared to close the door as if that answer were conclusive.

Reynolds was not so easily rebuffed. Indeed, he rather welcomed the delay, since it offered a fresh opportunity. Many a useful clue had he found by a little careful conversation with a servant.

"As my business is important, I think I had better wait until Mrs. Casinier can see me," he said in a pleasant but decisive manner. "I will sit in the hall, then she will not be disturbed."

"Very well, sir," the butler rather grudgingly conceded, "although I cannot promise that madam will receive you. What name, please?"

"Inspector Reynolds of New Scotland Yard." The butler's face became a shade less wooden as he indicated a chair.

With inward amusement Reynolds fancied that he could rouse it to still further animation. Very few people could resist curiosity where a crime was concerned. In all probability this man had not yet been told of Vanda's death, even though his master was aware of it. It was worth a trial anyhow.

"My visit is about Miss Vanda Quayne who has been dancing at the Regis cabaret," he said confidentially. "You've heard of her, of course."

The butler raised his eyebrows a fraction, as if surprised by the loquacity of the visitor.

"I have heard of the lady," he stated with hauteur.

Reynolds leaned forward.

"I'll bet you don't know that she was murdered during the night," he said, and saw that he had scored.

Gone was the supercilious mask of the trained servant. In its stead was an awed expression, avid for details.

"Murdered!" he exclaimed. "Was she stabbed or shot, sir?"

"There's a bit of a mystery about it," was the cautious reply."

"The boss—I mean, my master—will be in a rare state, seeing that Miss Quayne was one of his star performers. Does he know yet?"

"I have just come from the Regis," Reynolds told him, not mentioning that Casinier had known the news before he left his home.

"Better be careful how you tell madam," the butler advised.

"I expect she knows already. Mr. Casinier rang her up just before I called, didn't he?"

"Yes, sir. He also gave me instructions that she was not to be bothered by visitors. He can't have known you were coming, of course. What a shock it must have been to him to hear that news! He isn't too well to-day; scarcely touched his luncheon. He's a good quiet eater usually, and enjoys his food."

"Miss Quayne was a handsome woman," said the inspector. "Did she come here often?"

The butler shook his head.

"Only once to my knowledge, sir." The man gave a rueful smile. "I got into a row from the master for letting

Miss Quayne meet the mistress. That's why I'm wary about taking strangers to see her."

"I understand," Reynolds told him. "Perhaps Mr. Casinier didn't like Miss Quayne personally."

"I don't think he did. But that wasn't the reason in this case. The master thinks the world of madam, and doesn't like her to meet people of Miss Quayne's type, although he has to do so in the course of business. He says that they aren't of madam's social standard. Not that he's snobbish in any other way, but I'm sure he believes the angels are not good enough for her!"

"Rather a charming quality," Reynolds commented. "Naturally, holding those views, he would resent Miss Quayne's visit unless Mrs. Casinier had previously invited her."

"Madam certainly had not done so. Miss Quayne positively swept in, and insisted upon meeting her. Then the master was sent for from his study, and, my hat, he was furious. He and Miss Quayne had a talk in the library; hot words, too. When she went, he told me off properly." The butler stopped in confusion as he remembered the murder and that he was confiding— perhaps unwisely—in a representative of the law. "Mr. Casinier would be angry with any visitor who annoyed the mistress," he added quickly.

"Quite." Reynolds's tone was urbane and gave no hint that the butler's revelation was of the utmost importance. "Will you ask Mrs. Casinier to see me for a few minutes? I've several calls to make and time is getting on."

"Yes, sir." The man bit his lip. "I'm afraid I shall get into serious trouble if the master or mistress knows that I've been discussing their affairs."

"Leave that to me," Reynolds said with a reassuring smile. "I've never got an innocent man into trouble yet, and I don't propose to start. Take my card to Mrs. Casinier."

In a minute or two he was facing the lady of the house in the drawing-room.

"Please sit down, Inspector—" she paused and consulted the card—"Reynolds, and tell me what can do for you."

Her manner was a trifle distant but not forbidding, the inspector noticed. In this cold, impersonal way, Mrs. Casinier probably interviewed tradesmen and servants. It undoubtedly had its uses, but, for his purpose, this was not one of them. Witnesses of such a type were very difficult to handle, since their reserve of control was almost inexhaustible. Open antagonism was far less formidable.

Bracing himself, Reynolds went straight to the attack.

"Are you aware that Miss Vanda Quayne was murdered late last night?" he asked.

Mrs. Casinier bowed.

"Yes. My husband told me after Ferrari had telephoned the news to him."

"Naturally you were shocked as you knew Miss Quayne," he observed.

"I am shocked to hear of any violent death; but you are mistaken, inspector, I did not know Miss Quayne in the sense that you imply."

"Yet she called upon you a day or so ago." Mrs. Casinier stiffened.

"It would be more exact to say that Miss Quayne intruded upon me."

Pride had caused her to make her first slip. Reynolds seized upon it.

"Why?" he demanded blankly.

"I can only imagine that she wanted to meet her employer's wife socially."

It was a weak reply that did not deceive Reynolds.

"The interview was pleasant?" he inquired.

"Neither pleasant nor otherwise. Miss Quayne and I had nothing in common, and I was at a loss to account for her visit."

"But your husband resented it."

An air of frigidity crept over Mrs. Casinier's face.

"Are you stating facts or asking questions?" she demanded. "My husband was annoyed that one of his cabaret artistes came to his private residence uninvited. It was a natural attitude on his part."

Her explanation fitted in with the butler's statement, Reynolds reflected.

"Last evening you rested in Miss Quayne's dressing-room after a heart-attack."

"That is so."

As if the interview were ended, Reynolds rose, hoping to put the lady off her guard. Vanda had posted a letter which was addressed to Mrs. Casinier, according to Phil Ingram.

"Oh, about the letter that Miss Quayne wrote to you," he remarked casually, and was delighted to find that he had scored.

Mrs. Casinier moistened her lips.

"It has been destroyed," she said, after a moment's hesitation.

"That is a pity." Reynolds's tone was grave. "What did Mr. Casinier say about it?"

"We have not discussed the matter."

"Miss Quayne called for you and took you to the Regis last night," Reynolds chanced.

"She did not call. At her suggestion, I met her outside this house." Mrs. Casinier pressed the bell as she spoke. "I shall answer no more questions without the advice of my husband, inspector," she said coldly.

Reynolds's eyes had a steely hardness.

"It will save time, madam, if you assure me that neither you nor your husband left this house after midnight last night."

Mrs. Casinier ignored his words and turned to the butler, who had answered her summons.

"Show Inspector Reynolds out," she ordered.

XXXVI. Sanctuary

Sunday, November 28th.

THE inspector chuckled to himself as he walked away. He had a keen sense of humour and enoyed the novelty of being shown the door as if he were an importunate beggar. Neither was he disturbed because Mrs. Casinier had retreated to high ground and declined to answer his last question.

He had learnt far more than she guessed from his interview. He had brought out the fact that the dead woman had written what was probably an abusive or threatening letter to Mrs. Casinier. Vanda was far too astute to have done that without a substantial motive, he was sure. She must, too, have insisted upon Mrs. Casinier accompanying her to the Regis.

Also, Reynolds had gleaned from the butler useful information concerning Vanda's visit, and the subsequent row with Casinier. Did the dancer have some hold on her employer or his wife? If so, in view of Casinier's almost fanatical devotion to his wife, here might be a motive for the crime. The creeping tentacles of blackmail had strangled the happiness of many people, whose lives had apparently been built on as solid a foundation as was that of Julian Casinier.

Meanwhile, as the lady had refused to say if she or her husband had left the house after midnight, Reynolds decided to try and find out by other means.

Not far from the Casiniers' house was a taxi rank. The inspector strolled over and chatted with the drivers on general topics for a while.

"You fellows must get weary of such late hours," he remarked. "There can't be much doing here after midnight in a district where everyone owns private cars."

"You've hit it, guv'ner," one of the men complained. "They either uses their own car or walks. Except for last night, we haven't had a call this week. I often pack up early and go home."

"Perhaps the fares last night couldn't afford to own a car," Reynolds suggested.

The man laughed.

"Not afford it! Why, it was old Casinier I drove—the bloke that's worth millions. He's got three cars. I s'pose his chauffeurs was off duty at that hour."

"Probably," Reynolds agreed. "Most chauffeurs don't care to work until midnight."

"It was a good bit later than that," the driver told him. "He was in such a darned hurry to get out that he dropped some money and didn't stop to pick it up. You bet I did, though."

"You'd be in a hurry too if you were chasing your missus!" laughed his mate. "That's what Casinier was doing. P'raps he was scared of her going off in a common taxi alone when she was used to a Rolls!"

"Were you the one who drove her to her destination?" Reynolds inquired of the last speaker.

The man nodded.

"I did, sir—if you can call a street corner a destination. Funny place to drop a wealthy woman at that time—it must have been nigh on two in the morning. No wonder her husband went tearing after her. My mate," he indicated his companion, "drove him to the same spot a bit later."

"Out St. John's Wood way, wasn't it?" Reynolds's tone was casual, but he was tense with eagerness for the answer.

"That's right, guv'ner: you're a good guesser." The man grinned. "Wish you'd pick me a winner for the two-thirty to-morrow."

"If I could, I'd pick one for myself," Reynolds replied. "It wasn't exactly a guess. I met Mr. Casinier last evening at a house in Warne Road and wondered if he and his wife were going back there."

"I expect so, sir, because I dropped the lady at the corner of that road."

"And her guv'ner made me pull up about the same spot," put in the first man.

"You didn't see anything more of them?" Reynolds questioned.

The men shook their heads and stated that they'd gone home for the night after that.

"It was queer you should come along and talk about night jobs and know them folks we drove," one added.

Reynolds noted the numbers of their badges, reflecting that it was a lucky chance which had enabled him to establish the fact of Mr. and Mrs. Casinier's return to Warne Road the previous flight. Altogether, the Casinier interlude had produced far better results than he had anticipated.

Engaging one of the taxis, he was driven to Stephen Talbot's address. It was six o'clock when he arrived.

After ringing the bell, Reynolds fancied that he could hear footsteps and murmuring inside the flat before Talbot came to the door.

"Hello, inspector," was the young man's greeting. "Come in. Sorry to keep you waiting. This being Sunday, my man is out and I was half asleep over the fire. Leave your things in the hall."

Never was Reynolds so slow in removing his overcoat, and never did his brain work faster as during his leisurely movements he took in every detail of the hall.

Aside from the excellent furnishings, there was plain black coat, a short umbrella and two dark suitcases with old Continental labels on them. A man's mackintosh— probably belonging to Stephen—was hung where it more or less concealed these interesting objects.

There were three closed doors on either side of the hall and one at the far end. Behind which of them lurked the owner of these goods? Reynolds wondered. For Stephen Talbot's excuse about being half asleep did not tally with the sounds that he had heard. The inspector had a great longing to look inside the rooms and see who the secret visitor was. The suitcases might belong to a man, but the black coat and umbrella were obviously the property of a woman.

"This seems to be quite a large flat," Reynolds remarked.

"Dining-room, lounge, bathroom, kitchen, my bedroom, and a small one for my manservant to change in," Talbot enumerated. "He sleeps out, but I couldn't do with less space."

"I suppose not."

"The rooms are mostly smallish, but the lounge is a decent size. Come in and see it and meet my pal."

Reynolds's spirits rose at the frank. invitation. This, of course, was the explanation of the luggage in the hall. His face grew blank, however, when his host gravely introduced a soft-eyed spaniel who was curled up on a couch beside the fire.

"This is Barry, inspector. He's shamefully spoilt but grand company."

Reynolds sat down beside the dog and fondled its silky ears, regretting the limitations of canine conversation. He and Barry could have had a chatty five minutes.

"Do you know why I have called, Mr. Talbot?" he asked.

Stephen nodded and held out a box of cigarettes.

"Yes. About Miss Quayne, I suppose."

"How and when did you hear the news?"

"Her secretary, Miss Marsh, rang me up this morning. She gave me no details."

"You have not called at Briar Lodge to-day?" Stephen gave a whimsical smile.

"No. I thought better to await the visit which I was sure you would pay me."

"What made you expect me?"

"I knew Vanda many years ago, was in her dressing-room at the Regis last evening, and went back to her house afterwards, as you are aware. Being one of the last to see her alive, I naturally thought you would wish to question me."

"Can you help me in any way about her murder?" Reynolds's tone was blunt and direct.

"I regard that as being solely your affair. If I attempted to do so, I might throw suspicion on to an innocent person. I will answer any questions, of course, that relate to myself."

It was an ingenious answer, Reynolds reflected; one that might be either frank or cunning.

"Very well, Mr. Talbot. Will you tell me if you went back to Briar Lodge after you left it with the other guests last night?"

A cynical expression crossed Talbot's face.

"Does it matter what I say?" he demanded. "I've no alibi and you've only my word which you won't believe unless you can check it up."

"Can't your man help me to do that?"

"No. He doesn't come until eight in the morning." Reynolds was silent for a moment.

"Is there a night-porter or a lift-boy?"

"No, we don't run to those luxuries. Each tenant has a key to the outer door and works the lift himself if he needs it."

"It's a pity you have no one to corroborate your statement," Reynolds commented.

Stephen frowned.

"I've made no statement, inspector, for the reason that I've given you," he said shortly. "Apart from your duties, I believe you're a darned good fellow. But, to me, you have a detestable job, and you mustn't expect any sympathy from me."

"I'm asking for facts and not sympathy, Mr. Talbot. If you refuse to answer my questions now, as you have the right to do, you can be compelled to answer them elsewhere. And meanwhile," Reynolds's face was severe, "you are perhaps helping a criminal to escape by handicapping me. I presume that your dislike for my job doesn't run to the extreme of protecting a murderer."

Stephen's expression relaxed to a smile.

"I might even do that, if the circumstances were sufficiently extenuating."

"Are they in this case?" Reynolds demanded curtly. His eyes were on the spaniel who had sat up alertly, watching the door.

"I don't understand you," Stephen said with reserve.

"You implied that you were alone in this flat."

"What of it?"

Reynolds hurried to the lounge door and flung it open.

In the hall was a woman, clad in the black coat that had been hanging up, with a suitcase in each hand, obviously about to depart. It was Osmond.

She gave a startled cry as she saw Reynolds.

"What are you doing here?" he asked sternly.

"You must not blame Mr. Talbot," was the agitated answer. "I had nowhere to go, and he kindly allowed me to stay here."

Reynolds took the bags from her and set them down.

"I think you'd better tell me everything," he said, and followed her into the sitting-room. "Mr. Talbot, I shall be glad to know your explanation for harbouring and concealing Osmond, Miss Quayne's personal maid."

Stephen appeared to be unmoved by the inspector's tone.

"Sit down, Osmond, and don't be alarmed," he said kindly, and turned to Reynolds. "If a strange, frightened dog came to your door, inspector, would you turn it away?"

Of course not, but—"

Talbot interrupted him.

"Exactly. I regard a human being as being worthy of even more sympathy than a dog. Osmond is a stranger in this country. She ran away from Briar Lodge in alarm, friendless. I feel honoured that she trusted me enough to come here for refuge."

"There are hotels if she had no reason for hiding. When did she arrive here?"

Osmond would have replied but Talbot checked her with a sentence spoken in rapid French.

Unfortunately for his intentions, the inspector was an excellent French scholar, and heard Talbot tell her to say nothing yet lest she may involve others. Keeping his knowledge to himself, he requested Osmond to accompany him back to Briar Lodge at once.

Her face was calm but there was a shrinking look in her eyes.

"As monsieur wishes," she agreed. "Does Monsieur Talbot come also?"

"No," Reynolds said firmly. "I will see Mr. Talbot later."

XXXVII. The Nurse's Story

Sunday, November 28th.

AT Briar Lodge, Naomi and Phil had had a strenuous afternoon. The news of Vanda's death had leaked out, and reporters, eager to get details for the Monday morning newspapers, had not hesitated to pester the girls by telephone and personal calls.

"One of those news-hounds was in the kitchen a few minutes ago, talking to Skinny Gibbs," Phil said in irate tones.

Naomi gave a weary sigh.

"Anyhow, what does it matter? This tragedy has happened, and it certainly can't be kept dark."

"Can't it?" There was a significant intonation in Phil's voice. "You've not done much talking, I notice; and the less you say, the better."

Naomi made no comment. Her face looked wan and strained as she stood gazing out of the studio window into the grey November dusk.

Suddenly she jerked the curtains across.

"Turn on the lights, Phil," she urged. "This gloom gives me the blues."

"Sure that's the only reason you want the lights on— and the curtains drawn?" Again Phil's tone had a significant inflexion.

Naomi turned round with the desperation of a hunted animal at bay.

"Why are you tormenting me like this?" she demanded. "Haven't I enough trouble already?"

Phil raised her eyebrows.

"You know best about your difficulties. You've never confided in me."

"Remember that I tried to do so and you checked me. Let it go at that. I'm secretive, and you're frank. Is that what you wish to say?" Naomi asked bitterly.

"Isn't it true? I know nothing about you and you know all about me."

"Do I?" Naomi was silent for a moment. "Maybe this is the moment for me to change my ways. The inspector should be here very soon."

Phil caught her friend by the arm.

"You mean you're going to tell him what you know?" There was anxiety in her voice.

"I may be forced to do so," Naomi replied steadily. "That's all I can tell you, Phil. You'd better act as you think wisest."

"And you'd better prepare for the consequences, if you talk," Phil snapped, as she swung from the room and ran upstairs.

Naomi waited until she heard a door close overhead. Then, opening the French window, she stepped out on to the garden path and peered into the semi-darkness.

A hand grasped her arm, and a man's voice spoke quietly.

"Hush!" she whispered. "Don't say anything here. We can be overheard. Follow me."

She led him through the studio to a small pantry at the back of the hall, and locked the door when they were inside.

"Keep your voice down," she urged. "No one will come here, though you ran a great risk. How did you get past the policeman at the gate?"

The man gave a low chuckle.

"I went into the next garden and, climbing over the dividing wall, hid behind the shed. Did that girl you were with in the studio see me?"

"I don't think so. But her manner was suspicious when I pulled the curtains." Naomi spoke hurriedly to him for a few minutes, adding at last, "Tell me what I ought to do. The inspector may return at any moment."

The man gave her certain instructions.

"That's the line you must follow," he concluded, "or you'll be in a ghastly hole. You had no right to be mixed up in this mess; it's not a woman's job. Even at this stage I don't know where it will end."

"I'm not frightened now. Please go. Can you ring me up later to let me know that you got away safely?"

"The line is probably being tapped by the police, and any call of mine might land you into fresh danger," was his reply. "Be on your guard. If you can get out of the house, you know where to find me. I shan't go away yet."

Naomi's visitor had only been gone a few, minutes when Detective-Sergeant Jenkins arrived. On his heels came the inspector with Osmond.

"I see you've had luck, sir," Jenkins observed to his superior officer.

"Of a kind," Reynolds agreed, and explained where he had found Vanda's maid. "Did you see Cyril Wyburn?"

Jenkins told him briefly of his interview with Wyburn's mother and of his discovery of the pendant.

"His house is being watched and our man will telephone to Briar Lodge when Wyburn gets back," he added.

"I'll tackle that young man later. Meanwhile," Reynolds stated, "I've got the others covered. Also a man is posted outside Nicola's lodgings. Keep your eye on Osmond. I'm going up to see how the nurse is." He turned as he saw Naomi come from the studio. "Where's your friend, Miss Marsh?"

"Miss Ingram is upstairs in the room we occupied last night, inspector. Do you want her?"

"Not yet, but I shall be glad if you will both remain in the house."

Naomi raised her head proudly.

"We have been in all day and are not likely to go out until you give permission," she replied. "I shall be in the dining-room when you need me."

Reynolds knocked softly at the door of the boudoir upstairs. His summons was answered by a middle-aged woman in uniform.

"I am Sister McLaren," she explained when Reynolds had told her his name. "Dr. Hawthorn said you might talk to nurse for five minutes. She is a little better, but very far from well. Please don't distress or agitate her. The doctor told her of Miss Quayne's death."

Lying on the couch, supported by pillows, was the nurse whose statement might mean so much to him.

"I am very sorry that you have suffered this dastardly attack," Reynolds said with genuine sympathy. "Do you feel able to tell me what happened?"

"I'll try, but the murder," she shivered, "must have taken place after I was unconscious."

"Probably. Go back to the beginning and take your time."

Reynolds waited patiently while she placed a trembling hand on her forehead in an effort to collect her thoughts. He dared not hurry her.

"Miss Quayne was asleep," I the nurse began, "and I was reading in the boudoir with the door into the bedroom open. I could see her from where I sat. Both doors leading to the landing were locked on the inside, as you had wished, inspector. Suddenly she roused, and in quite a normal manner said she wanted to see her secretary at once. I asked her to wait until the morning, but she insisted, and would have been angry had I refused. Her words were, 'If you won't go, I'll get up and call her myself. I'm perfectly well.' I unlocked the bedroom door, and crossing the landing, knocked at the room opposite."

"Did you notice the time?"

"Of course. I had to keep a chart for the doctor. It was ten minutes to two when Miss Quayne awoke."

"Was Miss Marsh asleep?"

The nurse hesitated for a moment.

"I'm not sure, but thought I heard her talking to her friend before I knocked the first time. There was silence, so I knocked again. Miss Marsh came out presently and I told her that Miss Quayne wished to speak to her. I also begged her not to stay long. She nodded and came across to the bedroom with me. Probably Miss Marsh has told you about that interview, inspector."

Probably that was the last thing Miss Marsh wanted to do, Reynolds reflected grimly. Aloud he said: "I'd like to hear everything that occurred from your lips, nurse, regardless of what I know already."

The nurse smiled faintly.

"There isn't much more that I can tell you, I'm afraid. Directly Miss Marsh came in, Miss Quayne ordered me peremptorily to go into the boudoir, and shut the door between the two rooms. Again I had to obey her."

"Did you overhear any of their conversation?"

"Nothing of importance. I heard Miss Marsh say she would fetch a pen from her bedroom. While she went across the landing, I ventured to go to my patient and again urge her to wait until the morning. Miss Quayne waa extremely annoyed with me for a moment. Then she calmed down and asked me to go to the kitchen and heat some milk which she promised to take later. She added, 'Make yourself a pot of tea too, nurse, and don't be a fool. I'm all right now. There's nothing to worry about." It seemed a wise suggestion. I went downstairs, leaving her with her secretary. I think now that it was a ruse to prevent me from listening to, or disturbing the conversation."

"Was Miss Marsh's bedroom door open or closed when you passed it to go downstairs?"

"It was half open, but she was with Miss Quayne." The nurse looked surprised at the question.

"Was there any sound of strange movements while you were in the kitchen?"

"Nothing strange. Miss Marsh came down to the studio, and was there for perhaps three or four minutes. When she went upstairs, she was carrying a small case. I watched her from the kitchen door: she didn't notice me."

"So that for the period of three or four minutes, Miss Quayne was entirely alone," Reynolds summed up. "How long were you in the kitchen?"

"Twelve minutes exactly. I timed myself to be certain that my patient should not over-tire herself. I put the glass of hot milk on my tea-tray and carried it up. Miss Marsh was sitting beside the bed writing when I entered the room, and the case she had fetched was in Miss Quayne's hands."

"Did you open the boudoir door leading to the landing?"

"No, I went and returned by the bedroom."

"Did you give the milk to your patient?" The nurse shook her head.

"I had no chance to do so. Miss Quayne pointed to the boudoir and said in a cold, hard voice, 'Take it in there and shut the door, nurse. When I want you, I'll call. If you attempt to disturb me, you will leave the house at once.' Again, I could only do a she requested." The nurse gazed at Reynolds pitifully. "I might have prevented the murder if I had not obeyed her."

"On the contrary, nurse," Reynolds assured her in brisk, comforting tones, "there would probably have been two murders instead of one. When you came up to the landing with the tray, did you notice if Miss Marsh's door or any other door was open?"

"Miss Marsh's door was ajar as it had been previously, and her room was in darkness: possibly she did not want to keep her friend awake. The other doors were closed, but there was a light on in the personal maid's room. Perhaps, Osmond had been roused when I called Miss Marsh."

"Perhaps," Reynolds agreed dryly. "What happened after you shut yourself in the boudoir? No detail is too small, remember."

"I set the tray on the table, covered the milk to keep it hot, and poured myself out a cup of tea. It was five minutes past two and I was feeling anxious about my patient. I drank a little tea, and took up my book again, but could not read as my mind was on Miss Quayne. I was just going to write up my report for the doctor when I heard a slight sound behind me. Suddenly I felt a horrible pain in my head and I knew nothing more until a while ago when Dr. Hawthorn told me what had happened."

"You saw no one in the boudoir when you entered with the tray?"

"No. The small shaded table lamp left most of the room in darkness. Someone could easily have been hiding behind the thick curtains, but of course I did not suspect such a thing. I was sitting there," the nurse indicated an arm-chair with its back to the window, "facing the entrance into Miss Quayne's room. When the door was open, as it was, earlier last night, I could see my patient from where I sat as I told you."

"There are two more important questions that I should like to ask before I leave you to rest. During those few minutes immediately preceding the attack upon you, was Miss Marsh still in the bedroom with your patient?"

The nurse looked at him with candid eyes.

"I cannot possibly be sure. I could hear no voices, but Miss Marsh might have been writing something. On the other hand, I have a distinct recollection of hearing a door being closed softly. It might have been my patient's door as Miss Marsh left her; or Miss Marsh's door, as she went back to her bedroom."

"Or even the maid Osmond's door?" suggested Reynolds.

"Yes, though I had not thought of her. What is your other question, inspector?"

"Can you possibly tell if you uttered a cry when you were attacked?"

"I don't think so. Probably I just crumpled up and slid on to this thick carpet. I am sure Miss Marsh would have rushed in if she had heard a scream," the nurse ended.

"Always supposing she was still in the other room," Reynolds observed. Adding to himself, "and was not in collusion with the assailant."

He thanked the nurse, and going into the adjoining bedroom, measured the distance between the dividing door and the bed. It was a large room, heavily carpeted, and the walls and door were of the solid old-fashioned variety. If the nurse had not screamed, her fall might have passed unnoticed, he decided.

Crossing the landing, he tapped softly on the door of the room where Phil and Naomi had slept.

It was opened by the former.

"What do you want?" came her abrupt question.

"When Miss Marsh was called by the nurse last night, did you remain in this room?" the inspector inquired.

"I don't know what you're talking about," Phil declared. "I went to bed and slept, as I always do. I've told you so once already."

Reynolds's face was expressionless.

"In view of the nurse's evidence, I thought you might like to revise your statement, Miss Ingram." Phil gave a scornful laugh.

"If you want fairy tales, give me time and I'll think up some good ones, inspector."

"Thank you, I only want facts," Reynolds said evenly. "Do you still say you heard nothing at all during the night? Neither the nurse knocking on your door, footsteps on the stairs, doors opening, voices?"

"Again I tell you I went to bed and slept until Anderson the parlourmaid woke us this morning to announce that Miss Quayne was dead."

"You heard Anderson knocking but not nurse?" he questioned sharply.

"Yes. It was half-past seven. I usually wake about that time. Eight hours' sleep I need, and eight hours I always have. In between, I'm dead to the world."

Reynolds gave her a measuring glance.

"You didn't get your full quota last night, did you? It must have been nearly one when you and Miss Marsh retired. That would make your normal waking time nine o'clock. As you say you are dead to the world in between, would you not have been as likely to wake at ten minutes to two when nurse knocked twice, as at seven-thirty when Anderson knocked?"

A flame of colour rose to Phil's face.

"I'm not going to be tricked into altering my words by any clever questions of yours, inspector."

"Neither must you conceal the truth out of mistaken loyalty for your friend," Reynolds observed calmly.

In a very disturbed frame of mind, he went down to the dining-room to see Naomi. All this secrecy was hindering his progress badly. Had it not been for the nurse, he might never have discovered the vital information about Naomi's visit to her employer during the night.

XXXVIII. The Strange Visitor

Sunday, November 28th.

NAOMI was sitting at the table with her head buried in her hands when Reynolds appeared. She glanced up, with eyes that searched his, in an unspoken question.

"Yes, I've spoken to the nurse and heard her story, Miss Marsh," he said gravely. "Are you prepared now to tell me yours?"

"Perhaps it would be easier for me if you asked me what you wish to know," Naomi said faintly.

It was evident to Reynolds that she was suffering from intense strain, yet not altogether fear.

"Nurse tells me that she called you at Miss Quayne's request at ten minutes to two last night."

"That is true, although I did not know the exact time."

"Were you and your friend asleep then?" Naomi swallowed.

"I was awake. Miss Ingram must speak for herself."

"Nurse thought she heard you both talking," Reynolds told her.

"Perhaps she imagined it. Surely it is unimportant."

Reynolds's manner stiffened.

"You must allow me to judge what is important, Miss Marsh."

"In that case, I'm sorry, but I can give you no answers involving Miss Ingram. You must question her as you think best."

"Corroboration of a statement is essential to my work, Miss Marsh."

"Then I'm afraid you will find my replies of no assistance," was Naomi's steady retort.

Reynolds paused for a moment.

"What was the nature of your urgent interview with Miss Quayne?" he asked.

Naomi met his gaze calmly.

"Miss Quayne was my employer, and even though she is no longer alive, I shall respect the trust she reposed in me as her secretary." Her tone was dignified and final.

"You refuse to tell me what passed between you?"

"I do. Being too exhausted to write personally, Miss Quayne dictated a private letter to someone she cared for deeply. She signed what I had written. I will tell you nothing more."

A flash of admiration rose in the C.I.D. man's eyes at the girl's determined answer. He was big enough to appreciate loyalty, even though it hampered his work.

"We will not discuss that further for the moment," he conceded. "Leaving Miss Quayne's door open, you went downstairs to fetch something for her." He smiled whimsically. "Perhaps you can tell me about that without any breach of faith!"

"Of course," Naomi agreed with relief. "Miss Quayne asked me to fetch a locked letter-case."

Reynolds decided to take a chance shot.

"Why did you enter your bedroom first?" he asked mildly.

"Only to tell Miss Ingram that nothing was wrong."

"But you said she was asleep."

Naomi shook her head, realizing her slip.

"I didn't say she was asleep or awake, inspector. Our door was open. My bed was near the door, Miss Ingram's by the far wall. There was no movement, so I said nothing, but went downstairs."

"How long were you away from Miss Quayne?"

"A few minutes: possibly five."

Reynolds leaned forward and lowered his voice dramatically.

"That was a long time in which to fetch a letter-case, Miss Marsh. In those five minutes a great deal occurred. Someone entered Miss Quayne's room—with or without her knowledge—and concealed himself in the boudoir during the nurse's absence in the kitchen."

The girl gave a gasp. There was a touch of fear in her eyes.

"It took me some while to find the letter-case," she said.

"Where was it?"

"In a locked drawer of the dining-room bureau. I thought it was in a cabinet in the studio."

"You of course went to the studio first?"

"Naturally." Naomi evidently thought the question a stupid one.

"Who kept the keys of the dining-room bureau and studio cabinet?"

"I did." Her face flushed as she saw a trap into which he had led her.

"Not expecting Miss Quayne's summons, or knowing her requirements, you had to fetch your keys, I suppose?" he said inquiringly.

"Yes."

"To do so, you had to put on the light in your room."

"For a moment only."

"So that was why you entered your room before going downstairs! Didn't Miss Ingram rouse and ask you what you wanted?"

"We did not speak at all. I took the keys from my bag and ran down for the letter-case."

A smile crinkled the corners of Reynolds's lips.

"I wonder why you didn't mind answering a question concerning your friend that time!" he observed. "Even if she did not hear the knocking and running about the house, surely the light being put on in her room must have awakened her—if—" He stopped deliberately, and saw the colour which had previously flamed in Naomi's cheeks in anger, drain away, leaving an ashen pallor.

"Had you drugged Miss Ingram for any reason?" he demanded.

Naomi's expression was one of utter astonishment. "Of course not," she said indignantly.

His eyes twinkled.

"With so much drugging going on, the question had to be asked. Miss Quayne was drugged in her dressing-room; she died later from the effect of more drugs, and the nurse was drugged after she had been stunned." Reynolds related these points almost nonchalantly. Suddenly he demanded, "Have you a hypodermic syringe?"

Again Naomi's eyes held desperation

"Yes," she admitted. She paused, adding wearily, "I don't suppose you will believe me if I tell you I took it away some time ago from someone who was using drugs—one of my previous employers."

"Why should I not believe you if you have been telling me the truth, the whole truth, and nothing but the truth." Reynolds's voice had a solemn note.

"Have you, Miss Marsh?"

"The truth, yes."

"With reservations?"

She nodded.

"Yes." Her fingers clenched tightly.

"Thank you for that admission. It may help more than you know or wish. Is your hypodermic syringe here?"

"No. It's in my flat probably."

"We'll fetch it."

"I suppose Miss Ingram is in her room at Briar Lodge," he said as they left the house.

Naomi drew in a long breath.

"Yes."

In silence they walked upstairs and entered her flat.

Reynolds held out his hands which were soiled.

"The rail of your staircase needs dusting," he said. "May I wash in your bathroom while you find the hypodermic?"

He was in the sitting-room looking at a picture when she returned from her search.

"I don't know where it is," she said a little breathlessly. "Perhaps it has been thrown away."

"Never mind." His tone expressed indifference. "That's a fine painting you have here. I'm a great admirer of sea-scapes."

He discoursed amiably on art in general until they were back in Briar Lodge. Then his manner became brisk and a trifle peremptory.

"Please stay in the dining-room, Miss Marsh," he requested. "You will be good enough to have no conversation with anyone until I see you again."

Naomi bit her lip.

"May I go into the studio instead?" she asked. Reynolds glanced at her keenly.

"Very well. Osmond shall wait in the dining-room."

"I suppose you do not want your witnesses to be in collusion," she remarked cynically.

"Something like that," he agreed.

In the hall Jenkins greeted his superior officer eagerly.

"We've got the number of the car belonging to Nicola's landlord, sir. Nicola went off with them! The car has been traced to Brighton. A police officer is accompanying them back. They might be here at any minute."

"Excellent. Now, on no account is Miss Marsh to have a chance to concoct a story with Miss Ingram or Osmond. Do you understand?"

"Right, sir. I'll keep them apart," Jenkins promised. "Have you any fresh clues?"

"None that can be proved yet. I'm going to follow up a forlorn hope."

He was turning away when the telephone bell rang in the hall.

"Answer," he ordered his assistant.

Presently Jenkins laid the receiver down on the table.

"It's Mr. Talbot. He wants to speak to Miss Marsh."

"All right. Let her take the call here, keep out of the hall, and say I've gone. After that, leave her alone in the studio. It's important."

As Jenkins obeyed, Reynolds slipped into the alcove behind the staircase.

In a moment Naomi came out and lifting the receiver, gave her name.

"Yes, I'm alone," she replied over the wire. There was a pause while she listened.

"No, no, Stephen, don't come here yet. I can't explain. . . . Very well, if you insist, but it's unwise, if not dangerous. I'll expect you in half an hour. The inspector questioned me. I said as little as possible, but I'm sure he suspects—" Her voice was very low and Reynolds missed the end of that sentence.

When the girl had gone back to the studio, the inspector opened the front door and walked quietly up the side-path which led to the rear of the house. Careful to make no noise, he took shelter behind some shrubs near the studio. Only one shaded lamp was switched on. By its aid he could see Naomi, standing there alone, looking out into the dark garden.

Presently she glanced at her watch, and opening the French window, stepped out on to the path.

Securely hidden, Reynolds watched her, silhouetted by the light from the studio, peer anxiously into the silent gloom.

The minutes dragged by. At length there was a scrambling sound only a few yards from where he was concealed. It was followed by the crackling of shrubs.

"I was afraid the policeman had caught you," Naomi said breathlessly to the newcomer.

"Don't worry about me. Have you acted as I told you?" the man demanded.

Reynolds could not hear the rest of the conversation, and ventured a little nearer. As he moved, his foot touched a loose stone.

Instantly the man sprang towards him. Reynolds felt a strong hand grip his arm and pull him forward to the light. Naomi had vanished.

"Why were you skulking in the shrubs?" demanded the man. "Who are you?"

Reynolds surveyed the strongly built figure and firm, rugged face of his captor with interest.

"My name will be sufficient to answer both your questions," he said calmly. "I am Inspector Reynolds of New Scotland Yard."

The man loosened his grasp.

"In that case, I apologize," he said with equal calmness. His mouth twisted ironically. "I guess it's your turn to do a bit of catechism, inspector."

"Your sudden appearance over the wall does call for a little explanation," agreed Reynolds in a dry tone. "It's cold and dark here. Go into the studio, please."

The man preceded him without hesitation, and waited until Reynolds had closed and locked the French window. Naomi was not there.

"Well, the fat's in the fire earlier than I expected," commented the strange visitor, "but maybe it's for the best."

His deep voice had the trace of an American accent. He was perhaps forty years of age, with rather tragic dark eyes; eyes that reminded Reynolds vaguely of someone else whose name he could not recall. The man was well-dressed in good tweeds and a heavy travelling overcoat.

He pulled off his beret, revealing thick black hair streaked with silver, and again Reynolds puzzled his brain to know whom this man resembled.

The caller apparently was not at all disconcerted by this scrutiny; nor, judging by the easy manner in which he selected a chair and sat down, by the whole situation.

"Before you third degree me, inspector," he began, "I want to clear the air with regard to Naomi. You must cross her right out in this business. My being here is not her fault."

Reynolds raised his eyebrows as he took a seat facing the man.

"I gather that you know Miss Marsh well, as you use her Christian name."

"Very well," the man replied with a swift smile that transformed his face.

"In that case, I wonder you didn't use the front door if you wished to see her."

The man screwed up his mouth comically.

"I mightn't have got that far," he said with frankness. "One of your under-dogs in blue has charge of the gate."

"H'm. As Miss Marsh was watching for you, this presumably was not your first trip over the wall."

"Nor my second," the man admitted. "I'd been to the house before, or rather to the back door, a day or two ago." He laughed. "I looked less respectable then. The chef gave me a bob or so to brush the garden paths. I had to act the part of a down-and-out. Naomi, poor kid, saw me and had a ghastly shock."

"Why?" Reynolds asked bluntly.

"Because she thought I was a few thousand miles away, and not free to be here."

"Not free?"

"She thought I was in gaol. I wasn't. But that's another story and nobody's business but hers and mine."

Reynolds longed to know the man's name. He realized, however, the wisdom of not antagonizing him at the moment by over-hasty inquiries which might stop this pleasing conversation.

"It's odd that Miss Marsh has such interest in your affairs," he remarked.

"It would be odder still if she hadn't." The man grinned. "I'm her husband. We've been married for four years."

"Indeed! You're not British, are you?"

"My name's Jim Gordon, and I'm a citizen of the United States, though I wasn't born there. Rather unpleasant business called me to another country two years ago. I couldn't explain things to Naomi, and she was naturally hurt and annoyed. In a fit of pride, she left New York, came to England, and got a job. She didn't receive my letters and heard I'd been landed in a mess, which had ended in prison. When I discovered by whom she was employed, I was furious. It was mad of her to work for Vanda."

"You knew and disliked Miss Quayne?"

Gordon's lips set to a tight line.

"I doubt if anyone knew her better or detested her more," he said decidedly.

There was an alert expression in Reynolds's eyes. Frankness did not necessarily mean innocence. He was alive to that possibility. Gordon's words had the ring of fearless truth, but his actions had been distinctly suspicious and required much explanation.

"Did you come here last night? After midnight, I mean, to see your wife or Miss Quayne?"

"Yes: via the wall. To see Naomi, not Vanda. I had told her I might do so, and hoped she would come down. I waited over half an hour for her. Then I noticed the studio light turned on, and saw Naomi. She was hunting for something. The poor kid was terribly scared when I tapped at the window."

"Did you enter the house?"

"No, we talked for a minute or two in a whisper and I begged her to come with me, then and there. She refused and closed the window. I waited for a while in case she came back, but I had no luck. I also came here earlier this evening and told her how to act."

"Why did she insist on remaining here instead of going with you, her husband?"

"Because she had a crazy idea of clearing my name. That's a long-ago story, and doesn't matter two hoots to me. All I care about is Naomi, and all she cares about is me, plus what she calls my honour."

"And you assure me, Mr. Gordon, that that story has nothing to do with the murder of Miss Quayne?" There was a stern note in Reynolds's voice.

"Everything to do with Vanda, but nothing to do with her murder." Gordon's tone held an equal sternness. "There were plenty of motives—and reasonable ones—for that."

"Will you tell me some of them?" Reynolds inquired.

"To boil down the facts, I held a fairly high position in a bank in Rio," Gordon replied. "I was in charge of the safe deposit. Years before I married Naomi, jewels were placed there by a foreign Royal visitor, who was a gay young spark. Some of 'em vanished. Actually the Royal bird, after a binge, gave one or two priceless bits to Vanda. Possibly he regretted his gifts, or more likely his family insisted upon them being returned."

"Vanda refused to give them up?"

"She certainly did," Gordon said emphatically. "Then the fun began, if you've a sense of humour. I hadn't. Neither had the Royal lad. He turned nasty and said he'd never heard of Vanda! Bribed all kinds of folk to back him up too: you can buy quite a lot in Rio with money, inspector! The police are not quite so 'wonderful' as they are in this country."

Reynolds smiled.

"We may be 'dumb,' but most of us try to be honest, Mr. Gordon. What happened next?"

"The Royal person insisted that those in charge of the safe deposit must have been in league with Vanda, and given the jewels to her. Half a dozen of us, all English except me, came under suspicion. That's what Naomi has been putting up a fight about. Like a fool, I told her of it when we were married, and never told her I was going back to Rio to see if I could trace the missing bracelet."

"So Vanda had to return the things?"

Gordon gave a grim chuckle.

"She was caught in her own net! Two of the pieces of jewellery were found in her room. All might have been hushed up, but unfortunately a very valuable diamond bracelet was missing. Vanda was arrested, and at her trial, when she was charged with the theft of the bracelet, witnesses proved that they had seen her wearing it. Vanda admitted having had it, denied the theft, and declared that it had since been stolen from her."

"Was Miss Quayne telling the truth?"

Gordon nodded.

"For once, yes. Nobody believed her, however, and there's irony in the fact that she was sentenced for a theft she didn't commit, while she escaped the law for taking many things, more or less unlawfully, from men who were doped or drunk in her gambling den."

"What occurred when she was released?"

"I had quit Rio before then, with suspicion still resting upon me, and settled in America, where I later met Naomi who was out for a trip. Vanda, too, left Rio when she was free, and became famous. But her one passion was for revenge on the man who stole the bracelet and thus caused her to be prosecuted."

"Did she find him?"

Gordon shook his head.

"She would have done so, had she lived. She didn't know who he was until last evening when she called on Filmer in the hospital. He was the only man who knew. If Vanda hadn't been murdered last night, she would certainly have committed murder to-day."

"You know this man Filmer? He was attacked in a cab on his way to see Miss Quayne."

"Yes. He was the chief croupier in her Rio gambling den."

"Where is that bracelet, Mr. Gordon?"

"On its way by special messenger back to its Royal owner," Gordon stated. "I won't tell Naomi until I've got the receipt for its safe delivery."

"Did the man who stole it from Vanda give it up to you?"

Gordon chuckled.

"I kind of persuaded him to. If you won't arrest me for carrying firearms without a licence, I'll show you." He drew a revolver from his pocket and levelled it at Reynolds's head. "Stick 'em up, or I'll shoot," he ordered suddenly.

Not a muscle of the C.I.D. man's face moved as he stared into the muzzle.

"Better put it down, Mr. Gordon, or I really might have to enforce the law," he said lightly.

Gordon laid the weapon on a table.

"You've got pluck, inspector. I only wanted to test your nerve. Well," he resumed his normal tone, "that's how I got the bracelet. There was a girl with him, but she had a bit of sense under her red hair and kept quiet."

Reynolds drew in his breath. Could it be that his intuition had been right? Was the queer chance of this man's visit to Naomi to be the means of verifying his suspicion?

"Does this man know to whom you are married?"

"No," Gordon declared, "or he might try to get back the bracelet through her. He doesn't guess that I've already sent it to its owner. He was a wild young daredevil when he was in the bank at Rio. Fearing he might find out that Naomi was my wife, I wanted her to come away last night. She's not safe in this house where anything can happen. As a matter of fact she only came to work for Vanda in the hope of tracking down the truth for my sake."

"Your anxiety is natural; I shall do nothing to add to it," Reynolds promised. "If you will write down this man's name and address and that of the girl who was with him, you may take your wife away directly. I have proved your statements and received a satisfactory answer to another question."

Gordon scribbled on a piece of paper and folding it up, handed it to the inspector.

"Look at it when I've gone. I don't know the girl's name, but I've described her appearance," he said. "There may be a cable already at my hotel—I'm at the Waldorf if you want me—saying that the bracelet has reached its destination. What's the question you want to ask?"

The C.I.D. man gazed at Gordon keenly. Much depended on the truthfulness of this man's reply, much depended on Reynolds's ability in dissecting candour from bold lies, for there might be little opportunity for proving Gordon's veracity.

"You say you knew Miss Quayne well and disliked her, even more," Reynolds began in slow, deliberate tones. "Were you responsible—either directly or indirectly—for her death?"

"I was not." Gordon's voice was firm and emphatic. A grim smile twisted his lips. "My mother, whom I adored and who was killed years ago, would not have wished ill to Vanda. That alone would have kept me from violence, if there had not been another reason." He paused. "Vanda Quayne was my half-sister, inspector."

XXXIX. MOTIVE FOR MURDER

Sunday, November 28th.

SUDDENLY Reynolds realized whom this man resembled. In eyes and mouth there was a strong likeness between him and the dead woman. The inspector drew from his pocket the old photograph of half a dozen men marked "To Vanda Quayne, with warning from her circle of enemies," which Jenkins had found in Vanda's jewel-box. Gordon was undoubtedly one of that group.

"Are these the people who were in your bank?" Reynolds asked, holding up the picture so that the inscription could not be seen.

"Yes."

"All right," said the inspector. "Go on with your story."

"Vanda and I were brought up together. Our mother and her father—a Mexican—were killed during a brawl in the gambling den which he ran in Rio. I was employed in the bank of which I told you. I was twenty and Vanda, who was then about sixteen, inherited the den. A man bought it; a splendid chap. He tried to keep Vanda on the rails, but failed. In a year or two when he saw that she was using the place to entice youngsters to drink and dope and give her jewellery—which they had obtained honestly or otherwise—he left. Having a lot of shares in our bank, he became managing director of it. Will you believe it, he was nearly ruined by Vanda over that jewellery deposit case?"

"How?"

"Because she swore at her trial, out of sheer spite, that he had unlocked the vaults and given her the jewels! Her statement could not be proved, but his fellow-directors, knowing he had once owned the gambling den, made it impossible for him. He had to clear out with a smirch on his name and losing a lot of money. That's what he got for being kind to my sister. You can bet he has good reason for hating her!"

"Where is this man now?" Reynolds asked.

"Here in London; made a pile, I'm glad to say. Naomi got a job in his office on purpose to play detective, thinking that perhaps he had the bracelet. Poor kid, as if she could clear my name by that means! I mean to look him up and have a good laugh about it soon."

Reynolds decided that he also would look up the gentleman shortly, but that it would not be an occasion for merriment.

"Who was the man who bought the gambling den?" he inquired.

"You've probably met him, inspector," Gordon replied readily. "Everyone in London knows Julian Casinier, I believe. He owns all kinds of things, from ships to beauty parlours. Why, he even owns the Regis where Vanda had the nerve to dance although she had ruined Casinier once! She was cruel enough to have ruined him again if she could."

Julian Casinier! At last Reynolds saw the pattern evolving as the pieces of this human jig-saw puzzle were fitted into position.

Restraining his eagerness, he asked: "Why should your sister have wished to be vindictive to Mr. Casinier from whom you say she had received much kindness?"

Gordon made a grimace.

"I'm no psychologist, inspector, but some women don't take kindly to being turned down. You see, Vanda always loved Julian Casinier, and when he showed her that he had no interest in her, out came her venom. I wouldn't mind betting that she was raging with jealousy when she heard that he was happily married. It's a good thing for him that Vanda is dead, or he would never have felt safe."

So that was it! Vanda's visits to Mrs. Casinier were explained. Probably the dancer had made some vicious threat to damage Julian Casinier by bringing up the past, and he had taken desperate means to protect his home.

"Thank you for your help, Mr. Gordon," said Reynolds. "Your story explains a great deal that has been puzzling me. You and Mr. Casinier seem to have suffered a lot through Miss Quayne and those jewels."

Gordon stroked his chin.

"Perhaps he and I suffered most. But of course several of the English fellows in our banks lost their jobs too; or rather they had to resign, which is almost the same thing. Vanda was attractive and popular, and they had often gambled in her place. They were suspected, as Casinier and I were, though perhaps not quite so much. Remember that a bank employee must be above suspicion. He gets no second chance in that profession. At the time, they formed themselves into a band and called it 'Vanda's enemies.' One youngster felt the disgrace pretty badly, but his uncle left him a packet. Vanda liked him better than anyone except Casinier, although he didn't care two hoots about her. We used to call Talbot her second fiddle!"

"Talbot!" Reynolds exclaimed. "What kind of a man was he?"

"Stephen Talbot was a cheery boy of about twenty then," Gordon replied. "Full of pranks and a bit lawless. Yet he felt that business worse than any of us. I remember he said he had determined to make Vanda pay for what she'd done. I guess he made her pay when he lifted that bracelet from her out in Rio. I never knew until a day or so ago that he was the man who had it."

"How did you find out?"

"I forced Filmer to tell me," Gordon replied.

The inspector's face was like that of, a sphinx. Talbot had taken the bracelet! Vanda had vowed vengeance on that man, and Filmer spilt the beans. Although intuition had led the inspector elsewhere, the facts that he had just learnt had to be faced. He swung round when Detective-Sergeant Jenkins opened the door.

"Mr. Talbot has called to see Miss Marsh, sir," he told his chief.

"I want to see him first," the inspector said decisively. "Where is he?"

"In the dining-room alone, reading a letter which Miss Marsh gave him a minute ago," Jenkins replied. "She evidently heard his voice when he asked for her."

"They had no time for conversation?"

Jenkins shook his head.

"No. Talbot said, 'Hello. I was asking for you.' Miss Marsh handed him the letter and merely said, "This is for you. Do what you wish with it,' and left him. She also gave him a white silk scarf. By the way, sir, I've news for you about Filmer, who is much better. He said that an old lag called Corney shot him. One of our men has since found Corney and arrested him."

Reynolds nodded. In a few, words he made his assistant aware of the new development.

"Very good, sir," said Jenkins, and hurried out of the room.

"Now," the inspector turned to Gordon, "come with me. I may need you."

Picking up his revolver, Gordon followed Reynolds.

XL. A Confession

Sunday, November 28th.

IN the hall Jenkins beckoned a constable who had
been standing behind the staircase out of sight.

"Watch your step, sir," he warned his chief. "Talbot
perhaps carries a gun."

Gordon exhibited his own revolver.

"So do I," he said. Holding it well in view, he followed
Reynolds into the dining-room.

Stephen Talbot was perched on the corner of the table
reading a letter. He put it away as the two men entered
and glanced at them and the gun amusedly.

"Hello, inspector," he observed in his usual airy
manner. "Brought a friend in for a firework display?" His
hand went slowly towards his pocket as he spoke.

"Put your hands up, Talbot," the inspector ordered,
while Gordon levelled his revolver quickly and covered
the young man.

"Why not?" Stephen demanded cheerfully. "By the
way, I haven't a gun, if that's what you imagine." He
extended his arms above his head. "Search me, if you
like."

Reynolds did

"You can lower your revolver, Mr. Gordon," he said.

"Can I have a cigarette now?" Stephen inquired, and
lighted up after receiving consent. "Before you ask any
questions, I want to tell you about Vanda's maid,
Osmond, in case you suspect her. She and Nicola are
married and I can assure you that neither of them had
any hand in Vanda's death. Osmond admits that she and
Nicola searched Vanda's attaché ease to see whether she
had given Nicola a fair contract. That was all. They're a
couple of poor Russian refugees. Osmond noticed that an

emerald pendant was missing from Vanda's dressing-
room and was very upset. When she heard strange
sounds during the night it finished her and she crept out
in alarm. She sat in a railway station waiting-room until
it was morning and then went to Nicola's address to say
she had run away. He wasn't there and the house was
locked up. Terrified, she came to my flat where you found
her."

"Thank you, Mr. Talbot. What made you return to this
house late last night?" Reynolds asked.

"So you've discovered that," Stephen observed.

"Did you cause Vanda Quayne's death?"

Reynolds's question came like the crack of a whip.

"Yes, I must have done so."

Reynolds pointed to a chair.

"Sit down and tell me what you wish, Mr. Talbot."

"Vanda always used drugs and carried a box of mixed
dope round with her," Stephen said. "In her dressing-
room she told me to fill her hypodermic; said she wanted
to put some life into her show. I must have given her the
wrong stuff. As she jabbed the syringe into her arm, she
said, 'I've seen Filmer and know that you took the
bracelet, Stephen. Next to Julian, I cared more for you
than for any other man. Maybe I'll forgive you one day
because you felt you were justified. But I'll kill Julian
Casinier's wife if I live long, enough. Filmer says she was
aware that you'd taken the bracelet when she was out in
Rio, and the she-devil let me suffer in prison.'"

Stephen drew in his breath sharply.

"There must have been morphia in that syringe,
inspector," he went on "Otherwise she would have lived:
lived to kill Julian's wife probably." He stared hard at the
man with Reynolds. "Why, you're Jim Gordon of my old
bank, surely!"

Gordon broke in as he saw the inspector's perplexed
look.

"Here, Talbot, let me explain." He turned to Reynolds.
"You wonder why this youngster was so concerned about

Julian Casinier's wife. Well, Mrs. Casinier was a Miss Talbot; Stephen's elder sister. She was in Rio years ago on a visit when this fuss about the jewels broke loose, and Stephen told her everything. That's where she met Julian; they were married in England later."

"How did Filmer know what you'd done?" Reynolds asked the young man.

"The little skunk overheard me telling my sister at a café in Rio."

"Filmer told me the same thing," Gordon put in.

"Now you undatand why I hid behind the dressing curtains last night, inspector," Stephen said. "I didn't want my sister to think that I was friendly with Vanda and running into danger."

"Did you return to Briar Lodge late last night?" Reynolds inquired.

"I did"

"Why?"

"Because Julian rang me up in great alarm, saying that his wife had gone out, and he feared that she might have come here. I chased along and caught her up near the gate of this house."

"What time was that?" Reynolds asked.

"About two o'clock, I think. I noticed a light flash in the dining-room window."

"Did you enter the house?"

Stephen shook his head.

"No. I was too worried about my sister to do that. She looked very ill and half-demented. Vanda had terrified her by saying she could ruin Julian's good name by dragging up the past. She wanted to appeal to Vanda, she said. I took her arm and we walked slowly up Warne Road, and then, thank heaven, we met Julian who had come in search of her."

"What happened next?" Reynolds asked.

"They went home and I returned to my flat," Stephen answered "You can imagine how staggered I was when Naomi phoned me to-day, saying that Vanda was dead. I thought she was going on all right: I suppose her heart collapsed." He paused, as if weighing up something.

"Go on, please," Reynolds urged.

"I feel pretty sick," Stephen continued, "because Miss Marsh gave me a letter just now. It was from Vanda—dictated by her last night. Probably the last thing she did before she died. She forgave me for being the cause of her arrest." He hesitated. "I hate to tell you this, but feel I ought to do so."

"It certainly explains Miss Marsh's loyal reticence in the matter," Reynolds observed.

Gordon leaned forward.

"What on earth made you take the bracelet, Talbot? Vanda wasn't worth the risk you ran." Stephen shrugged his, shoulders.

"I've always been 'agin the law,' and as it seemed that Vanda would escape scot free, while we bank chaps were in a hole, I decided to fix things so that she was arrested. None of the bank bunch seemed to have the pluck. By the way, inspector, last night in her dressing-room it was my whispered 'Ill?' that surprised you. I thought Vanda had only fainted. Then I knew I was the cause."

"Did you send her threatening letters?" Reynolds asked.

"I did, hoping to scare her from coming to London, where I knew she'd try to hurt my sister. And I got the Weazel to try to frighten her secretary off."

"Said secretary being my wife," Gordon remarked, "and a darned pig-headed honey she is too."

"Naomi's a peach, and I congratulate you," Stephen told him. "Indirectly I was watching your interests, Gordon, for although I didn't know Naomi until we met on the boat, I pulled every string to make her give up Vandals job."

"I see your point," the inspector agreed. "If Vanda heard that her secretary was afraid to enter her service, Vanda might not have come to London." His eyes twinkled. "Considering that you had only just met Miss Marsh, you indeed worked hard in her interests."

Stephen chuckled.

"Wouldn't you do the same for a pretty girl?" he demanded. "I can't say that she overflowed with gratitude! Perhaps that is why she intrigued me. I was bound to admire her determination to stay with Vanda, although I did my best to hoof her out. My hat! How the Weazel threatened her over the telephone—by my orders."

"Naomi tells me that you took a packet, given her by Vanda, from her suitcase in the Paris hotel," Gordon remarked. "I guess you did it for Naomi's sake."

"You're right," Stephen said. "I saw that the wrapping was stained with blood: and although I didn't know what had happened, I realized that bloodstains were nasty things to explain away. It was like Vanda to dump trouble on to someone else, so I—er—purloined it, so to speak." He pressed his hand to his head. "If only that nurse had called the doctor, Vanda might have been alive now, and I wouldn't be in this predicament."

"Do you know that the nurse was attacked during the night, Mr. Talbot?" Reynolds studied the young man's face as he spoke.

"Great Scott, no," exclaimed Stephen. "What a senseless thing to do. Was it to prevent her from calling for help for her patient?"

Reynolds nodded.

"Undoubtedly. It must have been someone whom Miss Quayne knew, because the person had to cross her bedroom in order to enter the boudoir. The nurse was first stunned by a leaden weight in a man's glove, and then drugged."

Stephen started to his feet.

"But that's a repetition of what happened in Paris a week ago to-day," he exclaimed. "Someone threw a leaden weight at Vanda as she was interviewing Naomi; and that same person attacked a maid who was wearing

Vanda's fur coat, in the convent hospital gardens. The maid is getting better. I've made inquiries by cable to the Paris hospital. Vanda was curiously concerned about her."

"Did Miss Quayne tell you this?" the inspector demanded.

"Part of it. She said she admired Naomi's courage at the time."

"Who told you the other part?" Reynolds insisted.

Stephen looked at Reynolds squarely.

"I can't see what all this has to do with Vanda's death, which I admit I must have caused, but I had nothing to do with the affair in Paris, as my taximan and the nasty little trailer can prove. They were with me all the time that I was waiting for Naomi."

"Who told you the other part about Henriette's accident in Paris?" the inspector asked again.

Stephen appealed to Gordon.

"Do you mind if I speak to the inspector only?" he requested.

When Gordon had walked to the other side of the room, Stephen lowered his voice so that only Reynolds could hear.

"Waiting outside the convent hospital last Sunday I saw a girl in a heavy cloak arrive. After poking round, she slipped inside the garden by the little door in the wall. Her movements seemed rather surreptitious and I was curious. A while after, she came out and hurried away. I caught her up and, so that I could get a look at her, asked the way to some place. A few days later I discovered that the girl was Naomi's friend, Phil! She pretended not to recognize me. Later she came to my flat and explained that she'd been anxious about Naomi and had impulsively flown to Paris. She begged me to tell no one. She said she had seen someone throw something at Vanda and knock down the maid. Phil said she'd be suspected if I mentioned it. I promised not to tell."

"Why should you promise that?"

"Because I was sorry for her. She said her life had been spoilt by a tragedy. Her father committed suicide. Well, I had had my early life spoilt too, and I agreed to say nothing. After all, she had a right to fly to Paris if she wished. While we were talking—" Stephen stopped abruptly. "That's quite another angle though."

"This girl had no oilier reasons for secrecy?" Reynolds questioned, ignoring Stephen's broken sentence—for the moment.

"So far as I know," Stephen stated. "Definitely she was not in Vanda's dressing-room last night, so you can't link Phil with my nasty work with the morphia." He called to the older man. "The secrets are out, Gordon; you can join the party. Now, inspector, do you handcuff me or what? I'll go quietly anyhow, and, I hope, take my medicine like a little gentleman." He saluted Gordon. "So long, old lad. Never thought your pal would kill your sister, even though it was an accident, did you?"

"No," said Gordon stoutly. "And I don't think so now. By the way," his lips twitched, "you gave up that bracelet pretty easily."

"I was darned glad to get rid of the thing," Stephen declared. He frowned. "Hi, how do you know about that business?"

"Because," said Gordon, "I happened to be the man who collected it. I expected resistance from you—hence the gun and the attempt at disguise."

"You fooled me completely," Stephen admitted. "You might have frightened Phil, though."

"Was that the girl who opened the door to me? You called her your 'red-haired confederate,' I remember."

"Yes, that was Phil." Stephen grinned. "I called her my confederate because she had a little secret that she wanted me to keep,, and when you dropped in, it looked as if I also had one for her to keep quiet'

"She was a cool-headed, determined person, not at all alarmed by me or my gun! " Gordon observed. "Does my wife know her?"

Stephen smiled.

"Know her! Why, she and Naomi share a flat. Hasn't she told you of Phil Ingram?"

"Naomi and I have had no time for anything except grim business," Gordon assured him. His forehead wrinkled. "Ingram! I've only run across two or three other people with that name before in my life. There was a Philip Ingram, manager of our bank in Rio. Through Vanda's jewel affair he lost his job and shot himself. You remember him, Talbot? Why, what's the matter, inspector?" he inquired as Reynolds hurried to the door and called his assistant sharply.

"Where's Miss Marsh?" he demanded.

"In her room, sir. You were engaged and I didn't like to ask if you would mind. Miss Ingram called her, saying Miss Marsh was to come up at once."

"Keep Mr. Talbot down here," Reynolds told him, and raced upstairs.

XLI. THE LAST STAND

Sunday, November 28th.

THE inspector paused outside the room in which Phil and Naomi had slept the previous night. He knocked imperatively. There was no answer to his summons, and no sound from within.

Grasping the handle, he found the door was locked. "Open the door, Miss Marsh," he called.

As he spoke, Gordon dashed up to him. "Anything wrong, inspector?" he demanded.

"Both Miss Marsh and Miss Ingram are locked in there," was the significant reply.

Gordon's jaw set squarely.

"Unfasten the door," he shouted, "or I shall burst it open."

There was a click as the key was turned on the other side. A second later, the two men were confronted with the muzzle of a revolver, held in a girl's determined hand. It was Phil Ingram.

"Come in—both of you," she ordered, "and keep quiet—if you value your lives. Get over there beside Naomi."

Phil slammed the door and set her back against it as the inspector and Gordon crossed the room to the girl who sat, white and silent, on one of the beds.

"You'd better put that gun down, Miss Ingram," Reynolds warned. He shifted his position slightly so that for the moment he blocked Gordon from her view. "Against two men you haven't much chance."

"Both of 'em unarmed," Phil scoffed. "Ah! So that's the idea, is it?" she added quickly as she saw Gordon snatch his revolver from his pocket and raise it. "Well, you asked for this."

Naomi hid her eyes as two shots rang out in sharp succession.

The revolver dropped from Phil's hand and her teeth clenched hard as she gripped her right forearm.

"Her shot went wide," Gordon explained. "She won't score any more bull's-eyes this season. You look after her, inspector. I've got my own job to see to." He put his arm around Naomi.

"All right, honey?" he asked her tenderly.

Naomi nodded. Her eyes slowly filled with tears as she watched the inspector tear up a towel and put a tourniquet on Phil Ingram's arm.

"Chin up, Naomi," Gordon steadied her. "It had to be her or me. She isn't badly hurt. Well, you've tried your hand at detective work and found out that it's not your *métier*. Perhaps you'll let your husband look after you now. Lie down and rest. Nobody's going to worry you again."

Naomi leaned back obediently but her attention was on the girl who had been her friend. Phil Ingram turned towards her, and for a second their eyes met in farewell.

Then, at the inspector's request, she went from the room, head held high and defiant.

"Go down to the dining-room, Miss Ingram," Reynolds ordered. Walking behind her, he examined her revolver which he had picked up.

"Well, the game's up," Phil declared coolly, presently. "I can still laugh at the way I fooled you all. The frank girl who had nothing to hide!" Her lips twisted to the vestige of a smile. "I'm sorry I had to scare Naomi to keep her silent: it was the primitive instinct of self-preservation being the first law, I suppose. She must have guessed who killed Vanda when Anderson broke the news this morning."

Reynolds laid the revolver on the table and looked at her.

"You called Miss Marsh to your bedroom a while ago. Will you tell me what passed between you?"

"Why not?" Phil said with a touch of her old flippancy. "Naomi said her husband was downstairs talking to you. Up to his appearance she did not know if he were involved in any way. When he arrived she knew that soon she would have to tell the truth about me."

She and Reynolds were standing at opposite ends of the table. As she spoke, she drew a little nearer to him.

"Why did you fly to Paris last Sunday?" he asked.

"I did it on an impulse," she stated. "It had this to justify it: I made that sudden effort to kill Vanda really on Naomi's behalf. I wanted to get it over before she was employed by that woman." Phil flung out her sound arm, the other being in a temporary sling. "I failed, and injured an innocent maid! Stephen Talbot saw me there. Possibly he imagined what I meant to do, and tried to get Naomi away."

"In the bathroom cupboard of your flat, Miss Ingram, I found Miss Quayne's box of drugs, the key of the boudoir and a hypodermic syringe concealed under a pile of towels. Those things could have been placed there by you to shield your friend or Talbot, or because you were guilty. I had no means of proving which theory was correct until now."

The girl rested her left hand on the table, as if she needed support.

"I know when I'm beaten," she said in a flattened tone. "I brought the case of drugs back in the ambulance last night and hid them in my flat this morning." She drew in her breath. "As a kid I worshipped my father. I had only just left school when he shot himself in Rio, but ever since then I was determined to get Vanda Quayne, and let nothing hinder me. Nothing," she emphasized. "That explains why I didn't allow the mistake I made in the convent garden, nor the nurse, nor even my friend Naomi Marsh to get in my way." She flung back her head. "It's funny to think of those fellows in the Rio bank banding themselves together as Vanda's enemies, ready to do her in! And when their courage failed, a girl did what they had threatened. Say, can we have some air? This wound makes me feel queer, I suppose."

Her eyes followed Reynolds closely. As he pushed the window up her fingers groped along the table.

"You are aware that you are not obliged to tell me anything," the inspector observed.

"Quite aware," she told him. "Strangely enough I'm rather enjoying this." An odd laugh broke from her. "It was so easy. Nurse fetched Naomi last night and then they went downstairs, as you've heard. Instantly I went in to Vanda and told her that I wanted to ask nurse for something to make me sleep. Vanda told me there were several sleeping drugs in her case. 'Carry it into the boudoir,' she said. 'Nurse will be back in a minute; she'll tell you what to take. Stay there and don't disturb me until I've finished with Miss Marsh.'"

"You took the case into the boudoir?" Reynolds asked.

"Yes. I hid behind the window curtains until the nurse returned. I stunned her and then injected morphia into her arm. Then I charged the syringe with treble the dose I'd given her and waiting until Naomi had gone back to our room, opened the boudoir door. Vanda was half asleep. It was simple to plunge the needle into her arm. I locked the boudoir door, took the key, and went to bed."

"Surely Miss Marsh was surprised that you had left your bedroom?"

"Not at all. Vanda told her that I was in the boudoir and explained the reason." Phil's fingers closed on the handle of the revolver. Suddenly she swung the weapon up in her left hand and aimed it at the C.I.D. man.

"This is why I talked," she said. "Stand where you are. If you move one step until I'm through that window, I shall fire."

Ignoring her threat, Reynolds walked towards her. There was a sharp click as she pressed the trigger, but no report followed.

"The gun has been unloaded," he told her. "I left it there to induce you to tell me the truth, knowing you would only do so if you thought you had a means of escape."

"A despicable trick," she declared.

"One that I was forced to play to protect innocent people who might otherwise have been involved," Reynolds replied. Laying his hand on his prisoner's arm he led her out to the waiting car.

THE END

Other Resurrected Press Books in *The Chief Inspector Pointer Mystery* Series

Murder at Bridge

When an afternoon bridge party attended by some of Hamilton's leading citizens ends with the hostess being murdered in her boudoir, Special Investigator Dundee of the District Attorney's office is called in. But one of the attendees is guilty? There are plenty of suspects: the victim's former lover, her current suitor, the retired judge who is being blackmailed, the victim's maid who had been horribly disfigured accidentally by the murdered woman, or any of the women who's husbands had flirted with the victim. Or was she murdered by an outsider whose motive had nothing to do with the town of Hamilton. Find the answer in... **Murder at Bridge**

One Drop of Blood

When Dr. Koenig, head of Mayfield Sanitarium is murdered, the District Attorney's Special Investigator, "Bonnie" Dundee must go undercover to find the killer. Were any of the inmates of the asylum insane enough to have committed the crime? Or, was it one of the staff, motivated by jealousy? And what was is the secret in the murdered man's past. Find the answer in... **One Drop of Blood**

AVAILABLE FROM RESURRECTED PRESS!

GEMS OF MYSTERY
LOST JEWELS FROM A MORE ELEGANT AGE

Three wonderful tales of mystery from some of the best known writers of the period before the First World War -

A foggy London night, a Russian princess who steals jewels, a corpse; a mysterious murder, an opera singer, and stolen pearls; two young people who crash a masked ball only to find themselves caught up in a daring theft of jewels; these are the subjects of this collection of entertaining tales of love, jewels, and mystery. This collection includes:

- **In the Fog - by Richard Harding Davis's**

- **The Affair at the Hotel Semiramis - by A.E.W. Mason**

- **Hearts and Masks - Harold MacGrath**

AVAILABLE FROM RESURRECTED PRESS!

THE EDWARDIAN DETECTIVES
LITERARY SLEUTHS OF THE EDWARDIAN ERA

The exploits of the great Victorian Detectives, Poe's C. Auguste Dupin, Gaboriau's Lecoq, and most famously, Arthur Conan Doyle's Sherlock Holmes, are well known. But what of those fictional detectives that came after, those of the Edwardian Age? The period between the death of Queen Victoria and the First World War had been called the Golden Age of the detective short story, but how familiar is the modern reader with the sleuths of this era? And such an extraordinary group they were, including in their numbers an unassuming English priest, a blind man, a master of disguises, a lecturer in medical jurisprudence, a noble woman working for Scotland Yard, and a savant so brilliant he was known as "The Thinking Machine."

To introduce readers to these detectives, Resurrected Press has assembled a collection of stories featuring these and other remarkable sleuths in The Edwardian Detectives.

- The Case of Laker, Absconded by Arthur Morrison
- The Fenchurch Street Mystery by Baroness Orczy
- The Crime of the French Café by Nick Carter
- The Man with Nailed Shoes by R Austin Freeman
- The Blue Cross by G. K. Chesterton
- The Case of the Pocket Diary Found in the Snow by Augusta Groner
- The Ninescore Mystery by Baroness Orczy
- The Riddle of the Ninth Finger by Thomas W. Hanshew
- The Knight's Cross Signal Problem by Ernest Bramah

- The Problem of Cell 13 by Jacques Futrelle
- The Conundrum of the Golf Links by Percy James Brebner
- The Silkworms of Florence by Clifford Ashdown
- The Gateway of the Monster by William Hope Hodgson
- The Affair at the Semiramis Hotel by A. E. W. Mason
- The Affair of the Avalanche Bicycle & Tyre Co., LTD by Arthur Morrison

RESURRECTED PRESS CLASSIC MYSTERY CATALOGUE

Journeys into Mystery
Travel and Mystery in a More Elegant Time

The Edwardian Detectives
Literary Sleuths of the Edwardian Era

Gems of Mystery
Lost Jewels from a More Elegant Age

E. C. Bentley
Trent's Last Case: The Woman in Black

Ernest Bramah
Max Carrados Resurrected:
The Detective Stories of Max Carrados

Agatha Christie
The Secret Adversary
The Mysterious Affair at Styles

Octavus Roy Cohen
Midnight

Freeman Wills Croft
The Ponson Case
The Pit Prop Syndicate

J. S. Fletcher
The Herapath Property
The Rayner-Slade Amalgamation
The Chestermarke Instinct
The Paradise Mystery
Dead Men's Money

The Middle of Things
Ravensdene Court
Scarhaven Keep
The Orange-Yellow Diamond
The Middle Temple Murder
The Tallyrand Maxim
The Borough Treasurer
In the Mayor's Parlour
The Saftey Pin

R. Austin Freeman
*The Mystery of 31 New Inn from the Dr. Thorndyke
Series*
*John Thorndyke's Cases from the Dr. Thorndyke
Series*
The Red Thumb Mark from The Dr. Thorndyke Series
The Eye of Osiris from The Dr. Thorndyke Series
A Silent Witness from the Dr. John Thorndyke Series
The Cat's Eye from the Dr. John Thorndyke Series
*Helen Vardon's Confession: A Dr. John Thorndyke
Story*
As a Thief in the Night: A Dr. John Thorndyke Story
*Mr. Pottermack's Oversight: A Dr. John Thorndyke
Story*
*Dr. Thorndyke Intervenes: A Dr. John Thorndyke
Story*
The Singing Bone: The Adventures of Dr. Thorndyke
The Stoneware Monkey: A Dr. John Thorndyke Story
*The Great Portrait Mystery, and Other Stories: A
Collection of Dr. John Thorndyke and Other Stories*
The Penrose Mystery: A Dr. John Thorndyke Story
The Uttermost Farthing: A Savant's Vendetta

Arthur Griffiths
The Passenger From Calais
The Rome Express

Fergus Hume
The Mystery of a Hansom Cab
The Green Mummy
The Silent House
The Secret Passage

Edgar Jepson
The Loudwater Mystery

A. E. W. Mason
At the Villa Rose

A. A. Milne
The Red House Mystery
Baroness Emma Orczy
The Old Man in the Corner

Edgar Allan Poe
The Detective Stories of Edgar Allan Poe

Arthur J. Rees
The Hampstead Mystery
The Shrieking Pit
The Hand In The Dark
The Moon Rock
The Mystery of the Downs

Mary Roberts Rinehart
Sight Unseen and The Confession

Dorothy L. Sayers
Whose Body?

Sir William Magnay
The Hunt Ball Mystery

Mabel and Paul Thorne
The Sheridan Road Mystery

Raoul Whitfield
Death in a Bowl

And much more!
Visit ResurrectedPress.com
for our complete catalogue

About Resurrected Press

A division of Intrepid Ink, LLC, Resurrected Press is dedicated to bringing high quality, vintage books back into publication. See our entire catalogue and find out more at www.ResurrectedPress.com.

About Intrepid Ink, LLC

Intrepid Ink, LLC provides full publishing services to authors of fiction and non-fiction books, eBooks and websites. From editing to formatting, from publishing to marketing, Intrepid Ink gets your creative works into the hands of the people who want to read them. Find out more at www.IntrepidInk.com.